ONE FOR THE MONEY

NICOLE S. GOODIN

One for the Money
Published by Nicole S. Goodin

ISBN: 978-0-473-61201-6

Copyright 2021 by Nicole S. Goodin
All rights reserved. ©

First published December 2021
Cover design by Nicole Goodin
Images purchased from Deposit Photos
Editing by Spell Bound

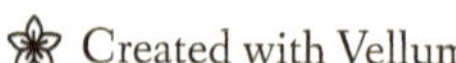 Created with Vellum

One For The MONEY

*To everyone who has taken a chance on my work,
thank you all so much.*

Nicole x

FOREWORD

This book has been written using UK English and
may contain euphemisms and slang words that form
part of the New Zealand spoken word.
Please remember that the words are not misspelled.
They are slang terms and form part of everyday, New
Zealand vernacular.
I.e: I'm from New Zealand and sometimes we say
weird things down here... please try and be cool
about it.

PROLOGUE

Tyler

NO ONE GOT the upper hand on me in this world. *My* world. *No one.*

I'd figured out how this Armageddon asshole had screwed me over within about thirty minutes, but that still didn't explain how I hadn't noticed when it mattered or *why* he was back causing trouble now.

The dude held a grudge – that much was clear.

What the hell was going on, I had no idea, but I was going to find out.

No one hacks me and gets away with it.

CHAPTER 1

Tyler
Two weeks later

AS I RAN, my feet pounding against the pavement, I contemplated my next move.

Armageddon had won the last round; that much I was certain of.

What I *wasn't* certain about in the slightest was *who* I was dealing with... I'd never really cared too much about my adversaries' real identities, but I'd also never been bested in such dramatic fashion.

I had no more idea now than I did a week ago about who this person was.

He was good at flying under the radar, I'd give him that much.

He'd fooled me – wound me in hook, line and sinker and played me like a fiddle.

I replayed the one, simple message he'd left for me.

You're getting sloppy, Watson.

The fact that he knew my name was enough to raise alarm bells. Actually, fuck alarm bells, it was more like a blaring tsunami siren.

I'd pissed off some real bad people over the years, and I prided myself on being digitally invisible.

It was glaringly obvious that I wasn't as imperceptible as I'd thought.

Not even close.

If he could find me, the *real* me, then I had problems.

All it would take is for someone to hire him – someone substantially scarier than Jasper Jones, someone who really wanted to see me burn – and I was a dead man walking.

My asshole brothers were always having a real good laugh about the fact that I sat behind a keyboard everyday while they were out there risking their lives with their extreme lifestyles, but as per usual, they were dead wrong.

I'd always said those two boys were dangerous creatures – as close to identical as it came, pretty faces, absolutely no fear and barely half a brain between them, but they had no idea who I was messing with on a daily basis. I'd screwed with men so scary they'd make getting a hiding in a boxing ring look like a walk in the park. Men so brutal, that flying around a racetrack at the speed of light may as well have been child's play.

I picked up the pace of my run, increasing my tempo and pushing my body to the limit until my lungs and legs were burning, protesting against the exertion.

This was my zone... the place where others dropped back and gave their body the rest it was craving was the place where I told mine to shut the hell up and endure it. No one ever got anywhere in life by giving up when things got tough. I was comfortable being uncomfortable.

Mind over matter.

That was true for most things.

If you didn't have your brain on board, you were fucked.

I glanced down at the alert on my smart watch, hopeful that it was the information I'd been waiting on.

I grinned in triumph as I skimmed the results of the search I'd had running and turned down the next block, cutting my run short, in a rush to get back to my apartment.

I was going to find out who this Armageddon asshole was if it killed me.

CHAPTER 2

Amarah

TYLER WATSON WAS COMING for me; I was sure of it.

I'd felt him virtually poking and prodding – sniffing his curious digital nose around the edges of my protection.

I was well prepared, this was in no way my first rodeo, but it wouldn't last long, not against a man who possessed the skill set he did.

I wasn't joking when I'd stated that he was the best there was. He may not have been the best there was in the *whole* world, but the world we were in... *undoubtedly*. It was his world, and we were just living in it.

The guy was yet to face something he couldn't

beat, one way or another, and there was no way in hell I was going to be the exception to that rule. I knew that. He knew that. Anyone with half a brain knew that. It was just a matter of time.

I'd made what was possibly an error in judgement by taunting him too, which would only make him stronger – more determined than ever to find me and beat me – show me who was boss. I hadn't really thought that through, but I hadn't been able to help myself.

He needed to beat me, to prove himself. It might have only been him and I who knew of his mistakes, but I'm sure as far as he was concerned, that was two people too many.

He'd gone from zero to hero in less than *one* day. I knew he wouldn't take that lightly, and I was right.

He was unreachable now.

If his security had been this impenetrable when Jasper Jones hired me to hack into his system, I would have been shit out of luck.

I was only still trying as a form of self-preservation.

Hunt or be hunted.

I'd found only one back door in the past week, but even that had thrown me for a loop.

I couldn't figure out how he had done it. He'd left me a slim, almost non-existent opening that looked nothing like any trap I'd ever seen before, drawn me in and then turned the tables on me before I even knew what had hit me.

One more press of a key on my keyboard and he would have had me.

It was the most genius use of a honey pot I'd ever seen.

If we weren't sworn enemies, I would have really liked to have asked him how he did it. I'd have been impressed if I wasn't so terrified.

Thankfully, I'd given in to my growing suspicion that it was just *too* easy and got the hell out of there. I knew he'd managed to extract something from my server; what he'd retrieved, I wasn't sure – but whatever it was, he'd use it against me. I knew that much.

I should have known better, I should be shutting down, starting over and never going near the digital fortress that was Tyler Watson again, but I was bored, stubborn and apparently had a death wish.

I'd been waiting for something, *anything* to happen since, but so far, radio silence.

It was making me nervous.

I was jumpy and off kilter all day, every day.

The cyber world didn't know who I really was – *nobody* did. I was confident that ninety-nine percent of my clients thought I was a man.

I'd revealed to Jasper that I was a female, because I trusted him. I considered him to be somewhat of a friend these days. He wasn't going to rat me out to anyone, and certainly not to Tyler, but that was still the most information I'd been willing to share with him. The mutual distaste we both had for the guy's antics was enough to reassure me that my secret was safe with him.

But he was the only one I'd trusted with that information so far in my career. Everyone else thought they were dealing with a male, and that's the way I liked it.

Being a female in the world of 'hackers' wasn't all that common. The image people conjure up of a bunch of geeky guys all huddled around a huge computer set up in their parents' basement wasn't exactly too far off the mark – I mean, sure, most of the set ups I'd come across were out of this world insane, but I was yet to find one that didn't have at least one of those geeky cliché guys, pushing his glasses up his nose, somewhere in the mix.

I preferred to work alone, and without personal recognition. I'd made a name for myself as being one of the best and most anonymous, and I was proud of that.

I hadn't crossed too many lines morally either, and I knew there weren't a lot of people in this industry that could say the same.

It was tempting at times; I would be the first to admit that. Draining some asshole's bank account wasn't exactly hard – neither was hacking into my ex-boyfriend's hard drive and changing all his pass-words, as petty as it was – but I wasn't about that life. I wanted to make an honest living, and for the most part, I'd been able to do that.

I'd only missed one opportunity in my career;

probably the one that would have had the biggest pay day too, and there was one man and one man only that I had to blame for that.

That's how I'd found myself in this sticky situation in the first place. I was stubborn as hell, and I held a grudge like no other. Tyler Watson may have been made to look like a fool at the mercy of my hands for only about thirty seconds, but given the skills of the guy, that was more than enough gratification for me given the way he'd screwed me over back then.

Now all I had to do was keep him out of my business. I had a pretty good feeling that was going to be easier said than done.

I'd struck the match myself, and now I had to desperately try and put out the fire.

The ringing of my phone startled me from my daydream, and I grinned at the name flashing across my screen.

I didn't have a lot of people in my life, even less that I trusted with my secrets, in fact, Jess was pretty much it. She was my person. She was my two-in-the-morning call when I needed a ride home, she was who I talked to about sex – not that I was having any of that currently, but she was my closest confidante and I was hers. We were two peas in a pod, and right now, she was hurting. Her dipshit ex-boyfriend had broken her heart... *again.*

Absolute douche bag.

I pressed the phone to my ear. "Hey, girl, how you doin'?"

"Rah-Rah, he's *such* an asshole."

I sighed heavily. I could already tell she'd been crying; I could hear it in her voice. She was upset, and he was the culprit. As per usual.

"Tell me what you want me to do, babe. I can drain his bank account and donate it all to charity, I can use his credit card to buy a collection of massive dildos and have them sent to his work, I can arrange to have a box of dog shit sent to him every day for a year. You tell me what you want, and I'll make it happen."

I knew damn well she was going to decline all the options I'd just given her, but it didn't mean I couldn't have a bit of fun imagining the look on his face.

She laughed a half-amused, half-miserable laugh.

"I mean it, Jessie, just say the word and I'll make him my bitch."

The laugh was more genuine this time.

"I knew I'd feel better when I called you."

I loved that we were that support for each other. I knew I could call her any time, day or night and she'd be there. I'd do anything for her in return. We were more like sisters than friends.

"What's he done now?" I question.

I knew he wouldn't go quietly. The guy was a grade A asshole and he liked nothing more than to make Jess' life a misery.

"He wants to take the dog."

"Tell him to get fucked. He doesn't even like the dog."

I spun my chair around and around in slow circles as I spoke.

"I know, right!" she agreed, snivelling.

"He's just trying to upset you; you didn't let him hear you cry, did you?"

"No. I started to crack and then I heard your voice in my ear telling me not to be a pussy and let him win."

"Good girl."

"And then I told him he could suck a bag of dicks, and I hung up on him."

I muffled a laugh. "Well, the maturity level obviously slipped, but I think we can still call that a win. I'm proud of you."

"He brings out my inner five-year-old, I swear."

"It *is* his mental age after all," I quipped.

"I think five is being generous."

"You're probably not wrong."

She took a deep breath before blowing it out heavily. "What if he really tries to take the dog?"

"You and I both know that lazy piece of shit isn't going to take the dog. The last thing he wants is to feed her and walk her every day. You should offer to drop her around to him; he'll backtrack faster than an old school cassette tape on rewind."

She sighed. "You're probably right."

"I'm *definitely* right."

She sighed again. "I should go, my sister just pulled up."

"Urgh. Way to kick a girl when she's down."

She laughed. Her sister was a complete bitch and we both knew it.

"Thanks for the pep talk."

"Anytime."

And I meant it. There was nothing I wouldn't do for this woman. She was my best friend.

"Talk to you later?"

"You know it."

"Oh, and if you wanted to send him a big, purple, glittery strap-on or something, I can't say I'd be upset about it," she teased.

I huffed out a laugh. "I'll see what I can do."

I knew she was only kidding, but I wasn't.

I hung up the phone and got to work. There was no way I'd only be sending him the one sex toy, *and* they'd be arriving to his work where all his workmates could see... but Jess couldn't be held responsible for something she didn't know about.

I grinned wickedly as I clicked on the biggest dildo I could find.

Karma's a bitch, Trent.

Turns out karma was about to be a bitch to me too, I just didn't know it yet.

CHAPTER 3

Tyler

I HAD HIM.

Well, not him *physically*, but I had an address, and that was the first step on the path to revenge.

He'd crept into my trap like a hungry bear, and the flash of a second before he'd figured out it was a trap was all I'd needed.

The data was scrambled to hell, but I'd never been afraid of a challenge, and I rarely failed at one either. This was no exception. It had taken me fucking days, but I'd got there.

I stared at the map on the screen in front of me.

An apartment block twenty-five minutes' drive from here.

I'd had a feeling he was close – I knew he was in

the country, most likely within state, but I had no idea just how close he really was.

It could have been a false location, but given the lengths he'd gone to protect it, I doubted that was the case. Armageddon was there. I could feel it.

I glanced at my keys sitting on the table next to me, and my fingers twitched with anticipation of hitting the road and tracking the guy down.

I didn't have a plan from here, but I could recognise that I needed one.

I still didn't know *who* this guy was. I couldn't rush in there all guns blazing, but I couldn't do nothing either – that wasn't in my nature – but I needed to be cautious.

He might be just a kid, or he could be old as shit.

I didn't have it in me to give an old dude a hiding. The more I thought about it, the more I realised a fist fight wasn't what I wanted anyway; I wanted revenge, not blood.

Right now, I just wanted to do *something*. I wanted information. In my life, information was power. Knowing who he was would give me back the edge.

I snagged the keys and headed for the door, a plan hatching in my mind.

First, I needed to know who this guy was, and then I needed to figure out what his weaknesses were... once I knew that, I could figure out precisely how to exploit them.

———

I pulled up outside the building at the address I had scribbled on the piece of paper in front of me and glanced around.

It was obvious that while this *Armageddon* might have been a total pain in my ass, he was also reasonably honest.

As professional 'hackers' we had opportunities every day to make choices that would benefit us financially. There were people in my profession with not even close to half my skill set who lived the cushiest lifestyle known to man.

I could rob people blind on a daily basis if I wanted to.

I *didn't*, but I *could*. And judging by the fact that this place was nothing special, neither did he. It was nice, but it wasn't The Ritz.

I glanced around the neighbourhood. Quiet street, tidy gardens. Perfectly respectable establishment.

Nothing out of place. Nothing to suggest the thorn in my side might be lurking around inside those walls.

I eyed the door to the apartment building from my stake-out spot across the street.

I felt like one of those detectives in a crime drama; all that was missing was the camera with a giant lens and a box of doughnuts.

Staking the place out.

Night was falling around me, and the streetlights flickered to life; a dull glow falling across the pavement.

Now I wait.

I was fully prepared to sleep in this car all night if I had to. There was no telling when this guy would appear, but if he was anything like me, he'd have to get out of his apartment and into the fresh air sooner or later. I always went batshit crazy if I didn't get out into the real world at least every six hours, no matter what time of day it was. Office hours were a foreign concept to me anyway.

I settled back in my seat and prepared myself to wait it out.

———

I rubbed my eyes and groaned.

When I'd committed to waiting out here all night, I didn't actually think I'd have to do it.

I'd sat out here for a solid twelve hours, and I still hadn't seen anything worth writing home about.

A mum and her kids had come back late last night; the kids were asleep, and the dad had come down to help her carry them up to their home.

A little old lady had taken her dog for a walk first thing this morning, but other than that, it was just a whole bunch of nothing. I might not have been sure who I was dealing with, but I was pretty fucking sure it wasn't Doris and her poodle from apartment six.

I glanced at my watch for what must have been the one millionth time and debated what to do. I hated to walk away empty-handed, but I had a shit tonne of work to get done today and I was getting exactly *nothing* done by sitting out here like some type of stalker. I was starving and I needed caffeine something chronic.

I didn't even know what I was going to do if a man came out that I considered *could* be the guy I was looking for... it wasn't like he was going to have a flashing neon sign above his head saying 'hacker'.

For all I knew, the dad carrying his sleeping kids up to bed late last night was the guy I was after. I was clutching at straws when it came down to it.

This was a stupid idea.

I shook my head at myself.

Guess I'm more like my meathead brothers than I thought.

I needed to get out of here before I lost my mind good and proper. I needed a better plan than 'sit and wait'. It was time to regroup.

I took one last look at the apartment building and froze at the sight in front of me.

Holy shit. Who the hell is that?

She was wearing the tiniest pair of black shorts I'd ever seen and a black and purple sports bra.

She was tall and exotic looking and had her long, dark hair in a braid that trailed down her back.

I held in a groan as I watched her stretch and twist her lithe body.

She was the sexiest woman I'd laid eyes on in a long time, maybe ever. She was tall and lean and gorgeous as hell.

I didn't have the faintest idea who she was, but I was suddenly *desperate* to know.

I caught sight of the scrap of paper I'd scrawled the address on as I reached for the door handle.

145 Ridge Lane.

Wait.

The tall, gorgeous woman lived here.

What if she's with him?

I grinned wickedly to myself.

Exploit his weakness...

If that woman was his, then I could take her from him.

Just how much of an asshole I was being struck me in that moment, and I snapped myself from my thoughts.

What the fuck is wrong with me?

I wasn't about to use a woman that way; whether she was involved with that prick or not. I wasn't a piece of shit, but that *was* a piece-of-shit thought.

Sleep deprivation. Blame it on that.

I needed to get the hell out of here before any other stupid ideas went through my brain.

I jabbed my finger at the start button and the engine spluttered and choked before falling silent.

This is not good.

"Motherfucker," I muttered to myself as I tried starting it again to no avail.

The car wheezed and rumbled before cutting out again.

Realisation hit that I was stuck outside what I presumed to be my arch nemesis's home, with no way to escape.

On top of that, I was making a total fool of myself in front of a drop-dead gorgeous woman, all because I'd gotten cold feet in the middle of the night and left the heater running for too long and my dying battery couldn't handle it.

I glanced out the window and cussed under my breath again.

She was headed my way.

CHAPTER 4

Amarah

I DARTED my eyes over again, doing my best to make it seem like I hadn't noticed what was going on across the street.

I *really* didn't want to go over there and see if whoever it was needed my help, but by the sounds of that car, I was going to have to.

The battery was dead as hell, and only a jump or a tow was going to fix that.

I didn't have a tow truck lying around unfortunately, but I could certainly help with the jumpstart.

I looked up again as the driver made one more feeble attempt to start the engine. I didn't know why they thought they had a shot at getting that thing going, given the sick sound the car was making, but God loves a trier, I guess.

The engine barely even made a noise as they tried and failed again.

"Dammit," I mumbled to myself before giving in and heading towards the driver's window.

This probably wasn't my smartest move. The windows were so tinted I couldn't see a damn thing through the glass. I hadn't a clue if I was dealing with a little old lady or the big bad wolf here, but I did seem to have a death wish lately, so why not stick with what I knew?

If only I had no morals, I could be out on my run by now.

I tapped on the window. "Need a jump?" I called out.

I'd been expecting the window to roll down – stupidly so, given that I was very aware the battery was flat, so when the door moved to open, I was already off balance, but even if I hadn't been, the sight before me could have knocked me clean over on its own merit.

Holy freaking crap.

I didn't care if he *was* the big bad wolf, he was *seriously* hot.

The early morning sun bounced off his brown hair, throwing flecks of red through it as he ran a hand through the strands.

I swallowed deeply as I regained my footing.

The man was a god.

He shot me a sheepish grin. "I'm kinda stuck, do you mind?"

He had on a pair of dark sunglasses, and as I stood there staring at him, I willed him to take them off so I could see his eyes.

Answer the question, Amarah.

"Sure, ah... no problem... let me go get my car."

———

"So, is this your car or your boyfriend's?" he asked.

I arched a brow at him. "*Seriously,* did you just fish around for boyfriend info?"

He chuckled and ran his hand through his hair again. "Guilty... and not sorry either."

I couldn't put my finger on what it was about this guy, but he looked vaguely familiar. I was sure I hadn't seen him around; I'd remember a body like that if it were wandering around the supermarket or the gym, but there was something tugging on my memories that I couldn't place.

"Good one, Mr. Smooth. Why don't you just ask the question you want to ask?"

"Have you got a boyfriend or not?" he tried again.

"Ooooh, that's direct," I teased as I clipped the red and black clips onto my battery. "I like it."

"You like it enough to give me an answer?" he probed as he took the other end of the leads from me and attached them to his own battery.

I rested my hip against his car as I watched him

move. The muscles in his arms tensed and bulged as he worked, and I had the urge to reach out and run my fingers over them.

Don't answer, my brain screamed, even though I knew damn well that I was going to. Biting my tongue had never been one of my strengths.

"No boyfriend."

"Good." He smiled at me, and my stomach filled with butterflies. "I don't have a girlfriend either," he confirmed.

"I would like to hope not, with the flirty, inappropriate questions and all."

He laughed again, and I decided then and there that it was a sound I wanted to hear more of.

"Is this your game plan or something? Pull up outside my house and run the battery flat, then hassle me until I agree to a date?"

He smirked at me. "So, you *will* agree to a date then?"

I rolled my eyes. "You don't even know my name."

"Tell me your name," he said without missing a beat.

"Taking the direct approach again, I see."

"Just trying to do what I'm told. So, about that name?"

"Wouldn't you like to know?"

He chuckled and shook his head. "Why do I get the feeling you're a real hard nut to crack?"

"Oh, baby, you've got no idea just how hard."

We were just standing out here now, staring at one another, neither of us doing anything other than flirting with the other.

"I think that's meant to be my line." He smirked again.

"Urgh," I groaned, "just start the car already."

The absolute last thing I needed to be doing was thinking about this guy and 'hard' in the same sentence... a girl only has so much self-control, and mine was wavering – big time.

He laughed loudly as I rounded the bonnet and turned the key in my ignition, starting the car.

He did the same, and this time his engine roared to life. Part of me couldn't wait for him to get out of here so I could breathe again, and the other half of me wished his car wouldn't go at all, so I could have a little more time with him.

He did a fist pump and jumped out of his vehicle.

I met him in the middle and held my hand out, palm up.

He raised his brows in question, not under-standing what I wanted.

"Give me your phone," I instructed.

He reached into his back pocket and pulled it out, unlocked it and handed it to me without so much as a second thought.

I typed my name and punched in my number, my heart pounding the entire time I did it.

I didn't do this – giving out my number to a stranger wasn't at all me, but there was something that pulled me to this guy, and I wanted to find out what it was.

"Give me yours." He held out his hand.

I passed his cell back to him. "Just text me tomorrow or something, mine's inside."

He shook his head. "What if I got into a crash on the way home and lost my memory, you'd spend forever thinking I never called."

"I'm not sure I'd spend *forever...*"

"You *would*," he insisted before reaching into his car and grabbing a scrap of paper and a pen.

He scrawled his number on the bottom of the paper, tore it off and passed it to me, his hand lingering in mine as he did. "You could have just text it to me right now, you know," I pointed out.

"I'll call you," he promised, ignoring my logic.

"I'll save your number as 'desperate flat battery guy'." I winked at him.

He laughed as he stepped away from me. His hand held onto mine until the distance between us made it drop.

My fingers tingled from the contact, and I resisted the urge to follow and touch him again. Maybe beg him to stay.

I needed to get a grip; this version of me was strange and unknown. I was as confused by it as I was intrigued.

"I'll talk to you soon," he repeated. "Real soon."

"Promises, promises," I replied, trying to sound casual.

"You bet it is." His reply came as he climbed back into his running car and closed the door behind him.

My stomach was still fluttering like crazy. Every single move he made was sexy as hell.

"Talk soon, Amarah."

The sound of my name in his deep, alluring voice was my absolute undoing. It was lucky he was pulling away, because had he still been standing before me, I probably would have thrown myself at him.

I was lusting after the man like crazy and I hadn't even seen his eyes yet.

He drove off down the street, his arm waving out the window. I waited until I couldn't see him anymore before I glanced down at the piece of paper in my hand.

0226745975

Tyler Watson

"Oh, *holy shit*," I breathed.

Tyler. Watson.

No. No, no, no, no, no, no.

"This is not good," I thought aloud.

My heart had already been racing, but now it was in a full gallop for an entirely different reason. This could *not* be happening. *That's* why he looked famil-iar. I hadn't spent virtually any time looking into his physical appearance, I was far more interested in his digital one, but I'd seen an old photo, years ago. He'd really grown into himself since then, but it was him.

I'd been conversing with the enemy.

Even worse, I'd just given the enemy my name

and number. Not only that, but he knew where I lived.

He *was* the big bad wolf after all, and I was so totally and utterly screwed.

He didn't come here by accident; there was no way in hell he was out the front of my building purely by coincidence. He came here for *me*.

He knew where to find me after all. *That's* what he'd gotten from my server.

He's playing me.

He *had* to be trying to screw with me. He'd come here with the intention of finding me and he'd done exactly that. He'd found me and now he was playing me.

Well game on, Watson.

I knew how to play too, and some pretty-boy computer genius wasn't about to get one up on me.

CHAPTER 5

Tyler

I MAY NOT HAVE GOT revenge, but damn, the possibility of what I did get was a hell of a lot better, far more satisfying and undoubtedly better to look at.

Amarah.

I'd memorised her number already, I'd looked at it so many times.

I wanted desperately to call her, but I didn't want to appear exactly that... *desperate.*

The twenty minutes I'd spent with her was the longest I'd gone without thinking about the mess my life currently was, and there was no way I was going to risk coming on too strong and scaring her off.

When she looked at me with those big dark eyes, all the radio static in my head faded away.

I scrolled back through my contacts and hit call when I found my brother's name.

"What up, dogggg?" Floyd drawled.

I rolled my eyes at his greeting. "There's something missing in your brain."

My brother wasn't actually as stupid as we all joked, neither of the twins were, but Floyd had petrol running in his veins and Louis had probably taken one too many knocks to the head, so at times, they really seemed like the meatheads I made them out to be.

"I'm sure you didn't call up just to insult me, so why don't you tell me what's on your mind, honey bun?"

I supressed a laugh.

"Well, *sugar fairy*, the battery on my car is fucked; you think you could do me a favour and fly on over here with a new one?"

None of us ever paid for stuff that had anything to do with cars. Floyd had a bunch of stores filled with beefed-up guys on steroids who practically jerked off anytime he set foot inside their doors. He could get anything he wanted, and they were just about paying him to take it off their hands. That's if he didn't already have it lying around the garage he had on his property. The thing was huge, probably bigger than my whole apartment building.

"You're a real inconvenience, you know that? I have a date tonight and I need to wash my hair."

"Stop being a girl and get over here."

"I'm telling Charlotte you said that." He chuckled.

"Go for it, she's still pissed with me anyway. What's another week of the silent treatment?"

My sister was furious with me, and it wasn't as though she didn't have good reason, but I was over it and it was about time she caught up. I missed talking to her.

"Ohhhh yeah, I forgot the golden boy had gotten himself into a spot of bother. I always told you Han was trouble, bro."

"And I always told *you*, and you know this as well as I do, that guys like us seem to have a way of attracting trouble."

"Speak for yourself. I'm not sure I want to be tarred with the same brush as you."

"*Unlikely*, you're the most troubled individual I've ever met."

"Me? *No...*" he replied as though the idea was ludicrous. "You must be thinking of my twin... tall guy, real handsome, not so bright?"

"We could literally do this *all* day," I deadpanned. "If you seriously have a date and need to paint your toenails or whatever, I can call Louis, see if he'll run down to Frank's and pretend to be you long enough to get me my battery."

He groaned. "Fuck *that* for a laugh. The last time I sent him down there he made me look like an *idiot*. What kind of halfwit doesn't know the difference between a V6 and a V8 engine for Christ's sake, and besides I've got about a hundred of the things lying around down here."

"So, you'll be here in about an hour then?"

He snorted in amusement. "An hour? I could be two towns over in an hour – I'll see you in twenty."

"Don't go breaking the law on my account," I drawled, already expecting nothing less.

Floyd always seemed to be racing an invisible clock wherever he went – that, or he was running from something. I wasn't sure if the guy was even capable of driving the speed limit anymore.

"Don't worry, mum, I'll wear my belt."

———

"You did something stupid, am I right?"

I raised a brow at him as he watched me switching out the battery in my SUV.

"Not by your standards." I smirked.

"I only get into trouble when a woman's involved." He chuckled. "I'm squeaky clean."

I chuckled. None of us were squeaky clean, that was for damn sure – but least of all Floyd.

"Oh yeah, a girl turned you into a getaway driver, did she?"

"Hey, hey, hey..." He held his hands up in surrender. "We're talking about you, not me... but since you brought up a woman, what's her name?"

I shook my head in amusement. "*You* brought up women."

"I'm not wrong though, am I?"

"I can assure you, I'm not in *any* trouble when it comes to a woman."

He raised his brows at me.

"Alright, correction, I'm not in any more trouble in regard to a woman than I was last week."

I'd gotten myself into somewhat of a sticky situation with my little sister Charlotte's best friend. I hadn't slept with her or anything, but I'd gone behind my sister's back, in what was probably a stupid decision, and I'd even managed to make a fool out of myself by telling Hannah how I felt about her.

I'd had feelings for her on and off for a long time, but I'd never acted on them until the spur of the moment, idiot choice I'd made... and now regretted.

She was married now, and obviously not to me.

I was okay with it, when I really thought about everything. Hannah was happy, and I knew I'd get over it. She wasn't 'the one' for me – if that concept even existed in my mind.

All I was worried about now was the wrath of Mrs. Charlotte Sloan. My sister could be a real hard ass when she wanted to be.

Floyd tsked at me in mock disappointment. "You know, it's a real wonder Lou and I turned out as good as we did with you as our role model."

I snorted in disagreement. "Oh yeah, you're a real upstanding citizen."

He worked away in silence for a moment, pissing around under my hood with God only knows what –

but as per usual, where Floyd was concerned, it didn't last long.

"So, what's on your mind, precious?"

He was a total pain in the ass, but he had my back, always. He could read me like a book too, it was a total inconvenience most of the time, but I appreciated that he cared enough to notice the small changes in my behaviour.

"I just don't like being out-done... and I was well and truly screwed over by this Armageddon dude, you know, the one Jasper hired to help him find Hannah?"

He nodded in recognition.

"I don't know who the guy is, but the whole thing reeks of a personal attack, and hell will freeze over before I'm going to let that slide."

He rubbed his hands together in excitement. "I feel a revenge plan hatching."

I chuckled. "I got his address. I went round there."

"That's next level." He joined me in laughter. "Even by *my* standards."

Bullshit.

"If I was anywhere near *your* standards, the building wouldn't still be standing."

"You drop a place once, and no one *ever* lets it go," he grumbled to himself with a roll of his eyes.

I chuckled as he slammed the bonnet shut.

"So, you find him?" he asked.

"*Nope.*" I shook my head. "Stayed there all night,

then decided it was a stupid plan since I don't have a clue who he is, *then* discovered I'd run my battery flat and had to get a jump start from what might be the sexiest woman I've ever seen."

"I'm not one to say I told you so, but I freakin' *told you* there was a woman."

"Trust me, man, she's not the issue... the only problem I had with her was that I wanted to toss her over my shoulder and take her home to bed."

"So, do it."

"What if it's the guy's sister, or his fuck buddy, or his daughter or some shit?"

"Two birds with one stone." He smirked, mirroring my less than moral thoughts from earlier in the day.

I shook my head. "I dunno, man, what if I like her? Then what? What if it actually goes somewhere and then I find out her brother has it in for me?"

He shrugged and leaned against his car door. "Grow a pair and ask her."

"I can't just come out and *ask* her if she knows a mastermind hacker. Then I'd have to tell her that I went to the building she lives in with the intention of finding the dude and doing I don't even know what to him when I did."

"So instead, you want to date the chick, have her fall in love with you, and then potentially find out her old man or whatever is out to get you? Good plan, jackass. He can walk her down the aisle and then punch you in the face."

He had a valid point, for once.

I strummed my fingers on the hood of my car. "Maybe I'll ask her out... sniff around a bit... find out if she lives alone or has any family in the area... that should give me something to go on."

"Not just a pretty face after all, are ya, cupcake?" He winked before pushing off the side of the hundred-thousand-dollar car he'd driven over here in. "I gotta go."

"Who's the hot date?"

"Wouldn't you like to know."

"Don't forget to wrap it, man; I don't know how the fuck you haven't got an illegitimate child out there somewhere."

He smirked and joked, "Who says I don't?"

"Double wrap it," I warned him as he slid into the driver's seat. "And thanks!"

He threw me a hang loose hand gesture – a common thing between us – before throwing the car into reverse and tearing off backwards. He then ripped the handbrake, swung the car around and went screaming off down the street.

I chuckled. The crazy bastard sure knew how to make a scene.

CHAPTER 6

Amarah

TYLER: **Hey… are you free for dinner tomorrow night? I want to take you out.**

I couldn't help the smile that broke out on my face when I read his message. I hadn't stopped thinking about our exchange. I'd been hoping I'd hear from him – whilst simultaneously knowing that life would be much simpler if I never heard from or saw that man again.

Amarah: Same day text, huh… you're awfully eager.

Tyler: You've got no idea. I've had itchy thumbs since the moment I walked in the

door. It shows real restraint that I've waited this long.

Amarah: I don't even want to know where your thumbs have been, thank you very much.

I rolled over on my bed and twisted my hair out of the way as I waited for him to respond. It didn't take long.

Tyler: I can't think of a witty reply, and you still haven't given me an answer…

I was going to say yes – I already knew that. After all, curiosity killed the cat, and I may as well have been meowing at this point.

Amarah: Sorry… memory like a gold-fish, what was the question?

Tyler: Ha. Ha. *sarcasm*… dinner tomorrow night? You know you want to.

I chewed on my lip as I thought of a way to stall. I was going in blind here and that was scary. All I knew about the guy – the *real* guy – not the man behind the screen, was that he was insanely good looking, and that was only going to be a problem, if anything.

Amarah: Ohhhh yeah, hmm, I don't know… it's kind of like stranger danger… I think I need 3 fun facts so we're not strangers anymore.

It didn't take him anywhere near as long as I'd

thought it might; his message came through after only a couple of minutes.

Tyler:

1. I read a newspaper from back to front.

2. My favourite part of a pizza is the crust.

3. I prefer cats over dogs.

I laughed as I read his reply. He was a seriously troubled individual by the sounds of this. I didn't know who in their right mind read something back to front, but I was going to find out.

Amarah: All these things disturb me greatly, I'm not so sure it'll work out after all, sorry.

Tyler: Only one way to find out. I'll pick you up at 6?

Amarah: What are we, 80 years old? Do you have to be home by 9? Make it at least 7.

I realised my mistake at the same moment his message came through. I'd just said yes without saying yes.

Tyler: Me and my saggy old man balls got you to agree to go though, didn't I…

Amarah: Touché. Well played, Mr. Watson, well played.

Credit where credit was due, he'd got me to agree

to this wild idea. And as stupid as I knew it was, I was already looking forward to it.

Tyler: Why thank you, and 7pm it is.
P.S. Cats rule.

I smirked as I typed my response.

Amarah: You do strike me as the kind of guy who appreciates a good pussy.

Tyler: I knew you were a smart girl. Your turn… I want 3 facts as well.

I thought for a minute about what I wanted to say. 'I'm your sworn enemy' came to mind, but I was fairly sure he already knew that, so I decided to leave it out. I could play the game.

Amarah:
1. When I eat ice-cream, I bite a hole in the bottom of the cone and suck the ice-cream through it.
2. I read things from front to back (shock horror).
3. I love cheesy pick-up lines.

I grinned as I read his speedy reply.

Tyler: You were right, this won't work out. Well, it was good while it lasted…

Amarah: Your sarcasm wounds me. You know they say it's the lowest form of humour, right?

**Tyler: I'll have to kiss it better then, won't I? (how was that for a cheesy pick-up

line?) and knock sarcasm all you want; I'm still going to use it. Sweet dreams, Amarah, I'll see you tomorrow – at 7, not 6.

I caught myself smiling at my phone and cursed myself.

I wasn't supposed to actually like the guy – *that* was not part of the little plan I was putting into motion here.

I had to admit though, he had surprised me. I didn't expect him to seem so... *warm.* He was funny, and I'd always been a sucker for a man with a sense of humour. It was becoming apparent he was going to be a hard guy to dislike, and that was going to be a problem – I could see that fact coming a mile away.

———

6.55pm

I glanced at myself one last time in the mirror and slung my bag over my shoulder.

Here goes nothing.

I hadn't told him which door to knock on, so I headed down to the front of the building where I'd first met him to wait.

It wouldn't have surprised me if he knew everything about my apartment, probably even which wall my bed was against, let alone something as straight forward as the number on the door, but if he didn't, and I could keep him away from here, for now at least, then I was going to. I was keen to prolong the inevitable in this particular situation.

The elevator door opened, and my breath caught in my throat.

There he is.

He was leaning against the hood of his car; in the very same spot he was parked yesterday.

His face broke out into a grin as he spotted me through the glass door, and as I pushed it open the breath got knocked clean out of me.

He was *so* gorgeous.

He glanced up and down the street before jogging across to meet me. I don't know when jogging became hot, but that was the situation I was dealing with.

Pull yourself together, woman.

I forced my legs to carry me forward, all the while trying to convince myself I *could* do this – I could dig around for info, try to figure out his game plan and *not* catch any feelings.

I've got this.

"*Amarah*," he said softly as he approached, his eyes never once leaving my face – no small feat for a straight man, especially considering the length of the dress I was currently wearing.

My mother had always told me 'dress to kill, and never assume you'll have to do anything less', so that's what I did. I dressed to impress, and I was always prepared for anything.

I took a deep, steadying breath and finally met his eyes, now that they weren't hiding behind his glasses.

Well damn.

They were the most beautiful shade of blue. In fact, he probably had the most amazing eyes I'd ever seen without the aid of photoshop.

If I wasn't already a total sucker for this man's looks, I would have been sunk after seeing those.

"Tyler Watson... two visits in as many days, what brings you here?" I teased, desperately trying to distract myself from the deep pools of blue.

"I'm here for a hot date." He smirked.

I glanced around for show. "Oh really? What's his name?" I grinned.

He glanced at his watch with a frown. "Big Brucey, and he's late."

I had to laugh at that.

Damn him.

"You look *incredible*," he breathed, his eyes finally raking over my entire body.

I wasn't usually the kind of girl to blush, but I was damn well blushing scarlet now.

His words were filled with such sincerity and truth that it was hard to believe he was here for anything other than to take me out to a nice dinner.

There was all this... *energy* between us that I couldn't explain.

"Thank you."

"What, no witty remark?" he questioned with a grin.

"Not this time. Now, *desperate flat battery guy*, are we getting out of here or what?"

"Be rude not to, I'm all dressed up and looking good."

"I mean, you look *alright*," I teased.

He looked a heck of a lot more than alright. He looked good enough to eat.

His navy button-down shirt set off his incredible eyes, and I was willing to bet that the dark jeans he had on clung to his ass in all the right places.

He chuckled. "I'll take it. Something tells me 'alright' is a compliment when it comes from you."

He wasn't far off the truth. I liked to keep my cards close to my chest, but he was testing my willpower, and that was a real problem.

He held his hand out to me, and I took it more than willingly like the total idiot I was proving myself to be.

CHAPTER 7

Tyler

"I'VE GOT to be honest; I didn't picture you for a Mexican food kinda guy."

I smirked at her and held out the chair for her to sit down.

I slung my thumb over my shoulder. "I'm not, but the basic white guy place down the street was all full up tonight."

She nodded in understanding, an amused smirk on her face. "Ahh... it's all making sense." Her eyes sparkled with mischief and made me think all kinds of wicked shit. Things like bending her over and pounding into her... things like staring into those eyes as I made her come.

I'd *never* experienced chemistry like this.

Amarah was entirely captivating. She had one hundred percent of my focus and attention just purely by existing.

This had never happened to me before – not like this – not this type of all-consuming attraction.

Normally, no matter what I was doing, I was multitasking.

I'd be in the supermarket whilst thinking about writing code, or how I was going to find my way into someone's system... but not with her.

All I could think about was the woman in front of me.

I didn't know what was happening to me, but I liked it. I was living for it.

This was a thrill, every time she smiled, or rubbed her lips together, or laughed, a bolt of warmth and excitement shot through me. Our connection had caught me totally off guard, but it was electrifying.

I still needed to confirm she wasn't in cahoots with the enemy, and as soon as I knew that for sure, everything would be perfect.

I'd long forgotten about revenge and ulterior motives at this point anyway – I wasn't thinking of *anything* but her.

I just wanted to enjoy my evening with this beautiful woman. Hell, she could have been best friends with my sworn enemy, and I probably still wouldn't have been willing to give her up.

She had me all kinds of fucked.

The waiter came and took our drink order and then we were left alone again.

"So, what do you do for a job?"

I didn't miss the momentary freeze of her whole body. It was only for a fraction of a second, but it was enough that I started to worry.

In my experience, there were only a handful of professions that would make a woman still in panic like that when asked what they did for a job.

I wasn't a particularly judgey sort of dude, but if she was a stripper or escort or some shit, we were probably going to have problems getting this thing off the ground.

When it comes to women, I don't share. No exceptions. No discussion. I'm hers and she's mine and everyone else can get fucked, as far as I'm concerned.

Each to their own, but I've always been of the solid belief that if you're not satisfied by what you already have, then you're probably doing something wrong. Power to the people who it works for, but that's not me.

She cleared her throat. "I build websites, you know, for businesses and stuff... online stores... that kinda thing..." Amarah answered, pulling me from my fucked-up conclusions, which low and behold, were wrong.

Not at all what I was expecting her to say.

"Really? That's cool. I sort of work in the same field."

I was surprised by her answer, and that surprise wasn't unpleasant, especially not when being compared to the possibility of her being a hooker.

"Yeah?" she questioned; her brow cocked.

"I'm a computer programmer."

She sipped her drink and eyed me up and down almost as though she was confused by my answer.

"*What?*" I asked curiously. Not many people really grasped what a computer programmer was, even some of my close mates assumed I was a glorified IT guy, but that was cool. Even 'computer programmer' wasn't really all that accurate, but 'hacker' didn't have the best ring to it. And besides, most of what I did these days was above board.

"Nothing," she answered with a smile. "I would have guessed you were a personal trainer or something. You're in pretty good shape for someone who sits behind a desk all day."

I chuckled and dipped my head to avoid her seeing how her words affected me.

I *was* in good shape. It was no secret.

I worked hard for this body.

Any chance I got, I was outside, pushing it to its limits or in the gym, hitting it hard, but running was my preference – the fresh air helped me think clearly.

That was the biggest downside to the job I had. I was stuck behind a screen, indoors, all the god damn time.

I was a lot like my brothers in the respect that I

liked to get out into the great outdoors. We all needed fresh air to keep our heads on straight and we all needed some type of release to keep from going crazy.

"Don't go getting all embarrassed on me now, hot shot." She smirked. "You've had this *confident, bordering-on-cocky* act perfected."

I cleared my throat and chuckled. "You know how to make a guy blush."

She eyed me as she took another drink, her eyes sparkling with what I was confident was excitement.

"You don't exactly look like someone who sits behind a computer all day either," I pointed out.

"I run, remember?" She raised her brows at me. "I was all set to go when you sabotaged your car to get a date."

I chuckled. "Scout's honour... the battery was buggered. I had to get my brother to bring over another one."

"So, you've got a brother?" she asked, her head tilting to the side.

"I wish it was just the one." I shook my head in mock outrage.

She raised her brows at me in confusion.

"I've got twin, batshit crazy, younger brothers," I offered. "And one sister – she's the baby of the family."

"You're the oldest?"

I nodded my head. "I am indeed."

"Twin brothers, huh?" She smiled in amusement. "I bet that was a handful to grow up with."

She was dead right. They were *more* than a handful. And given the fact that I practically raised my younger siblings half the time, I knew exactly just how much hard work they really were.

Those boys got themselves into sticky situation after sticky situation, and I was the one there to pick up the pieces and get them the hell out of it.

I could look back on it fondly now that they were old enough and financially well off enough to get themselves out of trouble – for the most part anyway.

"You have no idea." I laughed. "They're not just twin boys, they're daredevils too. One is a stunt driver and professional racer, and the other is a professional boxer. It's a deadly mix of too much adrenaline and not enough common sense."

She giggled. "That sounds like a whole lot of testosterone."

"I promise you; you've never seen anything like it."

"And your sister, where does she fit into this boys' club?"

"She's the total opposite of us. She's tiny, sweet, and feminine."

She smiled at me coyly. "I think you might be sweet too, Tyler Watson. You don't fool me."

I didn't answer, just watched her for a long moment. I enjoyed the way she made me feel. I enjoyed it far too much for two virtual strangers.

"Tell me about her," she prompted.

"My sister?"

She nodded.

"Her name's Charlotte... you actually might have heard of her... she's married to Parker Sloan, you know, the rock star from Exit Strategy..."

Her jaw fell open. "You're shitting me?"

I chuckled. "You've heard of *him* I take it?"

"The whole world has heard of him. *Your* little sister is the woman that tamed *Parker Sloan?*"

"The very one." I grinned.

She blew out a breath. "I'm *seriously* impressed."

"He's a really good guy. I've never seen my sister this happy."

Her eyes widened. "No shit, he's *Parker freaking Sloan.*"

I chuckled. "Remind me never to introduce the two of you, you'll only embarrass yourself."

Her hand snaked across the table and gripped mine. "Are you telling me there's a possibility I'd get to meet him if I keep seeing you?" She grinned, and I knew she was only joking, but *fuck*, I wouldn't be above using my brother-in-law as a bartering tool right now.

I wanted to see her again.

And again, and again...

I chuckled and twisted her hand so I could intertwine our fingers together.

"I'm not above blackmail, bribery and corruption, you know." My thumb skated down the side of her palm.

"I wouldn't imagine you are," she replied coyly as

she squeezed my hand. "And you should probably know that I'm not either."

"I'd only be disappointed if you were."

A moment of electricity passed between us. Sexual tension, excitement, possibilities... we were *clicking*, like two pieces made to fit together.

"What about you, do you have any brothers or sisters?" I pried.

"Nope," she replied simply. "It's just my mum, dad and me."

"Where are your folks?" I asked, hoping I sounded casual about the question, when in reality, I was hanging off her every word.

"Spain... that's where they're from. I moved back here about six years ago."

"Followed a man?" I questioned.

She snorted a laugh. "Do I strike you as the kind of woman who would chase a man across the world?"

Fuck no.

"You strike me as the kind of woman who'd do whatever the hell she wanted," I answered her honestly.

"You're a smart man, Tyler Watson, I'll give you that."

———

Tyler: I'm in the clear. Only child, parents live in Spain. No boyfriend, no roommate.

Floyd: Ding, ding, ding! Jackpot, baby… Can I be your best man?

Tyler: You'll have to fight your idiot brother for it.

Floyd: No deal – the big dumb bastard is a pro boxer, remember? I also appreciate your lack of denial for your impending nuptials. It takes a real man to admit he's in luuurrrrvvvve.

Tyler: I take it back, you're the idiot brother. Go play on the road or something.

Floyd: Gladly… peace out, sugar tits, I'll keep an eye on the mailbox for my save the date.

I stuffed my phone back in my pocket as I caught sight of her strolling across the room on her way back from the bathroom.

Jesus.

This woman was seriously beautiful. Those sexy legs were going to be the death of me.

She turned heads as she walked. One poor bastard even got a firm nudge in the ribs from his wife for looking a little bit too long.

I couldn't blame him. She was stunning, and I was the lucky man here with her. *And* I was in the clear – there was no reason I couldn't explore this further.

She smiled as she caught sight of me staring at her as she approached.

"You ready to get out of here?"

"Yeah." She sighed. "*No.*"

I chuckled.

She pouted. "I know we can't stay all night, but I'm not sure I'm ready for tonight to be over just yet."

I reached out for her hand and she held hers out for me to take.

I liked that. I'd always appreciated a woman who knows what she wants.

"You wanna go for a drive?" I asked hopefully, because I wasn't ready to take her home just yet either.

"Sounds perfect."

CHAPTER 8

Amarah

"YOU'RE NOT EVEN GOING to kiss me good-night?" The question flew out of my mouth before I could stop it.

He chuckled and turned around, continuing to walk backwards. "Nope," he replied smugly, "I'm saving that for next time."

"What do you mean *you're saving it?* I might not want another ride around the block if I don't know what I'm in for," I called after him. "There might not be a *next time.*"

"You don't fool me, Amarah García. I know how it is with you girls; gotta leave you wanting more." He smirked.

Truth be told, *I* didn't fool me either.

Not even a little bit.

I'd be seeing him again whether I wanted to or not.

"I'll call you," he yelled out to me. "*Soon.*"

I bit down on my lip and watched him as he jogged over to the door of his car and paused to turn back and look at me longingly one more time before jumping in and tearing off down the street with a wave of his hand out the open window.

He wanted to kiss me as badly as I wanted to kiss him. I could see it written all over his face.

Shit.

I hadn't intended to really like him. Not like this.

Hell, I didn't even *want* to like him, but at a certain point in the evening I'd forgotten why I was there. I was just a woman on a date with a man – an incredibly handsome, charming man at that.

He was engaging, witty, smart and sweet.

And he was interested in me.

I went into my building and up the elevator in a daze.

Whether or not that interest was genuine, or if it perhaps came with a hidden agenda, I wasn't sure anymore... For all I knew, this was just a charming act that he was putting on, but it certainly didn't seem that way.

If he was acting with me right now, then he was in the wrong profession.

That was the other thing that had caught me off guard. He hadn't gone into much detail, but when he said he was a computer programmer, I was shocked he had shared that information with me.

The guy was either totally clueless, or an absolute mastermind, and it terrified me that I couldn't figure out which of the two it was.

I didn't like the fact that I'd lied to him either.

It wasn't a *total* lie per se, but it sure as hell wasn't the whole truth, and that didn't sit too well with my morals.

Sure, I designed websites *sometimes*, but usually only as a means to an end.

The sites I designed were usually made to trap someone, or to get the information I needed for a client, but he didn't need to know that.

One thing I *was* going to have to do now was make a bunch of fake websites, just in case Tyler decided to look up my 'work'. I rolled my eyes as I thought about all the sites I was going to have to build, just to keep up appearances.

As if I don't already have enough to do.

I thought about the past hour as I walked down the hall and unlocked my door.

We'd just driven around, going nowhere in particular, but I'd enjoyed every second of it far more than I should have.

Tyler told me more about his brothers and sister, and I told him more about my family in Spain.

He only once mentioned his parents and it wasn't with fondness, so I wasn't about to push it and ask anything more. It seemed like the only family he needed was his siblings. He talked about them with love in his voice and light in his eyes. I'm not sure he even knew he was doing it, but it was obvious he loved them a lot. He seemed more like a parent talking about his kids than an older brother talking about his younger siblings.

We talked about everything and nothing.

It was the most fun I'd had in a long time.

I wasn't the girl who had a lot of friends, or people to talk to, but I felt comfortable with him right away – I already felt like I could tell him anything.

Anything except my *one* dirty secret.

I shut the door to my apartment behind me and leaned against the door, my heart still racing as I closed my eyes and thought over everything that had happened this evening.

I didn't know what Tyler Watson had done to me, but I'd *never* felt anything like this before.

"Well, you look like you had *quite* the evening."

My heart leapt and my eyes flew open in panic as my brain registered the voice in the same moment.

"Jessie, what the hell?" I clutched my chest as I tried to get the message to my thumping heart that everything was alright – that I wasn't about to be murdered and chopped into pieces in my own home.

"I let myself in," she replied casually from her spot on the couch.

She was flicking through a magazine and had an open bottle of wine next to her. She'd clearly made herself right at home.

"I can see that." I pushed off the door and crossed the room to join her. "You could have given me a heads up. I almost went into cardiac arrest."

"I hope you weren't this dramatic on your date; you'll scare him off."

I scowled at her and grabbed the wine. Apparently, she was drinking it straight from the bottle. I took a swig and winced as the red wine hit my taste buds. I tried to be an adult, I really did, but me and red wine had never really seen eye to eye. Room temperature liquid was a bizarre concept as far as I was concerned.

"So, what if I *did* scare him off?"

I was confident that the real events were quite the opposite, but I could mess with her for a bit. A girl had to have her fun.

She dropped the magazine and pinned me with her stare, those big golden eyes narrowing at me. "You better not have. You haven't had a boyfriend in *forever*. You need sex. Sex is good."

"Who said I don't have sex? I have Tinder, remember?"

She rolled her eyes and took the wine from me. "You hate Tinder and we both know it. In fact, I seem to recall you telling me it was a 'meat market' that made you want to puke... and stop changing the subject. I want to hear about your date."

My date. Where do I start?

"It was the best date I've ever been on in my entire life," I admitted with a defeated sigh.

She made an excited face before frowning. "Wait, why do you say that like it's a bad thing?"

I closed my eyes and dropped my head back with a groan.

She offered me the bottle and I took it, swigging back another horrendous mouthful.

"It's bad, because he's not just *some guy* I met."

She raised her brows at me, willing me to continue. I'd refrained from telling her this part of the story, out of worry that she'd think I was a terrible human.

"He's *the* guy. The one who I've been screwing with online. The universe hates me."

Her mouth formed an 'o'.

I nodded. "Exactly."

"How? *Why?*" She frowned, looking as confused as I felt. "I don't understand."

I ran my hands through my hair. "I don't know. I didn't know it was him when I met him, he was just hot as hell and outside my apartment and we connected. But it's *him*, Jess, *and* he was here, which means he knew where to find me... and I told myself I could go out with him to try and give me the edge, but I'm having feelings already. I never thought I'd really like the guy... and I don't know if he's playing me or if he really doesn't know who I am." The words came out in a jumbled, breathless rush.

"You need to calm down," she insisted. "But that's a lot."

"No shit," I exclaimed. "But I *like* him, Jessie. I

like him and I don't know if he knows who I am, and I don't know what to do now."

She took another drink from the bottle and tipped her head from side to side as she thought about it. "I think you just keep seeing him."

"But –"

"I wasn't done." She raised a brow at me in warning.

I huffed out a laugh. "*Sorry*. By all means, continue."

"I think you keep seeing him. Worst case, he's messing with you and maybe you have some hot revenge sex with a gorgeous man, and *best* case, he has no idea and you live happily ever after and have lots of pretty babies." She smiled at her own suggestion.

"You have a wild imagination."

"Untrue. It's basically all facts."

"Things can't be 'basically facts' they're either facts or they're not facts. End of story."

"Pffft." She waved away my logic with her hand.

"I love you to death, Jessie, but you're an absolute lunatic."

"Love you too, baby girl," she replied as she picked up her magazine again.

"Is that seriously all the advice I'm going to get out of you? 'Keep seeing him' and 'see what happens', that's all you've got?"

"You tell me," she murmured absently, "pretty sure we both know you're going to keep seeing him no matter what I say. You've got hearts in your eyes for God's sake."

"I might not... and there are *not* hearts in my eyes."

She paused from flicking the glossy pages for a minute. "I've never seen you look the way you do since you walked in that door. You're seeing him again. *That* is a fact."

I inhaled deeply. As much as I hated to admit it, she was right in this instance. It *was* a fact.

———

"When you said you'd call soon, I didn't think you meant quite *this* soon." I giggled as I climbed under my covers.

"You'll learn that I'm nothing if not literal." He chuckled, and the sound made me smile.

I didn't know what to say to that.

I hoped I'd get to learn a lot of things about him, but I needed to remember this wasn't as simple as girl meets boy.

This was some kind of twisted revenge attempt. This was a game. This was war.

I have to be careful.

It was tough though. He didn't seem like he was out to get me anywhere other than into his bed, maybe even into his life.

It was hard to keep your guard up with a man like Tyler knocking on the other side. I had a wall, what

I'd thought was a huge, impenetrable wall, and he was already making it crumble.

"What are you doing for lunch tomorrow?"

"You asking me out again already, Watson?"

"I'd ask you out again tonight if I could."

"That's awfully forward of you. I hope you don't scare me off," I teased.

"Something tells me you don't scare too easy, Amarah."

I almost sighed at the mention of my name in his sexy voice. I loved the way he made it sound.

I debated putting him off and playing a little bit hard to get, but I had a sinking feeling that where Tyler Watson was concerned, I was going to be incredibly easy to get.

"I don't have plans," I replied, my tone shy.

"You do now," he replied. "You want to meet me down at *The Blade?* You know, that spot down the beach?"

"I know it."

"Half twelve?" he suggested.

"Sounds great," I replied, trying desperately to keep my excitement about seeing him again under wraps.

"That'll get you another date under your belt."

"One step closer to getting to meet your famous family." I laughed.

"Whatever gets you there, baby, I'd let you use me any day of the week." I could hear the smile in his voice as he replied.

A nervous giggle escaped my mouth.

I didn't know if I was more caught off guard with his term of endearment, or the fact that I *was* using him, and he just didn't know it. That's what I was telling myself anyway, not that I was sure by any means about him being in the dark.

"I'll see you tomorrow?"

"You will," I half whispered. "Goodnight."

"Sweet dreams, Amarah," he said before the line went dead.

"Oh *God.*" I rolled over and buried my face in my pillow.

I was so utterly screwed.

CHAPTER 9

Tyler

WORK HAD NEVER interested me less.

Not even the idea of trying to lure out Armageddon could hold my concentration this morning.

My mind was already on a beach somewhere with a beautiful brunette by my side.

I was beyond intrigued by this girl, and that wasn't a normal reaction for me. I wanted to know everything there was to know about the exotic beauty who had fallen into my life.

My fingers hovered over my keyboard as I contemplated looking up her details. I already knew it was a bad idea. Amarah wasn't someone I wanted to play games with. I wanted to learn about her, *from her*, not from a computer screen or database.

I'd played enough games in my life and they hadn't got me anywhere worth going – not in my personal life anyway.

This needed to be a clean slate I decided. I pulled my hands away from the keys before I got myself into trouble.

My mind wandered back to Hannah and the stupid game I let her drag me into – actually *dragged* was definitely an incorrect statement; I went willingly... ran in headfirst even.

All that resulted from that little experiment was a stomped-on heart and my sister packing a shit with me.

Speaking of my sister, I was done with the silent treatment. I missed her. I missed our chats. I missed hanging out with her and Parker. I wanted my little redhead back.

I grabbed my phone off the desk and hit the number for Charlotte.

It rang over and over.

I huffed out a breath.

She was still ignoring me apparently.

Her voicemail cut in, and I scowled as I waited for the beep.

"Hey, short stuff, it's Tyler, but you know that already since you're still dodging my calls and all... look, can you call me back? I know you're pissed at me, and I'm sorry that I lied to you... I just want to talk to my sister again. Please, call me back. I love you."

I hung up the phone and tossed it on top of a stack of papers.

I knew I was in the wrong, and that's why Charlotte was pissed. I also knew I deserved it, but it had been over a month since Hannah and Jasper had been back home, and she still wouldn't speak to me.

I'd received the message loud and clear.

I *never* should have helped Hannah hide from Jasper... from *everyone*.

I made a mental note to myself that if anyone ever asked me for something that involved me lying to my family, the answer would be no. *Always*.

Hell freaking no.

I needed my family in my life – as crazy as my brothers were, my siblings were everything to me. Our parents were assholes. Charlotte and the boys were all I had.

I had to find a way to get back in my sister's good books, and sooner rather than later.

My phone rang loudly, and I grabbed for it, hopeful that Charlotte had finally decided to return my call.

No such fucking luck.

"What do you want?" I demanded by way of hello.

"Is that any way to greet your favourite brother?"

I rolled my eyes. "Floyd just hooked me up with a

new battery the other day, what have you done for me lately?"

"I'm hurt, bro," Louis replied, doing his best to sound wounded. "Here I was, thinking you'd be interested in coming with us to Exit Strategy in two weeks, thought you might have some much-needed grovelling to do, but since I'm not your favourite... maybe I'll flick the tickets online or something."

I sat up straight, suddenly interested.

"Woah, woah, woah, don't throw the fucking baby out with the bath water, dude."

He chuckled.

"I'm in. And I'm bringing a plus one, so you better have me covered."

"I've got you covered, but you have to say it."

"Say what?" I replied, even though I knew exactly what he was referring to.

"You know, sweet cheeks, *say it.*"

I groaned. One of these days, one of these man-children were going to push my stress levels through the roof and put me in an early grave.

"Fine. You're my favourite. Happy?"

"Told you! Bad luck, boy!" I heard Louis yell out.

"I'll remember this!" I heard Floyd's muffled voice yell from in the background.

"You've gotta up your game, little bro," Louis taunted him.

He was only two minutes older than Floyd, but apparently in the world of twins, a few minutes was cause to irritate your womb mate for the rest of eternity.

"I *created* the fucking game," Floyd argued.

"Can we get back to talking about the concert? I have shit to do today that doesn't involve listening to the two of you talk smack," I interrupted.

I heard them tussling in the background and then a groan before Louis came back on the line.

"So, who's the chick, DB?" DB was short for douche bag – something my charming brothers had been calling me for years.

"None of your god damn business, *that's* who."

He was silent for a beat, and I pinched the bridge of my nose. The absolute last thing I wanted to endure was an interrogation from Louis, but he had all the power and he knew it. I needed those tickets. Amarah was going to flip when I surprised her with them, and since Charlotte wasn't speaking to me, I couldn't go directly to her or Parker to get some. I could have asked Hannah, but I wasn't brave or stupid enough for that.

Dumb and dumber were my best shot.

"You want the tickets or not, Ty?" he taunted, knowing full well that he had me screwed.

I groaned. "Her name is Amarah, she's funny and smart and hot as fuck, and if you or your clone hit on her, I'll kick your ass."

He laughed. "I'd pay good money to see you try. And she can't be that smart, if she's spending time with you and your ugly mug."

I shook my head, exasperated. He was frustrating the fuck out of me, mostly because he was right. I didn't have a shot at beating him when it came to throwing punches – my threat was fairly empty.

"Fine," I drawled. "I'll hack into your server and leak a bunch of dick pics to the media or something."

"Got a big dick, bro," he replied without missing a beat, completely and utterly unfazed. "Do your worst. In fact, you might actually be doing me a favour."

"Just fucking do what you're told, alright? Jesus Christ, the two of you don't ever stop, do you?"

"Can stop when you're dead, Ty, look, I gotta go, but relax, I've got you hooked up and I'm looking forward to meeting this girl. I'll work on my pickup lines. Won't take her long to see she's with the wrong Watson brother."

I didn't even bother answering him, just hung up the phone and slid it into my pocket.

I loved those boys to death, but in small fucking doses.

This particular conversation was worth the mental exhaustion though. I now had concert tickets lined up, and I was going to score some serious brownie points with Amarah because of it.

I glanced at the time and hopped out of my chair. I had somewhere to be, and there was no way I was going to be late.

Just the idea of seeing her was already the highlight of my entire day, being near her was going to lift my entire week.

———

"Tell me I'm your favourite person in the world," I murmured in her ear.

She jumped, not having heard me come up behind her.

I chuckled as she clutched her chest and glared at me. "Fucking hell! That was next level creepy."

I laughed harder. "Sorry, might have played out differently in my head."

She narrowed her eyes further. "I'm not sure how lurking around and breathing down my neck could have played out any differently, but I'll bite anyway. Why would *you* be my favourite person in the world, Tyler Watson?"

I stepped in front of her and reached for her hands, pulling her to her feet. I held back a groan as I took in her outfit. Cut-off denim shorts and a skin-tight singlet. Her long, dark, glossy hair trailed down her back and spilled over her bare shoulders.

Sexiest fucking woman in the world.

"*Tyler?*" she prompted when I didn't answer, her full lips pushing out in a pout. "You okay?"

I groaned, a pained, desperate groan. "Do you have any idea how sexy you are?"

Her brows shot up and her teeth sunk into her bottom lip.

I groaned again. "That's not helping, beautiful."

I forced my eyes from her mouth; it was too easy to imagine doing bad things to her while I looked at that irresistible mouth.

"Good," she murmured as I stepped closer, so our bodies were pressed together.

Her chin lifted so our eyes didn't lose contact for even a fraction of a second. Those big dark pools were so damn beautiful, I could have stared into them forever and it still wouldn't have been long enough.

"What are you doing to me?" I asked as my hand came up to sweep some of the loose, long dark strands of hair behind her ear.

I'd never felt this consumed by *anything* before, let alone *anyone*, but there was something about her I couldn't figure out. This woman had me hook, line and sinker, and the most terrifying part about it was that she wasn't even trying. She was just being herself.

"I think it might be the same thing you're doing to me," she whispered, her voice vulnerable for the first time.

Fuck, I hoped that were true. I wanted her more than I'd ever wanted anything. More than revenge, more than God damn world peace, more than fucking oxygen.

Her hand trailed up my arm. "You said you were saving a kiss for me next time?"

I nodded, her touch doing crazy shit to my self-control.

"It's next time, Watson."

I had grand plans of making our first kiss something epic, but I realised there was nothing more perfect than this moment. The waves crashing behind us, the absolute beauty in my arms... the sizzling chemistry... I couldn't have created a more perfect moment if I'd planned it out on paper.

I gripped the back of her neck and pulled her towards me, closing the gap between our mouths and kissing her, softly at first, and then harder, with a passion that bordered on aggression.

She moaned into my mouth as her grip on my bicep tightened, and I couldn't help the smirk that twitched in the corners of my mouth. It appeared Amarah liked a firm hand.

My dream girl.

I tugged her bottom lip between my teeth and her free hand shot up to clutch my shirt in a death grip.

I groaned against her lips as she gave me back as good as she was getting, our mouths duelling for control in a way that had me hard as a rock in an instant.

My head was so clouded, I wasn't sure who pulled away first, but it was too soon, I knew that much. I couldn't imagine ever getting tired of doing that. Kissing her was like heaven.

"*Shit,*" she whispered, her forehead resting against mine.

"You okay, beautiful?" I questioned smugly as she inhaled deeply, knowing full well that she was struggling with this intense attraction as much as I was.

"Not when you're kissing me like that." Her reply was clouded with ragged breathing.

I chuckled deeply as my head spun. I was all fucked up, and I was okay with it – more than okay, I was embracing it. I should have been wary; Amarah was stealing a piece of my heart already, and I'd only known her all of five minutes. I'd been burned before and I thought I'd built a wall around my heart, but when she was around, that wall crumbled to the ground. One look in those big eyes and I melted.

"Kissing you like *what*, beautiful?" I murmured.

"Like you want to strip me naked and fuck me right here on this beach."

My head fell back as a groan slipped from between my lips. "You can't say shit like that to me right now."

She giggled, and when my eyes met hers again, there was amusement dancing in them.

"You think it's funny to make a man crazy?"

"You were doing the exact same to me and you know it."

I fucking liked the sound of that.

"I was?"

"You know you were. You *love* driving me crazy... tell me I'm wrong," she challenged, her chin lifting ever so slightly. "I'll wait."

A growl left my throat. I fucking *loved* a strong woman. Nothing flicked my switch quite like a woman who could give as good as she got. "This is going to be a battle of wills, and I fucking love it."

She smirked. "At *every* turn, you can count on that."

"Deal," I growled before claiming her mouth again in a kiss that was far too hot for a public place, but I didn't give a shit. I was taking what I could get. I kissed her until all the air was gone from my lungs and I was gasping for breath.

"I think you need to stop that." Her fingers skated across my shoulder, her nails digging in ever so slightly.

Fuck.

"I think you're *wrong*."

She giggled. "There are children around. I don't want to be responsible for giving them a sex education."

I chuckled. "Alright, fair call."

"And besides, I believe I was lured here under the pretence of food. Are you going to feed me or what?"

I had to stop myself from making some crude joke about having something she was welcome to put in her mouth. I was confident Amarah wasn't the sort of girl to get offended by that sort of thing, but I wasn't shooting the shit with my brothers in the garage right now – I was trying to get to know a beautiful woman – the dick jokes and sexual innuendos needed to be introduced at a more appropriate time.

"I think I can manage that."

She searched my eyes once again – I didn't know what she was looking for, but I wasn't complaining – before sighing deeply and stepping away.

I let my arm go with her, before skimming it down her side and taking her hand in mine.

I shook my head in disbelief as I took in her beauty once again.

"What?" she questioned shyly.

"Look at you." I shook my head again. "Just fucking look at you."

A light blush stained her cheeks and her eyes dropped, embarrassed.

"Come on, beautiful, let's eat."

CHAPTER 10

Amarah

THERE WAS nothing quite like the knowledge that just the mere sight of you was making a man die inside.

Tyler made absolutely no secret of the fact that he liked what he saw when he looked at me, and as much as I knew that looks were a superficial element, it was still a nice feeling nonetheless. It made me feel powerful, *sexy*. It gave me a boost of confidence I hadn't realised I needed.

Attraction was obviously important; it was the thing that drew me to him in the first place, and I wasn't about to deny that a physical connection between two people was important, but without that chemistry and connection, it didn't matter how handsome a man was, without a personality, I was never going to be interested.

I liked a man with confidence, but not arrogance. I liked a man who I could laugh with, and I wanted a man who thought I was something special. Tyler was ticking those boxes like he'd seen the list with his own eyes.

There was only one big black mark, and I still hadn't figured out what I was going to do about that.

He was my rival, my enemy, and I was quickly falling in love with him.

I was meant to be playing a game – acting my part, but I wasn't anymore. I hadn't been acting with him at all and it was scaring the shit out of me.

I'd screwed myself royally. Here I was, loving his company, letting my guard down... all the while I had a secret that was likely going to ruin us in the end.

This relationship was doomed, and it hadn't even begun yet.

I knew I either needed to end it, or come clean, which effectively would be ending it anyway. Owning up seemed counterproductive... I'd lose him *and* I'd have exposed myself to a man who could bury me professionally. I had to be smart, but with him looking at me with those brilliant blue eyes, it was *really* hard to be smart.

On paper, we were a perfect match. We had so much in common, we connected on a level I didn't know existed beyond the pages of a romance novel... but out here in the real world – or more specifically, in the digital world, we'd been sworn adversaries for a long time.

Coming clean wasn't something I was willing to do, so that left me only one choice – end things with him. Not something I wanted to do, but a necessary evil.

"You're deep in thought."

I blinked, trying and failing to pull myself from the spell he was casting over me.

I shrugged a shoulder. "Just work stuff."

He scanned my face. I don't know how he did it, but with one look, he seemed to be able to read me like a book. I was going to have a hard time keeping things from this man, that much was obvious.

"Nothing I can't handle," I added more convincingly, even though I was anything but convinced by my ability to handle a single thing right now. I was barely managing not to drool while I looked at him. I'd turned into one of those stupid girls you roll your eyes at in a romcom movie.

Who even am I?

"I doubt there's anything you *can't* handle," he replied, his eyes focused and his tone genuine.

That look made me want to cry in frustration. I'd dated dickhead after dickhead, men who treated me like shit – boys who didn't want to grow up, and here I was, sitting next to the man of my dreams, one who believed in me so quickly, one who I felt like I'd known forever, and there could never be any kind of future.

Karma was a bitch, and she was coming for me hard.

Tyler still could have been playing me himself – a possibility I'd all but ruled out at this point, but I almost wished he was – it would have done wonders for my own guilt.

I had to cut this off. Clean and simple, before I got any more invested than I already was. This was complicated and it was going to get messy if I let it go on any longer.

I opened my mouth to tell him, but I was interrupted by a deep hum in the back of his throat and his hand roughly cupping my jaw.

I was pressed to the ground, my back against the warm sand in the very next second, and his mouth was on mine, moving in a way that was so familiar, yet so new and exciting at the very same time.

I'd thought there wasn't anything much that could top the first kiss we'd shared only an hour or so ago, but I'd been wrong. Having his weight pressed against me while his tongue swept into my mouth was electric. My whole body was humming with awareness and every one of my senses was on high alert.

My hands moved of their own accord, pulling him down harder on top of me. His large frame was much bigger than mine, but I welcomed the extra weight pressing against my rib cage.

The scent of his cologne filled my nostrils, and I felt my eyes roll back in my head. He smelled like heaven. It didn't matter what I did now, I was *never* going to forget that smell.

I bit down on his bottom lip, dragging it roughly into my mouth, and he grunted, his hips flexing in unison with his noises.

I was only lying to myself if I really thought I was going to end things with him right here and now. I didn't have the willpower and I most certainly didn't have the self-control.

He felt too good – he made me feel *too* good.

That was what it really came down to – the way he made *me* feel... the looks he gave me were soul consuming.

"I can't get enough of you," he confessed as he ran the tip of his nose up the length of mine. "I don't know what's going on between us, but it excites me, Amarah."

It excited me too, as much as I didn't want it to.

It excited me so much that I let myself believe for a moment that maybe I wasn't playing with fire here – that maybe I could make something work between the two of us.

That maybe, just maybe, there was a way I could have my cake and eat it too. I knew I was wrong. That *never* worked, but at this point, I was desperate... and I really, *really* liked cake.

———

Tyler: I have a surprise for you.

Amarah: I hate surprises with the fiery passion of one thousand suns.

Tyler: Wow. That's an intense statement.

Amarah: It's an intense hatred.

Tyler: Forget the surprise. I'll just be over here hoping you don't unleash your fury on me. You're scary when you're mad.

Amarah: Don't make me beg, Watson.

Tyler: I could go for some begging if I'm being honest.

Amarah: You just like the idea of me on my knees.

Tyler: You're not wrong.

Amarah: I'm giving you the middle finger right now.

Tyler: I'm visualising it.

Amarah: Just tell me already!

Tyler: I mean, I could…

Amarah: TYLER WATSON, QUIT PLAYING WITH ME.

Tyler: Are you shouting at me already? Imagine how excited you're going to get at the Exit Strategy concert next weekend…

I re-read the text four times before hitting the call button next to his name. He better not have been playing with me, because *no one*, not even Tyler could joke about something this important.

He answered the call with a chuckle. "I thought that might get a reaction out of you."

"You better not be messing with me right now."

"Nope. We're going – if you want to?"

"*If I want to...* are you insane? *Of course* I want to. You seriously have tickets?"

"I sure do, but there's a catch...my brother hooked me up, so both of the twins are going to be there. You think you can handle that?"

"Pfft." I rolled my eyes. "I'd handle a screaming toddler and a raging bull if it meant I got to go to that concert. I tried to get tickets for an hour straight when they released, but I missed out. I'm not going to lie to you, I cried."

I'd even considered hitting up Jasper for a favour, but I'd decided against it. I didn't want him to think I was using him, and I definitely didn't want to risk him finding out who I really was.

"Well lucky for you, I have the insider hook up. It's a date, beautiful. And just so you know, a screaming toddler and a raging bull probably isn't far off the money when it comes to my brothers." He chuckled. "I was meant to tell you at the beach yesterday, but I got distracted by how fucking sexy you are."

If you'd asked me yesterday, I would have told you that Tyler Watson couldn't have got much better, but somehow, he'd just managed it. This was going to earn him some serious brownie points, and as much as it scared me, it also ensured his involvement in my life for another week. He'd already managed to get several more days than he should have through no other means than pure intrigue and sex appeal.

"I think I might love you," I joked, my voice clearly showing my excitement. I wasn't one of those girls who played it cool and coy; if I was excited about something, I said it, and I was excited as hell about this.

He chuckled again. "Well that was easy."

"*Wait*, why didn't you get them from your sister?" I questioned.

"Ummm...." He paused, his tone sheepish. "She's not exactly speaking to me right now."

"Spill, Watson, what'd you do?" I pried.

He groaned. "It's a boring story and one that paints me in an incredibly unflattering light, can we not?"

I sat down and got myself comfortable, something told me this was going to be quite the tale. "You and I both know we're going to discuss this whether you want to or not, so you may as well get started."

I was intrigued by this, I couldn't imagine Tyler doing anything to intentionally hurt or upset his sister. It was obvious he adored her – I imagined that feeling was mutual, so the fact that she wasn't speaking to him, made me think he'd really messed up in some way.

"I fucked up, thought I was helping out a friend, but I hurt Charlotte, and the people she cares about. It was a bad call."

"What's her name?"

"*Her* who?" he replied, confused.

"The 'friend' you were 'helping', who is she?"

"How'd you know it was a girl?"

"This isn't my first rodeo, big guy, and in my experience, when a guy does something stupid it's usually because he's thinking with his little head and not his big one."

He huffed out a laugh. "You think you've got me all figured out, huh?"

"Am I wrong?" I pried, already knowing I wasn't.

"Hannah," he answered after a few beats. "Her name is Hannah, and we're friends, well we *were* friends. I don't know what we are now."

My heart thudded in my chest. I don't know why I hadn't thought about this sooner. *Of course* Charlotte was mad at him for *this*.

"You wanted more?" I managed to get the question that I already knew the answer to, out, in a semi-normal tone.

He cleared his throat. "Yeah, I mean... I thought there might have been something there, but she's in love with Jasper and –"

"Hold up, Jasper Jones?" I interrupted him, playing along, but also desperately hoping I had it wrong and there was a different Hannah – a different situation that had nothing to do with me.

"Jasper Jones," he confirmed.

I shook my head, trying to make my voice level and even. "No offence, but you never stood a chance,

Watson. I've seen the way he talks about her in interviews. They're end game."

It was lucky we weren't having this conversation in person, because the shock on my face right now would have given me away for sure.

"Even got the wedding bands and bun in the oven to prove it."

I gaped. "Seriously?"

Now *this* was news to me.

I felt like a proud parent. I'd helped Jasper find Hannah and he'd gotten the girl after all. I just hadn't really considered the fact that Tyler had been so invested in Hannah. I knew he'd gone there to see her, that he'd had feelings for her; I guess I hadn't thought too much about how it related to the situation I currently found myself in.

I'd taken that job from Jasper partly because I could tell he was desperate and partly because I wanted the opportunity to beat Tyler when he least expected it. But I'd failed to think about the fact that I was now dating a man who had feelings for another woman. In my mind, that element of Jasper's story was entirely separate from me and the Tyler I knew, and I cursed myself for being so short sighted.

"*Shit,*" he muttered. "You didn't hear that from me. If the tabloids get a hold of that, Jasper will lose his shit. I don't know what it is about you, but I can't keep *anything* a secret when I'm talking to you."

A burst of butterflies followed quickly by a pang of guilt, hit me directly in the stomach.

I wished I could say the same to him.

I wished I could tell if he was being genuine.

I wished for a lot of things in this moment, but nothing more than I wished that we weren't both who we really were.

"Long story short, Han freaked and ran. She's kind of a head case, but whatever," he continued, oblivious to my inner turmoil, "she needed help to disappear, obviously money is no issue for guys like Jasper and Parker, and she knew that if she didn't get some help, they'd find her in about thirty seconds."

I focused on keeping my breathing even. I already knew about this. I was involved in this. I couldn't believe it, even though it should have been obvious. The reason his sister was mad with him, was because of *this*. I mean, it was fair enough, but I was still in disbelief.

"Why'd she want to hide?" I managed to ask the one question that had been bugging me from the moment I'd taken Jasper on as a client.

I could hear him moving around in the background. "The thing with Hannah is that she doesn't have the most confidence in the world. She overthinks and doubts herself. She knows Jasper loves her, but she's used to people that love her leaving her. I guess she just wanted to be sure."

"Seems like a kinda shitty thing to do to someone you love."

"Yeah. I guess it is, but if you know her and

understand her, you can see it comes from a place of self-preservation, not malice."

I felt oddly jealous listening to him talk about Hannah. It was obvious he cared a lot about this girl, and that bothered me. I wasn't a naturally jealous person, but Tyler was bringing out reactions in me that I wasn't accustomed to feeling.

I didn't like feeling jealous, envy-green was not a colour that looked good on me, but here I was, feeling that way regardless.

"It sounds like the two of you are close," I pried.

"Yeah... I mean... I *dunno*. I haven't talked to her in over a month. I guess I'll probably see her at the concert."

I wasn't sure how I felt about that either. I already thought the woman was a bit of a dick for the way she'd treated Jasper; he seemed like a really cool dude, and now that I knew the man I was dreaming about at night had been – maybe still was – in love with her, I liked her even less.

I wasn't usually so petty, and I was a big believer in things turning out the way they were meant to, so Tyler obviously wasn't destined to be with Hannah, but that didn't mean I wanted to feel like second best – even if I had much bigger problems to deal with than that.

Like the fact that I'm his secret enemy.

I needed to remember what I was – what *we* were. It was starting to become too easy to fall into whatever this was with Tyler, I had to try and keep some semblance of a guard up, or I was going to end up hurt... we both were.

"Amarah?" Tyler questioned.

I realised at the mention of my name that I'd fallen silent. "I'm here, sorry. Do you think things will be awkward between you two?"

"I'm pretty sure it's going to be awkward all round. Charlotte is pissed, Parker will be pissed purely because she's pissed, Jasper probably wants to knock my teeth in, and I bet Hannah feels sorry for me. You sure you still want to come?" he asked with a nervous chuckle. His laugh didn't fool me. He might have been trying to make light of the situation, but he was worried.

"You sure come with a lot of baggage," I teased.

"Tell me about it."

"I'll be there if you want me to be," I told him sincerely.

"I honestly couldn't think of anyone else I'd rather have standing next to me."

I bit down on my bottom lip, the genuine tone in his voice erasing my jealously, insecurities and my fears – for the moment at least.

"Then it's a date," I replied softly. "And your sister will get over it. I'm sure she loves you, no matter how much you piss her off."

"I hope so."

I didn't need to hope, I already knew she'd come around. It was becoming harder by the second *not* to love him. His sister didn't stand a chance.

CHAPTER 11

Tyler

I WAS GOING to reach out one more time, and if that didn't work, I was going to corner my sister at this concert and force her to talk to me.

She could yell at me if she wanted to, not that making a scene was really her style, but I would take it on the chin. I'd fucked up. I knew that. I owned it. I'd take whatever she had to say. Hell, I'd take *anything* over this silent treatment.

I couldn't handle the phone ringing and ringing again, so I decided to text her instead. That way, she could mull it over, think about what she wanted to say, and then hopefully reply for the first time in over a month.

Tyler: Hey, sis, I miss you. I don't know

if the boys told you, but I'm coming to the concert tomorrow night. I'm bringing someone with me, her name is Amarah and she's... important. I love you. Ty.

I couldn't think of a better word to describe Amarah other than *important*. In such a short time, she'd become one of the main focal points of my life. I went to sleep at night with her on my mind and woke up the same way.

Work had been absolutely mental for both of us this past week, and I'd only managed to see her for a quick coffee date a couple of days ago, but we'd talked on the phone every night as I lay in my bed, my exhausted brain fighting sleep so I could communicate with her for a few minutes longer. I missed her – which made no sense given that a month ago, I didn't even know her.

We talked about everything and nothing, and it calmed my soul in a way that nothing else ever had. Bantering back and forth about complete nonsense was way more fun than it should have been when it was her voice on the other end of the line. I had a pretty good idea that I could have sat next to that woman in total silence, and it still would have been the highlight of my week.

I had it *bad*. I was smitten and I was fully willing to admit that.

I had it so bad that I didn't even have it in me to go after Armageddon right now. I'd all but given up on that rivalry, and oddly enough, I hadn't seen so much as a glimpse of his online presence. No attacks on my servers. *Nothing*.

It was peaceful, but I was aware it was a ticking time bomb. We had beef, and that wasn't just going to disappear. We needed to end this thing, one way or another, but right now, I didn't have the patience or the desire to fight.

I was more interested in sorting shit out with my sister and spending time with my girl. Revenge could wait. I had nothing but time.

My phone beeped with a new message, and I just about dropped it, I was so surprised to see Charlotte's name on the screen.

Charlotte: You're seeing someone?

I didn't want to count my chickens before they hatched, but it was hard not to get excited when this was the first form of communication I'd had with her in nearly six weeks.

Tyler: Yeah, it's new, but it's exciting. She's beautiful and sweet. I already know you'll love her.

Charlotte: I can't wait to meet her.

I grinned. It might not have been much, and I knew Charlotte well enough to know that that was all I was going to get out of her for now, but I was so grateful to get a reply at all. Radio silence sucked.

Amarah might not have done anything directly, but she'd just scored herself another point in my book. Charlotte was a sucker for romance, and I was fully prepared to use that to my advantage if I had to.

I was okay with using tactics that might have been hitting a bit below the belt. If it got my sister back in my life, it would be worth it.

I tapped out a message to Amarah.

Tyler: My sister is looking forward to meeting you.

She replied a few minutes later.

Amarah: No pressure to be charming or anything.

Tyler: No pressure at all, but I really need her to love you so she starts speaking to me again, alright? That'd be really helpful. Thanks in advance.

Amarah: If you're going to insist that I be nice, I think I should get something in return.

Tyler: Seems fair. How about snacks and sexual favours?

Amarah: Pleasure doing business with you.

I chuckled. I loved the way she went toe to toe with me all the time. She could handle anything I threw at her. We hadn't even made it to second base yet – nothing but kisses had been shared between us, but she wasn't put off by talk of more sexually or emotionally.

That was the reality when I thought about this

woman, I could imagine *more* a little too easily. No amount of *more* seemed to be able to scare me.

I wasn't sure it could ever be too much; I was always going to want another part of her.

Amarah: I'm kinda nervous they won't like me.

That was the other thing I liked about this woman; she wasn't afraid to be vulnerable, and her honesty was important to me. You couldn't build a solid foundation on a pile of bullshit.

Tyler: They'll like you more than they like me. Trust me.

Amarah: Doesn't sound like that would be hard to achieve right now.

Tyler: Savage burn. But seriously, beautiful, they'll love you, how could they not?

Amarah: You're quite sweet when you want to be.

Tyler: Just don't say that in front of my brothers, they'll cut me down faster than a toddler can reject a phone call while watching YouTube.

Amarah: *laughing out loud*

I was fucking smiling like an idiot again. That was what she did to me, made me smile all the damn time, even when I wasn't talking to her, I was thinking about her – and then I was grinning.

What the hell has this woman done to me?

Amarah: Talk me through it... who's

going to be there tomorrow?

Tyler: Brace yourself. Parker and Jasper, obviously, Charlotte and Hannah will both be there I'm sure, plus my knucklehead brothers, and whatever poor women they've managed to drag along.

Amarah: I might need a family tree. Which twin is the boxer?

Tyler: Louis, but don't get him talking about it or you'll never get away from him. Floyd is the driver, and you'll never get away from him regardless of what you say or do.

Amarah: How am I meant to tell them apart?

Tyler: Floyd has a mole on his ass.

Amarah: You're hilarious. But seriously, how?

Tyler: You're not. I've been trying their whole lives and I still get it wrong most of the time. They pretend to be each other to mess with me too, so I don't even care which is which anymore. Charlotte is the only one who knows one hundred percent of the time and she refuses to share her secret.

Amarah: I bet she'll tell me.

Tyler: I bet she won't.

Amarah: Fifty bucks?

Tyler: Game on.

Amarah: You can bring me my $50 AND my snacks to the concert and I'll let you know when I'll require the sexual favours.

Tyler: Sounds like a party, I'll pick you up at six.

———

I pulled up at the curb outside her building just before six.

I was as nervous as I was excited, and I couldn't figure out why. I wasn't the kind of guy who got nervous, definitely not about a woman – in fact, the last time I could truly remember feeling nervous was when Louis fought for the world title in his weight division.

My little brother might have been more than capable of knocking ninety percent of the population out cold, but that hadn't stopped the nerves from seeping in as he stepped into that ring. It was terrifying watching him go shot for shot with the best boxer in the world, but I'd had nothing to worry about in the end. Sure, he might have come away with more than a few cuts and bruises, but he also came away with a shiny belt around his middle, and the title of champion.

I jumped out of the car and rounded the hood,

stopping when I reached the passenger side, and leant against the door of my SUV.

I liked to wait for her out here rather than at the door to her building. There were a few seconds when she stepped out of the lift, before she could see me – but I could see her. I probably should have been using the opportunity I had – asking to come up to her floor so I could snoop around for signs of my rival, but my head wasn't in the game. Maybe one day – but that day wasn't today.

No, today my focus was solely on the dark-haired beauty I'd somehow managed to convince to date me.

I loved watching the way she took a deep breath, smoothed down her clothes and then stepped forward, towards *me*.

I wasn't an egotistical man, but it was hard not to notice the way her eyes lit up when they met mine. I was sure mine did the same at the sight of her.

I was falling hard for this girl, and I'd only known her a hot minute. It wasn't like me. I didn't believe in love at first sight or any of that shit, but bit by bit, Amarah was making me question everything I thought I believed.

The doors to the lift inside her building slid open and there she was. I watched her through the glass window as she stepped out and paused, looking herself up and down. A smile crept onto my face as she closed her eyes and tipped her head back for a second before exhaling and taking another step.

She looked gorgeous as fuck. Cut-off denim

shorts, a black tank top and white converse. She was concert ready... absolutely perfect.

I hadn't told her yet that we not only had tickets to the gig, but also backstage passes to hang out with the guys after the show. I'd implied she'd be meeting my brothers and likely everyone else too, but I was yet to tell her she'd have the opportunity to check out the entire backstage setup like a real fangirl.

She was absolute perfection as her eyes searched for me, finding me waiting for her as she rounded the bend.

The corners of her mouth turned up into a smile as she flicked her long hair over her shoulder.

Perfection.

I didn't even believe in perfection – *no one* was perfect, but fuck, this woman just might have been perfect for me.

It was hard to argue with the concept when she was walking towards me looking like *that.*

Her dark eyes raked over me from head to toe, taking me in. I loved when she did that; I could feel her gaze like a caress as she did, and it sent tingles racing up and down my spine.

It made me want to grab her and tell her to never stop doing it.

She opened the door and stepped out into the warm afternoon air, her smile growing as the distance between us shortened.

"Hey, beautiful." I pushed off the car and strode towards her. "You look... *incredible.*"

She smirked at me. "You're exaggerating."

She was right in front of me now, sunglasses perched on her head and a small black bag slung over her shoulder.

"You're sexy as fuck, Amarah. I'm *never* exaggerating when I tell you that."

She swallowed slowly as I wrapped my arms around her middle. She tipped her face up to look at me, still unspeaking.

I ran my finger slowly down the side of her face until she shuddered, causing me to grin.

I loved the way she reacted to me. Her responses were directly caused by my touch, and it turned me on – drove me crazy.

"What?" she whispered as I stared deeply into her eyes.

I shook my head. "Nothing. Just looking."

Blush stained her cheeks, and a shy smile crept onto her lips.

"I'm getting my fill now since you're bound to ditch me after tonight," I teased.

She laughed. "*Absolutely*. I'm just using you for your connections and then I'm bolting like a cat on a hot tin roof."

"I figured as much."

She scrunched up her nose and gave me a light, playful shove in the chest. "Are we getting out of here or what, Watson? I've got some rock stars to fangirl over."

I rolled my eyes. "Your chariot awaits."

CHAPTER 12

Amarah

"WHERE ARE WE GOING?" I tugged on his hand, halting him, if only momentarily.

It was almost comical really, Tyler talked about his brothers and their endless streams of energy, but he was no better. Even when he was still, he somehow *wasn't...* his knee was bouncing, or his fingers were drumming out a beat on his leg. He was restless, *always*.

Like right now, as he towed me through the crowd of people packed in near the front of the stage, waiting for Exit Strategy to come on.

"To the front, right?" he replied, clearly confused by me questioning him.

"How'd you know I'd want to go right to the front?" I asked him.

He was dead right, I wanted to go *so close* that I could feel the body heat of Parker and Jasper, possibly even get sweat dripped on me, but I was curious about how he seemed to already know that piece of information without me telling him.

A slow smirk spread across his face; the same one I'd seen several times already, usually when he realised he'd figured something out about me without trying to.

"You just strike me as a mosh pit kind of girl."

I lifted a shoulder. "What can I say, sweaty bodies grinding against one another really does it for me," I replied, my tone suggestive.

His head fell back, and a pained groan escaped his throat before he brought those alluring blue eyes back to me.

"Can you not say shit like that to me while you're looking like that?" His nostrils flared, giving away just how much he was struggling to keep his hands off me in this moment.

I loved it when he struggled, because I was struggling too. Struggling with my emotions, my sexual desires... my morals.

His snug-fitting black t-shirt had taunted me the entire drive over here, showing off his defined biceps and broad chest.

It was only fair that I teased him back. I was the one out of my comfort zone, after all.

I hadn't met any of his family yet, our tickets were waiting for us out front when we arrived, and Tyler informed me that we'd be meeting up with them after the show. I was glad in a way; it was nerve wracking – the idea of meeting the people closest to him. It also made me feel guiltier than I already did about the secrets I was keeping.

He groaned again and squeezed my hand before he pulled me gently behind him. "C'mon, beautiful, I can't handle the look in your eyes right now. A man only has so much self-control."

I was tempted to tease him more, push it a little bit further, but that would require torturing myself too, and I wasn't one for self-torment, so I let him lead me away, weaving through the crowd as we snuck between too small gaps and pushed our way to the front like a couple of obnoxious teenagers who simply didn't give a shit.

I'd half expected him to have some security guard in his back pocket that would let us onto the other side of the barrier to cheat our way up there, so I was glad when we reached the front the old-fashioned way. I wanted the real concert experience. I had a feeling tonight was going to be a night I'd remember for a long time.

The pre-show entertainment came out onto the stage and the crowd went *crazy*, cheering and jumping around. Tyler ushered me forward, so I was pressed against the cool metal barrier, then positioned himself behind me, his firm arms coming around me protectively, his hands braced on the top bar to steady himself and stop me from being jostled.

Being in his arms was a feeling I couldn't describe. I'd never felt particularly at home unless I was back in Spain with my family, but right here, in his embrace – it was the closest I'd ever come... it just felt *right*. That realisation was something I was going to have to process another time, when I was at home, alone in my bed, because feeling that way about Tyler wasn't smart and it certainly wasn't going to end well... for either of us.

"Do you know this band?" I called to him, over my shoulder and the pounding music.

I'd never heard of them, but the rhythm of the music was catchy, and my body started swaying to the beat involuntarily.

"Cold Cut." He spoke directly into my ear, sending shivers up my spine.

He was too close, too big, too enticing. Tyler Watson was too much of everything, and yet, I couldn't get enough.

"I'm friends with the drummer. They're going to be massive."

Of course he's friends with them.

"Do you have any friends or relations that *aren't* famous?" I tipped my head back so I could catch a glimpse of his face.

He smirked at me and half shrugged. "Not really. Maybe one or two."

I rolled my eyes and turned my focus back to the

stage and the band rocking out. I didn't recognise their music, but I had a feeling Tyler was right about their potential; their tunes were easy to listen to, my body wanted to move when they played. Their lead singer had a set of pipes on him too – he was killing it.

I couldn't speak for anyone else here, but they had a new fan in me.

"I like them," I confirmed.

I felt, rather than heard him chuckle – the vibration of his throat on my neck. "I'm glad."

"He's no Parker, but I guess he's okay." I tipped my head towards the lead singer, who was saying thanks to the crowd.

"They'll be the next big thing, mark my words. I introduced Parker to them about six months ago and he was willing to give them a shot. They're on their way to the top." Tyler told me in the rare moment between sets when the noise wasn't so crazy loud.

He said it so casually, putting emphasis on the fact that it was Parker and Jasper who had given them a shot, but it was clear to me he was the one who made it happen.

That was the kind of man I was learning Tyler was; he wanted to do things for the people he cared about, and he expected nothing but respect in return. It wasn't a concept I was used to. In my past relationships, guys did something for me, because they wanted something specific back from me.

Tyler did things because he wanted to look after others – because he wanted other people to be happy.

The niggling feeling in the back of my mind appeared again, reminding me that this could all be an act – that maybe he was just playing some long, elaborate game with me, but when he pinned me with his stare, tipping my head back so those perfect lips of his could brush mine, the feeling disappeared entirely.

This *couldn't* be fake. It was too real.

"Here they come, baby," he murmured as the volume of the crowd hit a new high, screams and squeals hitting my eardrums and making me grin from ear to ear.

The noise was piercing, painful, but I was ready for it.

In fact, I was adding to it, screaming and cheering as Parker and Jasper walked out to the stage, waving to the crowd.

God, they were two fine men. Neither were particularly my type; I liked my men a little cleaner cut, a little broader built – but I wasn't blind, nor was I oblivious to the level of sexiness that had just taken up position behind the two mics.

Charlotte and Hannah sure were two lucky ladies.

"Good evening, beautiful people!" Jasper's voice filled the stadium, followed by more shrieking and cheering.

Tyler winced at the pitch. I grinned.

Parker began introducing each member of the

band as the excitement of the crowd continued to build.

We all knew we were in the midst of greatness.

"Fangirl." Tyler's voice taunted me in my ear.

I didn't reply. I was going to make him pay in another way.

Absolute torture.

I popped my butt and very intentionally ground my ass against his crotch as I danced to the music that was now filling the jam-packed arena.

I twisted my hips, teasing him more and more with each movement.

He groaned into my ear, his hips thrusting forward in the same moment to buck against my ass.

I grinned to myself. This was going to be fun.

———

Tyler nudged me in the ribs and pointed to the side of the stage. I followed his line of sight until I found what he was showing me.

Charlotte and Hannah.

I knew that for certain. This week I'd finally done the research I should have done a long time ago on Tyler and his friends and family.

I might have been caught off guard when I met Tyler for the first time – not even recognising the man – but it wasn't a mistake I was going to make twice.

I'd dropped the ball big time.

That had always been a bit of a flaw of mine – when I worked a job, I was thorough, but I refused to get caught up in irrelevant details of side characters, like who was dating who and where they went to get their nails done.

When I took the job from Jasper, I researched the hell out of that man. I knew every last detail of him down to each of the tattoos covering his body. I'd covered Hannah just as meticulously. Where I'd fallen short, was researching the connection between Jasper and Tyler.

In my excitement to win – which I had – I'd failed to do my homework.

I'd already known Tyler had no social media, no detectable online presence, I'd come across one photo of him once, years ago – but I'd barely glanced at it. The way my enemy looked had been irrelevant to me. It was almost a laughable concept to me now.

A foolish move.

If I'd done my research properly, I would have realised that his sister was now married to Parker, and that his brothers were very well known in each of their fields.

All things I knew now. Things that were easily found on the internet. Tyler featured heavily in articles and photos about Louis' boxing and Floyd's racing. The internet was a landmine for photos of the guy, if you knew where to look. He was smart though; he never had his name included – or he removed it from the internet himself; it was always 'my older brother'. He was clever.

I was still giving myself a hard time about not putting all the pieces together about Charlotte and Tyler being related, but I had all the facts now, and I'd learnt a valuable lesson for the future.

Information is power.

"They always watch from over there?" I spoke loud enough for him to hear.

"Mostly." His breath was warm on my cheek. A fine layer of sweat covered us both from dancing and singing to the music. "Hannah's probably not up for a mosh pit these days."

I eyed Hannah Jones from head to toe. She was gorgeous; there was absolutely no disputing that fact. Blonde and tanned, tall and slim – even with her small bump. She really did deserve the nickname Jasper had given her; she was as close to a real-life barbie as I'd ever seen.

Only now, she was 'knocked-up Barbie', a fact that didn't give me as much comfort as I thought it would.

This whole thing was stupid. Here I was, at a concert with a man I knew I could never have a real future with, and I was jealous over a woman who wasn't even his ex.

I was screwed, and it was about time I acknowledged and accepted that. I wasn't getting out of this, not easily anyway, and certainly not without someone's feelings getting seriously hurt.

And if this pang of jealousy was anything to go by, then that someone was probably going to be me.

I shifted my gaze to Charlotte. She was stunning, in a completely different way. Long, dark red hair hung around her shoulders in waves and her petite body swayed to the beat of her man's music, her eyes never leaving him as he moved around the stage.

I'd studied the bejesus out of her this past week, so I was well accustomed to the sight of her, but seeing her in the flesh was different. She had so much love in her eyes when she looked at Parker. She just looked like a good person, and they were the sweetest together.

I watched as he switched out his guitar between sets, his eyes meeting hers as he blew her a kiss.

"Shit they're cute."

Tyler chuckled, the sound giving me tingles. "I don't usually call grown men *cute*, but when it comes to the way he loves my sister, it is pretty fucking cute."

It was lucky for Parker too; I couldn't imagine Charlotte's three big brothers would settle for anything less than the absolute best for their little sister. I'd seen evidence to suggest they were all fiercely protective of her, and with a world champion boxer in the family, it would be in any man's best interest to keep her family on side.

"Are you having fun?" his voice came at my ear again.

I nodded furiously, my line of sight finally

shifting from the two women side of stage, and back to their husbands, who were front and centre again.

Unwarranted jealousy aside, I was having a great time. We hadn't run into either of Tyler's brothers yet though, and he'd said I was going to meet his sister too, so I figured the night was anything but over, even as Parker and Jasper announced that this was the final song in the set.

The boys played their last song, while I screamed and fangirled along with every other female in the crowded venue, then repeated more of the same when they came out for one more song for the encore.

I was going to have absolutely no voice tomorrow, but it'd be worth it.

So worth it.

Tyler stood behind me, his chin rested on my shoulder as people started to exit.

"Now what?" I prompted.

He chuckled. "Now we go backstage and see how badly you can embarrass yourself."

I shook my head as I spun around to face him. His arms stayed put, caging me. "There is no way we're going backstage."

"These backstage passes say differently." He slid his hand into his pocket and dragged out two laminated passes on lanyards.

"You better not be kidding, Tyler Watson. Going backstage at an Exit Strategy concert is not something to be joked about," I warned him, one finger pointed.

"I never kid when it comes to fangirls," he replied, a smirk on his lips.

I snagged the pass from his hand as a very un-chilled noise escaped me. "Oh my god. I'm basically a groupie. I'm going to embarrass myself *so* hard."

I hadn't given too much thought to when and where I'd meet his family, but I hadn't expected to go backstage. It was so rock and roll.

The lights came on, and I blinked against the harsh light. I probably looked like a hot mess, but I didn't care.

He nodded, a playful grimace on his face. "I think we both know that's a fact."

There were only a few groups of people left around us. It was surprising how quickly the place cleared out, given the absolutely packed state it had been only half an hour before.

He grabbed my hand and we walked parallel to the stage, weaving in and out of the few fans who hung around at the front.

We'd almost reached the side where a security guard was standing, arms folded, when I heard the yelling start.

"Looooover boy." Quickly followed by, "get your ass up here, DB!"

Tyler groaned as I glanced around. That's when I spotted them. It was like a glitch in the matrix. I was seeing double.

Louis and Floyd.

I couldn't help but grin as I made eye contact

with the one on the right. He winked at me, a shit-eating grin plastered across his face.

"Shit, Ty, she's way too pretty for you," the other one taunted him.

I shook my head in amusement.

Tyler tugged on my hand, and I saw that the guard had moved the barrier to allow us access. "You sure you're ready for this?" He grimaced as his brothers started another round of cat calling and whistling.

I was completely unprepared to meet all these people, but I was about to do it anyway.

I giggled and shrugged. "Let's do it."

CHAPTER 13

Tyler

"DON'T MAKE me do something we'll both regret," I warned Floyd, whose eyes hadn't left my girl's ass for the past thirty seconds.

He smirked, but his gaze didn't waver. "Like what?"

"Like rat you out to the cops."

That got his attention.

"For *what?*" he demanded.

"The options are endless, little brother." I grinned. "Safest bet would be not to try me."

I knew both of my brothers' dirty little secrets – they still loved to push my buttons, but it didn't hurt to give them a gentle reminder every now and then that I could fuck with them if I really wanted to.

I never would, but an empty threat was better than no threat at all where these two were concerned.

He scowled at me, and I chuckled.

Amarah had been talking animatedly with Charlotte and Louis for the past twenty minutes. She'd already met Parker and Jasper plus all the guys from Cold Cut, and blushed bright scarlet while doing it, but all in all, I'd been expecting worse. It wasn't every day that you got to meet two of your favourite musicians, not in her world anyway, mine was slightly different these days.

Floyd flipped me off and wandered off. I'd have been willing to bet he had no clue at all where he'd left the chick he'd brought with him, but knowing him, he probably didn't care that much either.

I took a swig of the beer in my hand and watched with what could only be described as great pleasure as Charlotte laughed at something Amarah said.

Charlotte glanced over at me, and I smiled. I almost stumbled back in shock when she returned my smile with an even bigger one.

I'd become so used to glacier glares or being ignored entirely – this felt like I'd entered some alternate dimension, and all she'd done was smile at me.

Amarah said something else, and Charlotte nodded before taking a step in my direction.

Finally.

My sister was *finally* going to talk to me. I'd been begging her for the chance for weeks, and I'd got virtually nothing but radio silence in return, but now that it was actually happening, I was shit scared.

My palms were sweaty as she closed the distance between us. I needed to get a grip; this was my sister for crying out loud, but it felt like I was dealing with a disappointed parent, which in a lot of ways, I was.

The boys always looked up to me a lot when we were growing up, Charlotte had too, but being a female, she was far more nurturing than I was, and I often found myself going to her for advice. Something I should have done the first moment Hannah contacted me with her ridiculous plan.

Hannah.

That was the other mess I had to untangle tonight. I hated that things were strained between us. I sensed she was steering as clear of me and Amarah as possible, but there was no need for it – sure, she'd shot me down, but I was over it now. It was something I'd barely even thought about lately.

"Hey, Ty," Charlotte said as she reached me.

I didn't get my usual hug upon greeting, but she was talking, and beggars couldn't be choosers.

"Hey, short stuff."

She stood next to me, watching the scene in front of us, the same way I did.

"She seems pretty great." She tipped her head towards Amarah, who was now being double teamed by both of my idiot brothers.

She looked like she was holding her own pretty well, to be fair.

"She is. I can't fault her."

Amarah threw her head back in laughter, and Louis looked proud as punch for having got such a reaction out of her. I knew how he felt; making her laugh was like striking gold. I felt a smile pulling at the corners of my lips.

"You really like her, don't you?" Charlotte questioned.

I turned to look at her and found her watching me closely.

I nodded. I was taking my vow of never lying to her again seriously. "There's just something about her that calls to me."

Parker chose that moment to walk back into view.

"I know the feeling," Charlotte mused, her focus on her husband.

Parker seemed to have some type of radar when it came to my sister; he never had trouble finding her in a crowd, and given her height, that was saying something. They were just so in tune with one another.

His eyes found hers, he looked her up and down, smiled and then called out to one of the guys in the band for something.

"Can we talk?" I asked in a rush. I knew it wasn't really the time or the place, but I was getting desperate.

Charlotte sighed. "You know, the twins keep telling me I'm being too hard on you and that I should give you a chance to say what you want to say."

I took that as a yes.

Part of me was pissed with Charlotte. She'd forgiven Hannah almost instantly for ghosting on everyone, and she hadn't even given me a shot at apologising, but I'd reminded myself that Hannah might have made some shitty calls, but she didn't lie directly to Charlotte's face the way that I did.

I'd made my bed, and I'd been lying in it, but I was sick of that now. I was getting up. Fuck that lying down shit – I owed her a proper apology and I was going to give it to her, and then we were going to get the fuck on with it.

"I really am sorry, Lotte. I'm not going to try and give you a bunch of excuses or try and explain why I did what I did. Long story short, I fucked up and I hurt you, and for that, I couldn't be more sorry. You're one of the most important people in my life, and I don't want anything to come between us ever again. You have my word that I'll never lie to you or keep anything from you again."

A few beats of silence passed.

"I know you won't," she replied quietly. "And I know I've been stubborn on this, but you really hurt me, Ty. You knew how worried I was about her, and I know you were just trying to do the right thing by Hannah, but we're family. Mum and Dad are useless, but I've always been able to rely on you... and it hurt me when I found out I couldn't."

I dropped my head in embarrassment. "I know."

"I've missed you so much. I miss our talks. Parker

misses you too. The twins came over for dinner last week and it wasn't the same without you."

"They tear the place apart like a couple of over-sized toddlers?"

"At an *alarming* rate," she joked, a smile on her lips as she shook her head in amusement.

Those boys were so much more to handle when they were together; it must have been some weird twin thing. They just went batshit crazy in each other's presence and reverted back to their teenage ways. I can only imagine how Parker and Charlotte would have handled that.

"I'll be there next time, tranquiliser gun in hand, if you'll let me."

"I'd like that."

I felt the weight lift off my shoulders. I knew I still had some making up to do, but we'd be okay. I knew that now.

"I do have one request..."

"Hit me with it."

"Talk to Hannah. She's worried that you hate her, even though I've told her she's being ridiculous. She's so hormonal... will you talk to her? I just want everything to go back to normal."

"I'll talk to her," I promised. "Right after I rescue my girl from those two."

I grimaced as Louis got his phone out to show Amarah something. God only knew what it was, but it wasn't likely to be anything good.

The last time he showed me something on his phone, it had been of a boxing buddy of his breaking his leg in training. The bone came through the skin and everything, it was definitely a visual I could have done without.

"Go, quick, before he shows her the video of him losing a tooth that time," Charlotte urged, shoving me in the direction of our siblings.

I took a step forward before quickly backtracking. I pulled her into my arms and squeezed her tight. I pressed a kiss to the top of her head. "I love you," I told her.

"I love you too, but seriously, you need to move fast."

I chuckled, released her and jogged over to Amarah. I slid my arms around her middle and lifted her clean off the ground, turning her away from my dipshit brothers.

"What are you doing?" she shrieked, holding back laughter.

"Saving your retinas from seeing things they can't unsee."

Louis and Floyd called out a string of objections and profanities after me, but I took no notice as I carried her away.

"Louis was going to show me something!" she moaned as I put her down in a private spot away from everyone else.

"That's exactly what worries me. You have got no

idea what could appear from the depths of that man's phone."

"If you're talking about pictures of his junk, I'd probably be willing to run the gauntlet."

I growled and tugged her against my body.

"Easy, tiger." She giggled. "I think one Watson brother is already more than I can handle."

I smirked at her, intentionally pressing my hips forward. "I think you've handled me just fine so far."

She breathed heavily. "I beg to differ."

I lowered my head, skimming my lips against the exposed skin on her neck. "What are we going to do about that then, huh, beautiful?" I murmured.

She shuddered under my touch. I didn't know if it was our surroundings that had her all off kilter, or if it was me, but either way, I was going to use it to my advantage. She was always so composed, so in control of herself. I liked seeing her a bit more exposed and vulnerable. It was sexy as hell.

I pressed my lips to her collarbone, over and over again.

I heard a hum in the back of her throat, the sound satisfied and pleasured. I smiled to myself.

Her hand found my hair and her fingers weaved through the strands, tugging slightly.

I felt like a bit of a rock star myself in that moment. There I was, with the most beautiful, sexy woman in the whole place, and I had her pressed up against a sub, side of stage at a massive concert venue.

I even had the band members strolling around and everything.

Her other hand reached between us and gripped the front of my shirt. She grasped it tightly and pulled me even closer to her.

Our mouths met in a flurry of heat and passion, our tongues duelled as she kissed me with even more heat and urgency than the first time our lips met.

I moaned into her mouth as her teeth sank into my bottom lip.

"Get a room, douche bag!" Floyd called out, or maybe it was Louis, I couldn't tell, and I didn't really care.

Amarah giggled and her grip on me loosened.

"Fucking pain in my ass," I grumbled.

———

"Pay up, Watson," she taunted from her spot on the couch in Parker and Jasper's dressing room. She was sandwiched between Floyd and Charlotte, looking inexplicably at home. "You owe me fifty bucks."

"I'll pay up when I see evidence that you've got the goods," I retorted.

She was claiming that she had the secret to telling the twins apart. I wasn't sure I believed her – Charlotte had always guarded that secret with her life – but Amarah's confidence had climbed at a rapid rate of knots. That could have had something to do with the half a dozen drinks she'd downed within a couple of hours, but the smug look on my sister's face, led me to believe that my girl's cocky attitude was down to the fact that she did indeed, have the secret.

"Fine, I'll prove it."

Floyd smirked. "I hate to point out the obvious, but it's hardly rocket science when we're dressed differently."

Amarah waved her hand dismissively. "So, swap clothes."

I chuckled. She really wanted to win this bet.

"I wouldn't be caught dead in that outfit." Louis scowled at Floyd, who flipped him off in return.

Everyone laughed.

Parker and Jasper had gone with Cold Cut to see the fans who had hung around outside, and Hannah had gone to take a nap, so it was just the five of us in here now.

I had no idea what had happened to Louis and Floyd's dates, but neither of them seemed particularly fazed by their sudden disappearances.

"This shirt is designer," Floyd replied, clearly insulted.

"Doesn't make it nice to look at, bro."

Floyd scowled. "You know what fucks me off the most about being twins? That I can't insult the way you look. Every part of me wanted to follow that up with a 'you're not nice to look at either, bro', but obviously you're too handsome for that kind of insult."

"You *do* have a decent mug on you," Louis agreed.

Amarah watched the banter back and forth between them with what I could only describe as delight.

"Would you two give it a rest? Go change clothes already. Or don't... surprise us, whatever, but Amarah needs to prove that she knows how to tell the difference," Charlotte insisted.

Both boys shot her a look but got to their feet to do as they were told.

"You've got to get two out of three to win, new girl." Floyd pointed a finger at Amarah, who just sat there grinning.

"Fine by me." She rubbed her hands together gleefully.

Charlotte looked like she was going to enjoy this a whole hell of a lot, a fact that *didn't* fill me with confidence as far as this bet was concerned.

"Hope you've got the cash ready, hot shot, because it's *all* mine." Amarah smirked at me.

The boys disappeared into the adjoining room and shut the door behind them.

Parker strode into the room, right as Floyd and Louis came out of the bathroom, dishevelled and grinning.

"What are these two idiots up to now, legs?" he grunted as he slid in next to Charlotte.

She beamed up at him. "Amarah is just about to take some money off Tyler's hands by proving she can tell the twins apart."

"Bullshit. Only you can tell those two knuckle-heads apart, and you refuse to share your secret."

"We'll see, won't we?" Charlotte replied, full of sass.

Uh oh.

I think I've been played.

"Hurry up and choose already," one of the twins, the one dressed in Floyd's clothes, demanded.

Amarah looked at them both carefully.

They'd swapped clothes, I was certain of it.

"Nice try, boys, but you're still wearing the same shit," Amarah announced.

No one reacted for half a second, and then Floyd, who apparently was still wearing his own clothes, grinned. "Well shit, the girl *might* know."

Charlotte held her hand up and Amarah high fived her.

"Lucky guess. Go again," I insisted.

Charlotte rolled her eyes. "She knows!"

"I don't believe you, short stuff. I've been hounding you for the secret your whole life and you've never come close to telling me. You haven't even told Parker and you worship the ground that man walks on. I don't buy it. It was a lucky guess."

"Go again then." Amarah raised one brow at me in challenge. "I could do this all day, Watson."

"I like her," Parker mused. "She's ballsy."

"I gotta be honest with you, *I* like her a little less right now," I interjected, smirking.

"Boys," Amarah prompted the twins, completely ignoring my grumbling. "If you would."

"Trained monkeys, at your service," one of them said as they exited the room again.

I'd practically given up trying to figure out which was which at this point. It seemed as though I was the only one in the room who had no idea.

The boys emerged a few minutes later, and I studied them carefully this time, but it wasn't the first time I'd tried to decipher this mystery. I'd been trying their whole lives to tell them apart and I sucked at it.

Usually, Louis had a black eye or a cut lip, but he wasn't in training right now. Sometimes Floyd had injuries from his crashes and close calls, but lately he'd been doing stunts in movies more than he'd been racing on the track.

They'd both had several broken noses, given their reckless lifestyles, so even the slight bump on the bridge of their noses was virtually identical. It was infuriating.

I glanced over at the girls, who were both watching me, waiting for my guess. I groaned and shrugged. "No fucking clue," I admitted.

Amarah shook her head at me in mock disappointment. "You really are a terrible brother, aren't you? It's pretty clear that they're still wearing the same clothes."

Charlotte laughed out loud. "Nailed it."

I looked to the boys for confirmation. They both

nodded. "Credit where credit's due. She's good," Floyd replied.

"Fuck's sake," I groaned. She'd already got two from three.

She wins.

Amarah jumped up out of her chair and strutted over to me, her hips swaying. "Pay up, Watson."

I leaned around her and glared at my brothers. "Seriously? You couldn't switch clothes even once?"

"Work smarter, not harder, sugar tits," Louis quipped.

"*Unbelievable*," I groaned.

Amarah stood before me, looking as sexy as sin, her hands planted firmly on her hips and a cocky expression on her face. "A bet's a bet."

I slid my hand into my pocket, my eyes never leaving hers, and pulled out my wallet. I'd hoped to win this bet. I was almost one hundred percent certain that Charlotte wouldn't give up her secret, but I'd come prepared. Just in case.

I stared at her hard, loving and hating at the same time how pleased she was with herself, before breaking our connection and locating the note I put in my wallet earlier.

I handed it to her, reluctantly letting go when she pulled on it.

She held it triumphantly above her head and everyone cheered and clapped.

I glared at every single one of them, giving my sister special attention. "I can't *believe* you told her."

She lifted one shoulder. "Us girls have got to stick together."

Amarah paraded around the room, collecting high fives from each person. I didn't miss the blush on her cheeks when Parker gave her one.

I shook my head in mock disbelief. I hated losing, but fuck, it just might have been worth it to see her so happy.

CHAPTER 14

Amarah

I LOVED CHARLOTTE ALREADY. She was *awesome.*

She'd welcomed me with open arms and made me feel so comfortable in their inner circle.

It was easy to see why Parker had changed his ways for her. She radiated love and kindness, and the love and adoration between the two of them was obvious for anyone to see. He gravitated towards her. I wasn't sure he even knew he was doing it, but he watched her constantly. He touched her continuously, and I think if he could have had his way, they'd have been virtually inseparable.

"He's been so much happier since Jasper joined

him," she continued, oblivious to my inner deciphering of her husband's love for her.

We'd been walking around, her showing me all the cool quirks of the venue and telling me the story of how Parker went from being Parker Sloan – rock god solo artist, to one half of the insanely popular Exit Strategy.

It was a pretty good story, I had to admit. I'd been a fan of that man for a long time, so I knew bits and pieces – the parts that made it to the gossip columns. I'd certainly seen him singing to get her back and watched clips of him singing to her live on stage at his concerts – something Charlotte seemed less than thrilled with.

Something told me she'd be perfectly comfortable living a quiet life, flying under the radar. Unfortunately for her, her choice of husband didn't allow for that.

"They're so good together. Their music is amazing."

She smiled wide. "They really are. Everyone always says you shouldn't work with friends, but I think the four of us are testament to that being bullshit. We basically live in each other's pockets, and we still never get sick of each other."

"Things will change a bit when the baby arrives, I guess?" I asked, as we strolled around side by side.

"Things will be different, but I can't imagine anything slowing Hannah down for long. She'll probably be back after a week with the kid strapped to her chest or something."

We rounded the corner, and I stopped dead in my tracks.

Down the far end of the corridor were Tyler and Hannah, they were in the middle of a conversation. I watched as his hand reached out and touched the bump protruding from her stomach.

I froze.

Charlotte walked a few more steps, still talking about something, before she noticed I was no longer next to her.

She looked at me in confusion, then followed my line of sight to her best friend and her brother.

My face must have told a story because she backtracked, grabbed my arm and turned me, then led me in the opposite direction. "Come on. We're going this way."

I followed along after her, letting her lead me.

I wasn't sure why this bothered me so much. I wasn't an overly jealous person, but something about Hannah presented itself as a threat to me.

A threat over a man I shouldn't even want. A threat over a man I couldn't ever really have.

The irony.

Charlotte took me out onto the now empty stage, right into the centre of it.

"Sit," she instructed as she lowered herself to the floor.

I followed suit.

"I'm not going to sit here and tell you what to feel, but I am going to tell you one thing, if that's okay?"

I nodded.

"I've never seen my brother the way he is when he's with you. He's a thirty-six-year-old, grown man, and I've never seen him with a woman and imagined that he'd have any type of real future with her. That all changed the moment I met you."

I liked what she was telling me far more than was smart.

"Are you just saying that because I'm being stupid and jealous?"

She laughed and shook her head. "*No.* I'm saying that because I understand why you feel jealous, but there's no need to be. He's never looked at her the way he's been looking at you. He had a crush on Hannah that he mistook for something more. I think that you could be that something more."

I had no idea how she'd done it, but I felt better. I was still jealous as hell, but I appreciated what she'd said. Even if it completely terrified me.

I'd never had any intentions of being something special to Tyler, even though he was quickly becoming something special to me. It was all so fucked up.

"Thank you." I squeezed her hand softly. I didn't know what else I could say.

"Should we get back to the others? Parker will send out the cavalry if I'm not back soon."

"I'm pretty sure he has at least one bodyguard tailing us," I laughed, "but let's get back. I've got more bragging to do anyway."

She laughed. "He's going to be salty about losing that bet for a *long* time."

"God, I hope so. Thanks for hooking me up."

She got to her feet and held out her hand to help me up – it was comical really, she was so tiny, I doubt she'd have a lot to offer in helping.

"Don't mention it, like I said, us girls have to stick together. But I'm warning you now, he's going to want to get a win under his belt, so don't go buying into any of his bullshit bets."

"I'll be on the lookout for any dodgy dealings." I laughed.

"Let's go, Hannah's obviously up from her nap, and I want you to get to know J better. You're going to love him."

She wasn't wrong about that. Jasper was great. We got on well. Only now, I had to pretend he was a total stranger to me.

I needed to remember where I was, and whose company I was in. I needed to keep my guard up.

Unfortunately for me, that was proving to be far easier said than done.

———

Tyler kissed my temple and slid his arm around me the second I walked into the room.

"Where'd you two disappear to? I was about to send out a search party."

His comment made me smile. I liked that it was in line with Charlotte's comments about Parker. The two men were more similar than they realised; both loyal, protective and sweet.

Only difference was that the man I'd come here with tonight had a personal vendetta against me, and me against him. It was hardly a romance story for the ages.

"Just girl talk," Charlotte answered before I could.

She went straight to her husband, who tugged her into his lap.

I'd totally been right about us being tailed; a bulky-looking man settled near the doorway, and I was confident he'd been following us the whole time.

Parker was a smart man, and I sensed that he was also a fiercely protective one, especially when it came to his wife – possibly even to the point of being wildly over the top, so it didn't surprise me that we were probably never ever really alone.

"I hope she hasn't been telling you horror stories from my teenage years," he murmured into my ear.

"What gets said during girl talk, stays there," I whispered.

He chuckled. "I don't think I like the idea of this friendship. You two are already ganging up on me."

That made me smile again. I liked the idea of

being friends with Charlotte. I could see us being close, given the chance.

Charlotte held up her hand to give me a virtual high five across the room. I obliged, smiling wider.

Stupid.

Stupid.

Stupid.

I was being naïve, but I decided right there and then, to allow myself to be fooled by my own hopes and dreams, if only for this one night. It was too easy to imagine being a permanent fixture in Tyler's world, and it scared me how big of a part of me wanted exactly that.

"Hannah wants to meet you properly," he whispered.

I knew that was coming. I'd managed to avoid it so far, but it was a ticking time bomb. I had to exchange more than a quick *hello* with the woman, it was inevitable. And more than that, I wanted to. I'd built her up to be this big thing in my mind, when really, she was just a woman. A pregnant woman who was very in love with her husband if the way they were snuggled up together on a couch, whispering to each other, was anything to go by.

Hannah hadn't done anything wrong here – other than abandon Jasper – but that was Armageddon's beef, not Amarah's.

I was just a website designer who met a guy on a whim and was now meeting everyone closest to him.

No big deal.

Tyler took my hand in his and led me over to where Jasper and Hannah were still oblivious to the world.

I wondered if this was weird for Tyler. Obviously, Hannah and Jasper both knew he'd had feelings for her, at least at a point in time, and now here he was, watching them kissing and growing a family, and with his new girl in tow.

They both looked up as we reached them, and a real, genuine smile crossed Hannah's face when she saw me. She looked absolutely over the moon at the mere sight of me.

I guess I'd be the same if a man I cared deeply for, but didn't love, had expressed unreciprocated feelings towards me. I'd be completely ecstatic at the idea of him moving on and forgetting all about loving me too.

I'd barely exchanged more than a few words with either Jasper or Hannah today, and I was nervous. They might not have been Tyler's best friends, but I still wanted to make a good impression on these people. Plus, Jasper was an uber hot rock star, and the mere thought of that had me threatening to blush and trip over my words. He was just a client over the phone – it was hard to have this level of sex appeal without a visual.

Tyler squeezed my hand and pulled me down onto the couch facing the couple before us.

"What's been happenin', Ty?" Jasper drawled.

The guy was so laid back it was almost unfathomable. Nothing much seemed to faze him at all.

A few members of crew had come around earlier with a problem with some of the gear that needed to be transported to the next venue they were playing – I didn't understand what was going on, but I didn't miss the fact that Parker lost his shit over it, and Jasper didn't so much as bat an eyelid. Charlotte had given her man a serious look, which had calmed him down in approximately a third of a second, and then she'd taken care of it herself. Like a total boss bitch.

"Nothing too outrageous," Tyler answered him.

The two men exchanged a look. It wasn't hostile as such, but it spoke of a mutual understanding.

One that I'd be willing to bet went something like 'you stay the hell away from my girl and we won't have any issues'.

I was sure Tyler was smart enough to comply. He was a big guy, strong and fit, but Jasper had this catlike edge to him that I'd never seen before, and I sure as hell wouldn't have wanted to mess with.

"Sorry I've been so useless tonight; morning sickness has been a real bitch this past week and I'm just so tired all the time," Hannah apologised, a sheepish expression on her face.

"Don't be silly," I replied quickly. "I can't even imagine growing a human, let alone actually doing it, you take all the naps you need."

Hannah beamed.

Dammit, I cursed myself. I could already see that she was going to be likeable too.

Where the hell were all the assholes that the media always painted in showbiz? I needed someone to hate, pronto.

"It's a tough gig, that's for sure," she agreed. "Pregnancy is definitely not all glowing skin and cute baby bumps."

Jasper played with her hand as she spoke, intertwining her fingers with his own.

"Have the paparazzi got hold of the story yet?" Tyler asked.

Hannah nodded. "Just this week. It was getting too hard to hide the bump, and there's no way I'm staying home for the next twenty weeks."

"Yeah, fuck that," I replied before I had a chance to filter my words.

Jasper chuckled. "That's exactly what she said when I suggested it."

"Great minds." Hannah laughed.

"What do you do for a job, Amarah?" Jasper questioned me.

"These days it's mostly website design," I prattled, "but I've dabbled in a bit of code writing and other design fields as well." I shrugged.

That was my pre-prepared answer I'd practised at home; I'd used it at least three times this evening already.

I'd also pulled an all-nighter a week or so ago to launch a business landing page and created a bunch of websites to use as client testimonials. It absolutely bored me to tears, but it had to be done, and I was good at it, so it wasn't all bad.

"That's cool," Hannah replied. "I bet you two have a lot in common, all that computer stuff no one understands."

"Something like that," I muttered.

We had more in common than anyone in this room could possibly comprehend.

I glanced at Jasper and was surprised to find him watching me, a curious expression on his face.

I smiled nervously. This was *so* weird. We'd had so many conversations over the phone – he was the only client I'd ever told that I was a female – yet here we sat, less than one metre away from one another and he had no idea who I really was or what I actually did for a living.

Tyler kissed the top of my head, drawing my attention away from the intense stare of the man across from me.

"What did you do before you started working for these guys?" I asked Hannah, eager to keep my focus somewhere other than on Jasper.

Hannah's eyes lit up. "I'm a hairdresser, me and Lotte still have our own business..."

I spent the next fifteen minutes listening to Hannah tell me all about the life she lived before she became part of team Exit Strategy. She was an impressive woman, I had to hand it to her. She and Charlotte had created an incredible business from virtually nothing, and they'd done hair and makeup for some of the most famous and well-paid celebrities on the planet.

I certainly was rubbing shoulders with the other half tonight.

Jasper didn't say much, just chimed in here and there, Tyler was much the same. Both men seemed content to allow Hannah and me to do all the talking.

It wasn't as awkward as I thought it'd be. In fact, it wasn't awkward at all between Hannah and me. I wasn't sure how I felt about that, but it was happening regardless of my feelings.

Hannah yawned, long and loud.

"Home time, Barbie," Jasper announced.

"I'm not that tired," she argued.

"You're so tired I bet you're going to fall asleep in the car on the way home."

"Are you going to carry me in yourself this time or call Sammy to do it?" She raised a brow at him.

He chuckled. "That was *one* time. And I had a sore shoulder."

"I think you just can't handle the extra weight."

"You're not going to bait me into commenting on your weight, Barbie. I might not be smart, but I'm not that stupid."

A giggle slipped out.

He was smart as far as I was concerned; commenting on a woman's weight was a no go at the best of times, let alone one who was growing a human.

"I reckon we should head off too," Tyler told me, getting to his feet.

I nodded eagerly. I'd had the most incredible night, but my head was starting to feel a little foggy and I was keen to quit while I was ahead.

The last thing I needed was another drink and to say something I shouldn't with a room full of witnesses.

"Let's do it," I replied.

CHAPTER 15

Tyler

"I APPRECIATE YOU BEING COOL, MAN." I held out my hand to Jasper.

We were out the back of the venue, waiting for Charlotte, Hannah and Amarah to stop fucking talking so we could finally go home.

It was quickly becoming a half-hour process.

Parker had got into the waiting car about ten minutes ago, when it became apparent the girls weren't going to wind things up anytime soon.

Floyd and Louis had taken off in Floyd's car as soon as we got out here. They'd probably crossed three borders by now, but I tried not to worry too much about it. Floyd was a maniac, but he was hands down the best driver in the country; probably one of the best in the world.

I was just glad neither of them drank very often anymore. They were full on enough when they were sober, but filled with booze, it was anyone's guess what was going to go down.

Jasper slowly reached out and took my hand in his, firmly shaking it. "I appreciate you getting on with your life and not trying to steal my wife."

As straight up as always.

Jasper and I may not have been mates, exactly, but I rated the way he operated. He was a good man. Hannah was lucky to have him.

"And it's not exactly hard to be cool when I came out on top." He smirked as he dropped my hand.

I deserved that. I knew I did.

"I'd say that everything worked out exactly the way it was meant to."

Amarah laughed, and my eyes found her right away. She made me smile, even though I wasn't in on the joke.

"She seems like a good one," Jasper said, dragging my focus back to him.

I nodded. "It's only early days, but I think I'm in love." I chuckled.

He raised his brow at me. "Well, I'm happy for you, bro. And it probably makes it sting a bit less too."

I furrowed my brow. "Makes what sting a bit less?"

"The fact that my guy beat you. From what I

hear, you two have some kind of beef... can't feel good to have him one up you."

I didn't reply.

"You didn't even see it coming. I'm just sayin', must make you lose sleep at night."

Jasper was baiting me. And it was working.

Bastard.

I hated knowing that Armageddon had one upped me. It had been pushed from my mind lately, all thoughts replaced by Amarah, but he was right, it *didn't* feel good, and I needed to get my head back in the game.

"You say that like it's over," I replied. "Who said I was done?"

Jasper didn't reply, just looked at me with an expression that was both amused and a little arrogant.

He clearly had faith in the guy he'd hired to help him find Hannah, and he was justified in that. I'd been sloppy and careless then, but no more. It was the slap in the face I'd needed to get my shit together and keep it tight.

I was on the top of my game now, and it was time I got to work. This was a back-and-forth battle that had to come to an end. The sooner the better.

Life was clearly being kind to me lately. I'd got the girl of my dreams, my sister was back in my life, neither of my brothers had hurt themselves or done anything illegal in the past month... but the real cherry on the top would be getting revenge.

It was time I made that happen.

Amarah sidled up next to me, her hip bumping my thigh. "You look deep in thought."

"Oh, so you're going to talk to me now that you're finished with your new best friends?" I teased.

She lifted a shoulder and smirked. "Well, I need a ride home, don't I?"

I chuckled. "You sure know the way to a man's heart."

"Nah, that's food and sex."

She's not wrong there.

I pulled her flush against me, my hands landing on her ass.

I needed to taste her... the way she'd been teasing me all night, looking so sexy – she was driving me crazy.

She looked up at me, those dark eyes wide as I lowered my mouth to hers.

Her lips were soft, and her tongue tasted like the fruity drinks she'd been sipping all night. Her mouth moved against mine with the same urgency I gave her.

I heard someone clear their throat, but I ignored it; they could fuck right off.

She sank her teeth into my bottom lip, and I let out a groan.

"All right, that's enough of that. Take it home, you two."

That was Charlotte's voice.

I felt Amarah smile against my lips.

I chuckled, the sound vibrating up my chest.

"Do you want to stay together tonight?" I asked her softly. I didn't want to pressure her, but I had absolutely zero intentions of sleeping anywhere that wasn't right next to her. I had even less intentions of taking no for a fucking answer.

"What do you think?"

"I think I rarely ask a question that I don't already know the answer to." I smirked.

"Well then, Watson, you tell me what I'm going to say."

I deliberated for a moment. "I think you would have gone with... 'Your place or mine?'" I asked with a smirk.

"Ooooh, I'm awfully forward in your narrative. I like it."

"Love me a woman who knows what she wants."

"Love me a man who knows how to take control," she replied.

"Good. My place. You can brush your teeth with your finger and sleep in one of my t-shirts. Under-wear optional."

I heard Charotte groan in disgust. Truth be told, I'd forgotten they were all still there. I was too wrapped up in Amarah... the little smirks, the batting of her lashes, the pout of her lips...

The idea of her in my bed.

"Sorry, short stuff. Maybe it's time we went our separate ways." I apologised to my sister without looking away from the brunette in my arms.

"I think it was probably time for that *before* you stuck your tongues down each other's throats."

"Sorry, Charlotte," I replied.

"I'd like it noted on the record that *I'm* not all that sorry," Amarah said with a giggle.

Charlotte laughed at that.

"The honeymoon phase. I remember those days," Parker said.

I glanced over just in time to see my sister glare at him as he emerged from the car, clearly bored of waiting.

"Are you saying it doesn't feel like that with me anymore?" Charlotte demanded.

He chuckled and dodged the jab she threw to his midsection.

He was just playing; we all knew that. Those two were almost sickening to be around.

"Fuck him up, Little Red," Jasper encouraged.

Charlotte made a few feeble attack attempts, and Parker let her think she had a shot, like the gentleman he was when it came to my sister.

"Well, this has been fun, but we're out of here," I announced.

I had more important things to do.

Far more important things.

Charlotte gave up stalking Parker and pulled Amarah away from me for a hug. "It was *so* good to meet you. We're hanging out again soon."

"Did we just become best friends?" Amarah replied animatedly.

"Did you just quote *Step Brothers?*" I demanded, interrupting their conversation.

She smirked over her shoulder at me, her expression said *of course I did.*

"Just when I thought you couldn't get any better," I muttered to myself.

She laughed, mockingly. "Oh, Watson... you've got *no* idea."

I held back a groan. That tone, the insinuation, the way she looked...

Damn.

I'm screwed.

———

"So, *this* is where the magic happens," Amarah said as she strolled around my living room, her gaze travelling over my computer setup.

"Depends what type of magic you're referring to." I smirked from my position in the doorway where I was watching her carefully.

I didn't really let anyone come inside my place unless they were family. I had a lot of secrets hidden within these servers and hard drives, secrets that could get me into a lot of shit, with a lot of important people – people that weren't to be messed with.

She rolled her eyes in an exaggerated gesture.

I held my hands up in surrender. "Oh, *come on,* you left me wide open for that one. It was almost too easy."

"Then have some discipline," she teased.

"Not one of my strong suits, unfortunately."

"I think that might be a generic trait within your family tree."

"Are you suggesting that my brothers aren't the absolute epitome of self-control?"

She grinned at me. "I'm more concerned about you, but I tell you what.... they're certainly *something*. I'm not sure I can actually figure either of them out."

"I wouldn't even try." I smirked. "They're balls to the wall insane. I've seen Louis be nothing but completely focused for weeks, months on end even when he's in camp for a big fight – weighing every portion of food, not doing anything that didn't serve his goal... but then I've also seen him eat nothing but peanut butter and chips for a week straight while he watches Oprah re-runs back-to-back."

She bit back a laugh.

"And Floyd," I continued, "he's even harder to decipher. On the surface he's this crazy, happy-go-lucky, nothing-fazes-me kind of guy, but he's got some secrets, man. I swear to God, that kid has seen some shit."

"At least your sister seems to know how to behave herself."

I shrugged. "She's been in her fair share of trouble. She dated this absolute fucker of a man once. He caused her some problems again a while back, but that's handled now. She's a good girl."

Amarah strolled across the room, slowly prowling towards me. "Let me guess... you took care of that problem?"

"What makes you say that?" I asked as she reached me.

She slid into the gap between my body and the door frame, and looked up at me, eyes wide. "Call it an educated guess. I think you've spent your life taking care of the three of them."

I raised a brow in question, waiting for more.

"You talk about them as though they're your children, not your siblings... there's a protective edge to your tone... that, and the fact that I've never heard you even mention your parents, suggests to me that it's just been the four of you for the most part."

"*Perceptive*," I breathed.

"Maybe you're not as hard to read as you'd like to think you are," she whispered, her fingers trailing a path down my chest, towards my stomach.

Fuck, maybe I wasn't after all. "What read are you getting on me right now?" I murmured.

I groaned as her lips found purchase on the skin just below my ear.

"I'd say you're thinking it's time for bed," she replied, her warm breath tickling my neck.

I had her in my arms, her ass gripped in my palms and her back flat against the door before she even managed another breath.

"Right again, beautiful," I said before I slammed

my lips to hers, kissing her with every last drop of built-up sexual tension I had in me.

It'd only been a few weeks, but it was a few weeks too many as far as I was concerned. I'd been fighting the urge to fuck her on the hood of my car since the minute I first laid eyes on her.

I'd been patient.

I was basically a saint.

I'd waited long enough, and if the breathy moans coming out of the beauty in my arms were anything to go by, she felt the same way.

She gave as good as she got, her lips and tongue pushing back against me, her body melded against mine.

I pulled her back from the wall before pushing her against it again, her back making contact with a thump.

She hummed deep in her throat; the sound full of appreciation.

Her hand wound into the strands of my hair, tugging hard and forcing my head back.

I growled.

Fuck, that's hot.

Our mouths separated and our eyes met. I saw everything I needed to see in hers; want, desire, passion... it was all there. I didn't need to see a mirror to know she'd be seeing the same in mine.

"I need to shower," she panted.

I didn't reply, just walked with her still wrapped around my waist, in the direction of my bathroom.

I flicked on the shower with one hand, before sliding her ass onto my vanity. Her legs stayed cinched around my waist as the bathroom slowly filled with steam around us.

"Fuck," I grunted as I looked at her swollen lips.

She was so fucking hot.

"Fuck," she mimicked, her tongue darting out to moisten her lips.

That was it. I snapped.

She gasped as I lifted her again, our lips meeting as I walked us both, fully clothed into the shower.

"Holy shit." She squealed as the hot water cascaded down on us, soaking through my t-shirt in an instant.

I captured her lips roughly at the same moment as her back connected with the tiled wall of the shower.

I kissed her until I was panting for breath and desperate for more. Water streamed between us, soaking us both to the skin.

"Tyler," she moaned as I moved lower, nipping at the skin on her neck and kissing along her collarbone.

I slid her onto the ledge in the shower wall and took a step back to look at her.

Holy shit.

Amarah was sex on legs on any given day, but soaking wet, her tank top plastered to her skin and her long hair dripping... she was unfathomably sexy.

"What?" she breathed as her eyes scanned my body, head to toe.

I shook my head. "*You*."

She leaned back and beckoned me forward. "Lose the shirt."

I didn't break eye contact until I pulled the shirt over my head, the soaking-wet fabric dropping to my feet with a splash.

I stepped forwards, between her legs and reached for the wet denim that covered her ass.

I took my time, enjoying every gasp and sharp intake of breath as my fingers intentionally brushed her pussy. I undid the button and lowered the zip as she watched me.

She lifted her ass as I tugged at the waist band and slid her shorts down her legs, discarding them in the same manner as my shirt.

I dropped to my knees in front of her, water running down my face as I leaned in, kissing her through her thin, lacy underwear – the white fabric was see-through from the water, and the sight before me had me instantly hard.

She let out a loud moan as I slid the fabric to the side and my tongue met her sexy-as-hell pussy.

"*Fuck*," I groaned as I tasted her for the first time.

"Oh my god," she gasped as I circled her clit with my tongue before sucking it gently.

Her hands gripped my hair, pulling me closer.

I chuckled against her, thoroughly enjoying how much *she* was enjoying this.

I slipped two fingers inside her, working her as I licked and sucked at the place that I could see made her squirm. She cried out as I slipped my fingers in and out, bringing her to a frenzy.

I wanted to fuck her so badly, my cock was nearly exploding out of my shorts.

"Oh my god, you're going to make me come." She half screamed the words at me.

"Come all over my face, beautiful."

She fell apart on my command, her body sagging as she rode out her release. I gripped her waist, holding her in place as she orgasmed.

"Holy shit," she breathed.

I looked up at her face. She was sated, her lids hooded, and her lips pouted. Steam filled the shower as the water continued to pour down around us, giving her an almost surreal aura.

I tugged on my zipper and dragged my jeans and boxer briefs down my legs.

"You on the pill?" I asked as I palmed my dick.

She nodded.

"Good," I grunted as I lined myself up and thrust deeply inside of her.

"Oh fuck," she choked out.

Oh fuck didn't even come close to covering it. She felt like heaven.

"You're so wet," I grunted as I stilled inside her.

"You did that."

"Fuck yes I did."

I claimed her mouth, tugging her bottom lip roughly into my mouth and sucking it hard. She kissed me back with just as much heat, her arms wrapped around my neck as she hung on for dear life, while I pounded relentlessly into her.

I lifted her off the ledge and spun her around. She didn't put up a fight as I bent her over and resumed fucking her from behind.

"Holy shit," she groaned as her hands ran down the shower walls, trying and failing to find purchase.

I took one hand off her hips and reached for her long, dark, soaking-wet hair, and gripped it in my hand, pulling it hard. Her head tipped back and her back arched.

"You like that?"

"Fuck yes," she replied.

I slammed into her over and over again, the pleasure so much I could almost see stars.

"I'm going to come in you."

"Fill me up," she cried.

I lost it.

I shuddered, my whole body shaking with my release as I spurted ropes of cum deep inside her sexy little pussy.

I moved slowly in and out of her, riding out the last of the tremors still racking through me.

That was... fuck.

That was the most intense orgasm of my life.

"Jesus Christ."

She was motionless, breathing heavily, my dick still inside her and the water from the shower beating down on us. I released her hair and rubbed my hand gently down her back.

"You all good, baby?"

She hummed deep in her throat, the sound one of pure satisfaction.

I chuckled.

I slipped out of her and pulled her right under the spray of the water with me, washing her and kissing her until I'd touched every inch of her body.

She kissed me back as her hands roamed over my skin, exploring every inch of me.

"Come out when you're ready," I told her as I got out, wrapping a towel around my waist.

She emerged a few minutes later, a towel wrapped around her body and her wet hair trailing down her back.

"That wasn't exactly what I had in mind when I said I needed a shower," she admitted sheepishly.

"Really? It was *exactly* what I had in mind." I smirked, a shit-eating grin stretching across my face.

She rolled her eyes at me as she slipped the shirt I handed her over her head, and holy shit; if I'd thought she looked irresistible before, it was *nothing* compared to how good she looked now.

Thirty seconds before, I'd been perfectly satisfied.... But that was short lived now that she was back in my line of sight.

I knew damn well I'd be having her again before the end of the night, and the look in her eyes told me she knew it too.

CHAPTER 16

Amarah

"I BET they're not as hot in real life as they look on TV."

"Not even close... they're *hotter*."

Jessie groaned. "This is such bullshit, you know that, right? I can't believe you went to that concert without me *and* got to go backstage and hang out with celebrities. You're the worst friend I ever had."

I huffed out a laugh at her sulky expression.

"You're such a whiny little bitch."

She flipped me off.

"Do you want to see what I got you or what?"

"If you offer me your ticket stubs, I'm legit going to start plotting your murder."

I laughed. "Way to overreact. And no, it's way

better than ticket stubs, but if you keep sulking, I'm going to auction it on e-bay and then spend the money while you watch."

She pretended to be unfazed. "Do whatever you need to do. Unless it's covered in Jasper's sweat, I'm not interested anyway."

"Well... coincidental that you mention *that* fact specifically..."

That got her attention. She put down the magazine she was pretending to read. It landed with a thud on my coffee table. "I'm listening."

I rolled my eyes and pulled the two t-shirts out of the bag at my feet.

"You got me concert tees?" she asked sceptically as I handed them to her.

"Nope." I smirked. "I got you the shirts off their backs. White is Parker's, grey is Jasper's. They're signed. You can thank me now."

She didn't move, instead she just gaped at me.

I sat back in my seat, prepared to wait her out.

She carefully unfolded each shirt, looked at the signatures, sniffed them both and then finally yelled, "Oh my fucking god!"

I clutched my chest as I scowled at her. "You scared the shit out of me."

"I'm not even sorry." She grinned. "I have the sweaty t-shirts they performed a live show in. I literally own some of their DNA."

I laughed at her overwhelming joy.

"That's not all I got you."

"I don't need anything more; my life is complete." She sighed dreamily as she hugged the shirts to her chest.

"Okay then, well I guess I could see if my hairdresser wants to go on a date with the drummer from Cold Cut if you're not interested."

The look in her eyes was something I'd never seen before in my life. "If you have Wilder Hansen's number, so help me god, I'm going to lose my mind."

"Prepare yourself to be mindless then, Jessie. He personally requested I give it to you."

"I don't believe you." She tossed the shirts aside, her prized possessions now one upped by the idea of a date with a rock star. "*Prove it.*"

"I told him you'd say that."

That was exactly why I'd got evidence. Jess was never going to believe that Wilder had actually asked for her number, but I had the footage to prove it.

I'd been raving about Cold Cut since we got back from the concert the night before last, and I'd successfully converted Jess into a lunatic fan in that short space of time too. When Jessie went in, she went *all* in. she knew everything the internet could tell her about the members of Cold Cut, and she also knew a few things she'd had me dig deeper for.

I was just *that* good of a friend.

I'd waited until now to tell her this piece of information though, I wanted to do it in person... there was no way I was willing to miss the look on her face when I showed her the video I was about to show her now.

I flicked through my phone until I found what I was looking for. I hit play and turned the screen around to face her.

Wilder's face came into view. "Hey, Jessie girl, I'm just here with my new BFF Amarah, and she's been pimping you out *hard*." He grunts as my elbow knocks him in the ribs, out of shot. "Anyway, I think you're hot as hell. Give me a call. I'm gonna take you out."

There's some ruckus in the background, which from memory, was the twins giving Wilder shit for 'telling instead of asking', and then the video cut out.

"I think I'm going into cardiac arrest."

Jess was frozen, staring at the now black screen of my phone as she clutched her chest.

"Is this what dying feels like?"

I couldn't blame her; Wilder Hansen was *seriously* hot. And it wasn't like I could judge; it'd taken me a solid twenty minutes to stop blushing and stuttering whenever Jasper, Parker or any of the other band members spoke to me – and none of them were even trying to date me. Her reaction was fair and justified, as far as I was concerned.

I took her phone from the seat next to her, retrieved his number from my phone and typed it into her contact list.

"If you don't text him, I'm disowning you," I warned her.

"Oh, I'll be texting him, alright. That man is my future husband, he just doesn't know it yet."

I laughed as she returned to her usual, animated, totally over-the-top self.

We spent ten minutes going back and forth between what she should and shouldn't say in her first message. She finally settled on, "so, where are you taking me?"

It was hardly going to make it into the flirting hall of fame, but with Jessie, less was definitely more.

"Tell me more about Tyler. How are things going with you two?"

I sighed, not an exasperated sigh, but a dreamy one.

He was dreamy.

The whole date was dreamy.

So much so, that I'd dreamed about him for the past two nights straight.

I was catching feelings, and I was catching them fast.

"He's too good to be true."

"Pffft." She rolled her eyes. "You're so unreasonable. You finally get hold of a decent guy, and you're going to convince yourself that he's *too* good. It's official, you're going to die alone."

"Gee thanks."

"It's okay though, you can spend holidays and special occasions with me and Wilder."

I ran my hands over my face in disbelief.

"Oooh, you can babysit for us when we want to go out for date nights."

"You have children now?"

She lifted her brows at me. "Two girls and a boy. *Obviously*."

"Obviously," I repeated, amused, if not a little concerned about her mental state.

"Seriously though, talk to me. What's his family like?"

"Crazy, but perfect. His brothers have a lot of energy, but they're really smart, driven guys when you get past all the madness. And his sister... she's amazing. Hands down the sweetest woman I've ever met."

"Rude and hurtful, but whatever," Jessie intercepted.

I shook my head at her. 'Sweet' was not the word you'd use to describe my best friend.

I ignored her. "The boys all love her to death, and somehow she can control them. Sort of."

"Do you think they liked you?"

I shrugged a shoulder. "The twins seemed to. Charlotte definitely did. She basically gave me her blessing to marry Ty."

"*Ty*, huh?" She raised a brow at me, amused at my use of a nickname for the man I was meant to be keeping my distance from. A task I was failing spectacularly at.

I shot her a sheepish look. "Must have rubbed off from his family."

"What's the go with him and Hannah? Did you meet her?"

As per usual, Jessie was in the loop with everything. She knew about Tyler and Hannah's history. We'd touched on the fact that I'd seen the two of them talking but given that she had a brand-new band to obsess over, and she also needed to extract every possible piece of information about Parker and Jasper that I had, we'd done nothing more than discuss it briefly. I still had a *lot* to tell her about the whole night.

"Yeah, I met her, and I didn't want to like her, but she's kinda cool. I don't think I trust her all that much, but she wasn't who I'd pictured her to be in my mind. Her and Jasper are so smitten. It's pretty adorable really."

"That doesn't excite me... doesn't sound like any drama at all."

Jess twisted her legs up under herself and gave me a look that told me she was looking for me to spill some tea.

"So, who's the villain then?"

I thought about it for a minute. I knew what she was talking about. There was *always* a villain. Some bitchy blonde or some salty brunette. Maybe a sleezy guy or a grumpy manager. These kinds of circles didn't have perfect harmony. That wasn't the world we lived in. Only, theirs was exactly that. There was no drama. They were tight – close knit – they had each other's backs. All except...

Shit.

"Me," I finally answered. "*I'm* the villain."

"Huh," she mused. "Well, I guess you kind of are."

The thought deflated my previously joyous mood.

"Or maybe *he* is," she offered, sensing my reaction.

I shook my head. "I'm as sure as I can be at this point, that he has *no idea* who I am. He came to my building looking for Armageddon, there's no doubt about that, but he doesn't know it's me. I could be wrong, but I really don't think I am."

So that only left me. *I* was the bad guy, and I was beginning to hate myself for it.

"Maybe you better get out of there before you do something crazy, like fall in love... or sleep with him."

I giggled nervously.

Her eyes flashed back to me. "Oh my god, *what?*"

"I slept with him... but I haven't fallen in love, I promise," I replied quickly.

She rolled her eyes. "Oh, *please*, you're a female – we all know that if you're sleeping with him, then you'll be falling in love in no time. That's how it works."

"Pffft."

"It's basic math, Rah Rah, I don't make the rules."

"That doesn't even make sense."

"Yet you know exactly what I mean, don't you? How's that for logic, huh?"

"Stop."

"I can't. You're already falling into his dick sand; I can feel it."

"*Stop*."

"Whatever, what do I care anyway? Not my monkey, not my circus. So how was it? Tell me allllll about it. I need details. Is he good? I bet he's *so* good, right? I can't believe you finally had sex! I've been feeling so bad for your poor vagina."

"Oh my god," I mouthed, falling back in my chair dramatically. "He was *so* good. We started in the shower, Jessie, can you imagine where it ended if we *started* in the shower?"

"This is the stuff dreams are made of."

"Yours and mine both, sister," I agreed.

"I'm going to tell you *all* about mine and Wilder's sex life, so prepare yourself for that."

"Oh, I'm already prepared to hear all about the sex you're not yet having." I crossed my legs at the ankles and rested them on the coffee table.

She gave me a 'what the fuck look'. "Listen to this bitch; has sex *once* and thinks she can throw shade at those of us who aren't so fortunate."

I smirked at her. "It's cute you think it was just once."

Her lips stretched into a full-blown grin. "Dayuu-uuum, girl. Why you gotta play me like that?"

"Go back to sniffing your groupie t-shirts and stop giving me shit."

She picked up the shirts and brought them to her

nose again. "Mmmmm. *So good,*" she moaned. "Seems unlikely that I'm going to stop giving you a hard time though, just so we're clear. What kind of friend would I be if I backed off now, when my bestie was finally getting some D, *and* was right on course to fall in luuuuuurve? No, sorry, I'm a better friend than that."

"You know what? I feel like I should be setting you up with one of the twins. You're on their wavelength currently, and that's reaaaaaalllly saying something, girlfriend."

"I don't know whether I should be proud or insulted," she mused aloud as she reached for the magazine she'd been pretending to read earlier and opened it, presumably to actually read it this time. "I guess that's a matter of opinion."I just rolled my eyes in response. Arguing with Jessie was akin to arguing with a brick wall.

I unlocked my phone and began mindlessly scrolling social media – the account wasn't in my name of course – I wasn't stupid, and I had no friends or followers on there, but I still enjoyed losing myself for an hour or two watching clips that had no relevance to my life.

A girl has to get her kicks.

———

It felt like an eternity had passed since Tyler had threatened to take me down, but here I was, desperately scrambling to recover what I could from the current job I was working.

The security company that had employed me would never know of the breach that just occurred – if I could work fast enough to get everything back in order – but *I'd* know.

Tyler had come too close, yet again, to ruining something good for me – and now that I could picture the man behind the screen, it felt all the more personal.

I tapped out seemingly endless lines of code, one after another, my rage growing every time my finger connected with a key.

My anger was misplaced. Obviously, we were rivals – I'd even go as far as to say that he was my nemesis. *Of course* he was going to try and take me down.

I'd done the very same to him without one ounce of remorse.

The mystery of 'Armageddon' would have been driving him insane, I'm sure it always had, but Tyler had come at me today with a renewed passion. I couldn't help but think that seeing Jasper and Hannah again had sparked something inside of him.

It had certainly been a strange experience for me. Jasper was almost like a friend to me, and it had been a challenge, especially with a few drinks in my system, to remember that Jasper was friends with Armageddon, *not* Amarah – and to the world, we were not the same person.

We were strangers, as far as he was concerned anyway.

My phone chimed on the desk next to me, and I allowed myself a moment to glance at the screen to see who it was.

Tyler.

I didn't quite catch the whole message before the screen flicked back to sleep mode, but I caught the gist of it. He was having a great day and he hoped I was too.

Fuck's sake.

I was *not* having a good day, and that was entirely down to him and the fact that he'd chosen the busiest day of my week to inconvenience me. It didn't surprise me that he was having a good day though; he'd been a total pain in my ass.

I didn't pick up my phone. Instead, shifted my focus back to the screen in front of me, my fingers flying faster over the keys now.

I was going to fix this, but the reality was that when I did, he was just going to come after me in some other way.

I needed something to get him off my case. Part of me wanted to shut down my entire system and start over – build a new one from scratch, but that would have taken time, and time was something I didn't have the luxury of wasting right now.

Business had come in thick and fast over the past two days, and I had every intention of fulfilling each and every contract. If Tyler would fuck off and let me do my job, that was.

I hit the enter key and breathed a sigh of relief that, for now at least, I had done enough.

My client's asset was safe and sound, and I was going to spend the rest of the morning locking that shit down so tight that *nothing* could get in again – not even Tyler Watson... not even Tyler Watson on speed.

He might have gotten into my pants, but he sure as shit wasn't getting into my business again – not in the next twenty-four hours at least.

I dropped my head back and breathed in deeply.

This was getting messy.

I was catching feelings for Tyler, *fast*, and as much as I tried to deny that fact, there was no point in lying to myself. I had real feelings for the guy. I wanted him in my life, I wanted *him*. And up until this very moment, I'd been able to believe that maybe I could keep the two ways in which our lives crossed paths separate, only now that I was actually dealing with it... I wasn't so convinced.

This stuff was who we were. I wanted to believe we could have some type of future, but it was becoming increasingly difficult to see how that could work with this secret between us.

The shrill ring of my work phone startled me, and I snapped forward, fumbling for it.

I flipped the screen over and was more than shocked by the name I saw.

Jasper Jones.

I was torn, I normally spoke to clients with a voice distortion app that made me sound like a male, but with Jasper, I'd ditched it. He knew I was a woman, but things were different now. I'd been in his presence in the weekend, and I was shitting myself that he'd put two and two together.

Another few seconds passed while I debated my decision, before finally settling on just being me. Being anything different would only arouse suspicion.

"*Jasper*, long time no chat..." I answered, "did you misplace another girlfriend?"

His chuckle filled the line. "Not bad, *A*. A little ruthless, but I can appreciate the humour."

I grinned. "To what do I owe the pleasure?"

"I actually thought I better give you a courtesy call... I've got a confession to make... I think I might have fucked up..."

My heartrate accelerated slightly.

He could have done *anything*. He could have told Tyler I was a girl. Even worse, that I was a girl with a hint of a Spanish accent... he could have fucked *everything* up.

I tried to breathe normally. "What did you do?"

He blew out a breath. "I dunno... I saw Tyler over the weekend..."

I knew this, I already knew this. I wanted to scream at him to get to the good part, but unless I wanted one of the world's biggest names in music to think I was wildly unhinged, I needed to keep my composure.

"I think I might have baited him," he confessed. "I was paying him out about how you beat him last time, with all that Hannah stuff, and he gave me the impression it wasn't over yet. I think he's going to be coming for you."

That's it?

I breathed a sigh of relief. Tyler was *always* going to be coming for me, this was nothing new. Poor, sweet, naïve Jasper was over here thinking he'd done something wrong – kicked something off, merely by stirring the pot a little bit.

I didn't even blame him for giving Tyler shit. He had every right to be pissed, and a little smug.

It did confirm my theory though... and explained why Tyler was gunning for me harder in the past eight hours than he had in the past month combined – his competitive nature had been poked, and I knew better than anyone that you didn't poke the bear and not expect to get bitten.

"I've actually had the pleasure of him trying to fuck with me, just this very morning... but you can relax. This is nothing new. We've been battling back and forth for *years*, you're just a minor player in a much bigger game, Jones."

"*Minor player?* That's all I am? You really know how to wound a guy."

A smile played on my lips. "I hate to break it to

you, but this isn't rock star land; you're a nobody in tech town."

He chuckled again. "The fact that you just referred to your professional industry as 'tech town' has made my day."

This was what I liked about Jasper. He was just a regular guy. You'd never guess from talking to him that he was one of the wealthiest celebrities on earth – or that he'd been voted into the top ten for 'sexiest man alive' last year. He was chill. It didn't appear that fame had changed him too much.

"Well, I guess my call was unnecessary after all, sounds like you can handle Tyler. Not that I ever had any doubt."

"I can definitely handle Tyler," I replied, my tone filled with a hell of a lot more confidence than I felt. "And it was nice to hear from you anyway. You don't need some type of crisis to reach out, you know."

"Yeah, I know, I know... it's been too long. I've had a bit on."

"Marital bliss and impending fatherhood, you mean?"

He chuckled in agreement.

"Two things I never saw happening for me," he mused, "not until her anyway."

I might not have been entirely convinced by Hannah, but I sure as hell was sold on the love between her and Jasper. They were two puzzle pieces that fit together perfectly.

"I'm happy for you. You two look so good together."

I realised my slip the moment it left my lips.

There was a pause, then, "You've seen us together?"

My mind scrambled, looking for a logical explanation. My gaze landed on a magazine on the table next to me.

"Only on the internet and in the gossip mags," I replied quickly, hoping like hell that they'd featured somewhere... *anywhere*, lately.

"Fucking paps," he grumbled, and I breathed a sigh of relief.

"Rather you than me," I agreed. "Anyway, I should let you go, but thanks for the heads up, no matter how unnecessary. It's very sweet and I appreciate it."

I was suddenly keen as hell to end this call before I went and said something else stupid, something that I couldn't talk myself out of so easily.

It was bound to happen. There was a good reason I preferred to work from behind a keyboard and not over the phone. I spoke before thinking, far too often.

"No worries," he replied. "And good luck with Tyler. I was hoping he'd give it up now that he's all loved up and distracted, but I guess the guy is more stubborn and proud than I thought."

"Loved up, huh?" I questioned, even though I knew I shouldn't.

"Yeah, he's got himself a woman. She seems cool.

Hannah hasn't stopped going on about how they're going to make pretty babies."

"Lucky lady," I mused.

"Lucky guy," he argued.

I smirked to myself. This was all too weird, but the one positive was that my secret was safe... for now at least.

CHAPTER 17

Tyler

I HEARD my cell phone ringing, but I ignored it. I was more interested in the woman next to me, and the stories she was telling me about growing up with her wild-sounding family. The world could wait.

The ringing stopped but started again immediately.

I groaned.

"I think you better answer that." Amarah nudged my knee.

I got to my feet and picked up my phone from the coffee table.

I frowned when I saw Parker's name flashing across the screen. Park hardly ever called me, and when he did, it was rarely just to have a chat.

"It's Parker," I told Amarah.

"I still can't believe that you have Parker Sloan's phone number," she gushed.

I chuckled at her before picking up the call.

"Park, what's up?" I answered.

"Turn on the news, *now*." His voice was borderline hysterical.

A knot formed in the pit of my stomach as I rushed to grab the remote control for my TV – there was only one thing that could get Parker to sound like that, and it was worry for my sister.

Amarah sensed my change of mood immediately and got to her feet.

"What is it?" I demanded at the same moment the screen flickered to life. I hit the channel and heard a gasp leave me.

There was a massive pile up on the highway. Cars were everywhere, some of them upside down, some of them smashed to pieces. There were helicopters circling and smoke filled the air.

"Charlotte is there."

No, no, no. She can't be.

"Have you talked to her?" I demanded. "Is she okay?"

Amarah tugged on my arm, but I was frozen to the spot, my eyes glued to the absolute carnage on the TV in front of me.

"I can't get her on the phone," he whispered.

No.

I heard a guttural sob. I didn't have a clue if it came from him or me.

"Ty?" a different voice came through the line. "It's Jasper. We thought there might be something you can do."

"Talk to me, Jasper," I demanded. "What the fuck happened?"

Amarah stepped in front of me, her eyes full of concern.

I pulled the phone from my ear and hit the speaker button. "Amarah is here too, you're on speaker."

"They're saying it's a live hostage situation. There was a bomb apparently, that's why there's so much fucking carnage. Parker was on the phone with Charlotte when it happened. She saw something up ahead and then the line went dead. She's with Sammy, and she's in the truck, but we don't know if they're okay or how far away they are from the site – cell service has been cut somehow."

"Fuck," I muttered.

Amarah covered her mouth with her hand – her shocked eyes darting between the phone in my hand and the absolute shit show on the news.

"Fuck!" I yelled.

My sister, my little sister – the most important woman in my life – was in the middle of *that*.

"What do we do?" I thought aloud.

Amarah shook her head. She had no more idea than I did.

"We don't know," Jasper replied, "but maybe you might be able to do something. Whoever the fuck is running this show has contact with the police, and the media are streaming the scene live, but every other cell phone in a two-mile radius is out. How the fuck are they doing that?"

"Stay on the line," I barked.

"I'm putting you on speaker too," Jasper replied.

I ran over to my computer setup and tossed the phone down onto my desk before I began frantically typing on my keyboard, pulling up updates about the situation and what the chatter on the web was about it.

"Have they made any demands?" I asked.

Amarah turned up the volume on the TV and then followed me over.

"I don't know, man. They showed their vehicle on the news before, and they've said that the police are in communication. There's people dead on the road..."

I could hear him starting to lose it.

"*Don't*," I snapped. "Don't even go there. Charlotte is going to be fine. She's got a bodyguard and she's in the most heavily armoured vehicle known to man – which I will never judge Parker for, *ever* again."

"I know," Jasper replied. "I know. She'll be okay, she has to be."

I nodded in agreement. Amarah squeezed my shoulder.

"I've found the police call audio."

"How?" Jasper questioned.

"Is now really the time for a lesson in hacking the nationwide police database?" I deadpanned.

He was silent.

Didn't think so.

I hit the play button and we all listened to the worthless pieces of shit making their demands to the police officers that had arrived at the scene. Jasper was right – they were still using their cell phones, but somehow had blocked everyone else's.

They also wanted to be seen, because they were making no move to block the camera crews' live feeds.

The sick pieces of shit wanted a show, and they obviously had someone in the know, on the ground with them – inside that armoured truck if I had to fathom a guess.

If it wasn't in our best interests to be able to see what was happening on the ground, I'd have found a way to cut the footage myself, just to fuck them off.

Their list of demands weren't ground-breaking. They told the police to stay back, they refused to allow medical assistance for the injured and they threatened to start killing civilians if their expecta-tions weren't met.

"What do they want?" Amarah whispered.

"To make a scene," I sneered. "Terrorist pricks. It's not about money, it's about putting their name to the havoc they're creating."

"What are we going to do?" she breathed.

I shrugged. Honestly, I had no fucking clue what we were going to do. I couldn't hack these asshole's brains and get them to stop being the scum of the earth... I couldn't do shit about shit.

Floyd couldn't drive in there, and Louis couldn't fight his way out of it.

We were all as helpless as one another right now.

"I need to know she's okay, Ty, I need to hear her fucking voice." Parker's voice came from somewhere on Jasper's end. "Can't you hack her cell?"

"I already tried," I replied.

I'd done that within about thirty seconds of sitting my ass in my chair.

"I've got her location and that's it. That doesn't help us right now, we already know where she is. But she is a little bit back from the terrorists, that's something at least."

It was nothing in the scheme of high-power weapons and bombs, but it was something, and something was the best we could hope for right now.

"Can't you just turn it back on?"

I refrained from rolling my eyes at Jasper. In theory, it probably seemed quite simple, but the reality was that we weren't dealing with some under-prepared halfwits here. These guys knew their stuff and while it was possible, it wouldn't be easy, especially from so far away.

"Um, Ty..." Amarah tapped my shoulder and then pointed at the television screen.

Half a dozen men with hoods and balaclavas on, climbed out of the back of the truck, all of them carrying what looked like automatic shotguns.

That was about the last thing I wanted to see.

I didn't even bother conversing with Jasper. I knew they'd be seeing exactly what I was seeing.

I got to work on trying to figure out what they were using to block the cell service in the area. I hacked into the nearest tower, but it was scrambled to hell. It was going to take too long and be next to impossible without getting closer.

"I'm putting you on hold," I barked.

I didn't wait for a response, just hit the button and then hit call on Floyd's number.

"Ty, what the fuck is going on?" he answered before the phone even had a chance to ring. "No one's picking up."

"How quickly can you get to my house?"

"I'm nearly at Parker and Charlotte's."

"Get to mine, now."

"On it," he replied. I heard the screech of his tyres as he turned back towards my place.

"See you in five."

The line went dead.

There was no way he should have been able to get here in only three hundred seconds or so, but I knew he would. He was fast, and these were desperate times.

I took Jasper off hold.

"Floyd is on his way to me. I want to get closer."

"What are you going to do?"

I started packing up my laptop, power packs, portable hard drives... anything I thought might be useful, even though I really had no fucking idea what this might take.

Amarah took things from me and stacked them in her arms.

She had no idea what we were doing, but the fact that she was up for whatever it was anyway, only made me fall for her more.

"What are you going to do?" Jasper demanded, having been ignored the first time.

"Honestly, man... I've got no fucking idea."

———

The door swung open wildly after only about four and a half minutes. "I'm here, what the fuck are we doing?"

"We're getting closer," I replied, already heading for the door he'd just entered. "You're driving."

"Obviously," he drawled.

I ignored him and marched out the door. Amarah followed.

"In the back with me," I told her as I held the door open.

Floyd jumped in the front seat and revved the engine.

Amarah's eyes were on me as I slid into the back seat after her. She looked a little scared. I could hardly blame her – there was a real shitty situation going down and we were about to go barrelling towards it.

"Put your seat belt on," I instructed at the same moment Floyd hit the gas and we took off down the street.

Her eyes widened and she scrambled to pull the seat belt around herself.

"Tell him not to crash," Jasper's voice came from my phone.

"Give me your phone." I held my hand out to Floyd and he dropped it in my hand without further question.

"Call me back on Floyd's phone," I told Jasper before hitting the red button to end the call.

It'd be more effective having Parker and Jasper on handsfree.

Ringing filled the car via the Bluetooth only a second later. "Hey," I answered.

"Hey." It was Parker's voice this time, from Jasper's number. "I want to keep my phone free... just in case she calls."

There was silence as I set up my laptop, with Amarah handing me each thing I needed without even having to be asked.

"We're only a few minutes away. What do you want me to do?"

I didn't answer.

Amarah laid her hand on my thigh. "Where do you need to go, Watson?"

I looked at her, helplessly. My head was a mess. I was normally so cool under pressure, but I was cracking, big time.

"Cell tower," she told Floyd, making the decision without me. "Get us as close to it as you can without losing signal."

She leant through the middle of the front seat and showed him the location of the tower I'd pointed out earlier.

He nodded once and then whipped down a side street, doing what I assumed was at least twice the legal limit.

"Got caught on a speeding camera on the way over to you; you reckon you could be a dear and wipe that for me?" he asked as he navigated gaps so tight I wouldn't have believed a car could fit if we hadn't just flown through them. "It'd be great if I didn't lose my licence today."

"I'll put it on my list," I muttered.

I glanced at Amarah, and she was gripping the handle on the door so tightly, her knuckles had turned white.

"It's better if you don't look," I whispered.

She pulled her eyes from the window and focused on me instead.

"I don't want to get too much closer or we might lose our connection." Floyd pointed up ahead. "But there it is."

We were on the other side of the highway. "Pull up on that rise over there," I instructed.

Amarah looked relieved when the car finally stopped. I didn't blame her. Floyd's driving always made me feel like I was going to hurl.

"Leave the car running."

He nodded.

He must have been freaking out – this was the quietest he'd ever been, and it reminded me that I had no idea of the location of his other, and just as reckless, clone.

"Where's Lou?" I demanded.

"He's at the gym. I sent one of my security guys to go pick him up and make sure he didn't do anything stupid... like get himself killed," Parker answered. "He'll bring him back here."

Parker was a smart man; I knew I liked him for a reason.

Having Louis trying to barge in there like a lunatic would only make things worse, but that's exactly what he'd want to do when he learnt that Charlotte was in harm's way.

It's what I felt like doing too, but I was smart enough to figure out that throwing punches was no match for weapons of mass destruction – I wasn't sure Lou had the same sense.

"Good," I replied.

"I've tried picking up the frequency from the tower, but I just keep getting bounced – it's a good hack, I'll give the prick that."

"Then try something else," Floyd snapped.

He was getting titchy too, now that we weren't in

motion – he'd always felt like a sitting duck when he was stationary.

Old habits die hard.

"Fuck, I hadn't thought of doing that," I snapped sarcastically.

I tapped away on my keyboard, trying everything I could think of and coming up empty at every avenue. It was fucking weird. If I wasn't looking at it with my own eyes, I could have sworn the cell tower was totally gone. It was nearly impossible to hack something that didn't exist.

"Could you hack the hacker's computer?" Amarah asked.

"I could, if I could get on the same network, we're running off a cell tower in that direction, and he's using the one in front of me. It's different to what I usually do, I can't pick up something like that, quickly. And time is of the essence."

I tried a few other things, but still, nothing.

"Cmon, man," Floyd grumbled.

"I think I have an idea," Amarah said.

"I'm all ears."

I wasn't filled with confidence that she was going to have the answer, but I was out of ideas of my own, and I'd have considered just about anything at this point.

I reached over and squeezed her hand.

She nodded, and then started talking and didn't stop. I ate up every single word she said, and most shockingly of all – it was a solid plan, something I hadn't even thought of, and more importantly, something that might actually let us get hold of my sister.

It was smart.

It was good.

And it was *way* above her pay grade.

She stopped talking suddenly – done with her explanation – and looked at me expectantly.

"How the hell do you know about all that shit?" I gaped at her.

She shifted nervously in her seat and shrugged a shoulder. "I saw it on some hero-saves-the-day kinda movie. No biggie. Watched it like ten times. Thought it might make me sound smart one day."

I eyed her curiously.

Floyd spun around in his chair to look at her in much the same way.

The silence stretched between us.

"Sounds like a woman with a plan," Jasper drawled through the phone.

That was an understatement.

CHAPTER 18

Amarah

I SMILED NERVOUSLY as both the boys stared at me in a state of semi shock. Floyd, probably because he had no idea what I'd said, and Ty, because he *did*.

I really hoped I hadn't just said more than I should have, but this was an emergency. I couldn't just sit there and say nothing... not when I had a possible solution.

I just had to hope that they bought my piss-weak explanation of how or why I knew this stuff.

A movie. As if.

"Do you think that could work?" I prompted, trying to fill the silence.

"I think it's worth a shot," Ty replied slowly.

The basic principle of my idea was to hack

into Charlotte's phone individually, rather than trying to tackle the entire network, and stop it from trying to connect to the current cell network, then, hopefully we could manually connect it to a weaker signal, or boost it off our own, *if* there was one close enough, if we could make all that happen, then at least we should have been able to speak to her, and put Parker and all the guys' minds at ease.

I'd done something similar to this once, but the factors were much different this time, and I wasn't sure it would work. I'd been searching for someone who was missing, I hadn't dealt with some prick actively wiping out a whole radius of service.

Tyler snapped out of his trance and began tapping away on his keyboard frantically, his fingers flying over the keys at a million miles an hour.

"Hmmm, that part won't work, but this might," he muttered to himself.

I was dying to see what he was doing; there was nothing like learning from the master, but I decided that I'd probably pushed my luck far enough for one day. The last thing I needed was to risk blowing my cover any further.

He typed away for a few more minutes before suddenly stopping. He hit one more key.

"It worked," he breathed, "her phone should be active again."

"Where's my fucking phone?"

That was Parker. We all waited with bated

breath as the line rang out. He had the call on speaker so we'd all hear if she answered.

I *needed* her to answer. What Tyler had done had worked – my idea had worked – her phone hadn't been ringing before, but now we needed her to pick up or I had a feeling that nothing would stop the boys from barrelling in there.

"Parker," Charlotte answered, her voice almost a sob.

"*Legs*," he choked out. "I'm here, baby, are you okay?"

"I'm okay. I'm fine."

"God, I love you, legs. I've been dying over here."

"I know. I love you too, rockstar."

The utter adoration in their voices had my throat feeling thick with emotion.

"Are you alright? Are you hurt?"

"I'm fine," she replied quickly. "I'm okay. I'm not hurt. How are you talking to me? The phones don't work."

"Tyler," Parker answered.

"Ty?" Charlotte whispered.

"I'm here, honey," Tyler replied. "We're all here."

I reached over and took Tyler's hand in mine. He had tears welling in his eyes. I knew how scared he'd been, and still was, for his sister.

"What's going on, Little Red, where are you?" Jasper questioned. "Is Sammy with you?"

"Sammy's here. We're still in the car. We're okay. Sammy can fill you in."

"We're about eight hundred meters from where the bomb went off. It wasn't a huge blast, but it was enough to have killed or hurt a lot of people," Sammy answered. "There's about six men walking around with guns, but they've only been this far out a handful of times. Traffic is jammed, I can't get us out of here, but I think things are slowly starting to move behind us, I can hear updates on the police scanner, and I've got binoculars to keep an eye on everything."

"Don't leave her side," Parker instructed, his emotions back in check. "Stay with her until she's in my arms."

"Wouldn't dream of it," Sammy replied. "No one will touch her. They'll have to go through me."

"He made me lie down on the backseat, even though the windows are tinted," Charlotte said.

"Good. Last thing we need is anyone getting wind of who you are."

I shuddered as I realised what he meant. If these guys wanted cash, Parker would pay *any* amount to get Charlotte back. If anyone figured it out, they'd take her.

"Just stay down and wait it out, legs."

"This thing is like a fortress on wheels. We'll be fine. I'll be home with you soon," she promised him, her voice soft as she tried to comfort the man she loved, from the total danger zone she herself sat in.

That was true love, I guess – always being more worried about the other person than you were about yourself.

"You haven't put holes in any of the walls, have you?" she asked him softly.

He chuckled. "Not yet, but that glass lion in the living room has had a restructure."

"Yeah, it went from being in one piece, to being in about five million," Jasper chimed in.

"If you break anything else, I'll come over there and kick your ass, Parker Sloan."

"You promise?" he asked, his tone vulnerable.

"I promise," she whispered. "Is Hannah there?"

"Nah, she's sleeping. She was up all night, so she has no idea that anything is wrong yet. You want me to go wake her?" Jasper questioned.

"*No*," Charlotte replied quickly. "Let her sleep. Just tell her I love her if she wakes up before I get home."

"I'll tell her, Little Red."

"I think we should cut it here, guys, I don't know who I'm dealing with in that van, and the last thing I want is him getting wind of a call going out and tracking Charlotte down," Tyler stated.

"Okay," she whispered.

"I'll reconnect every hour to check in, okay?" he promised.

"Okay. I love you guys, all of you."

"Love you too," Floyd answered quickly, as everyone else responded with much of the same.

"See you soon, baby, I love you more than anything," Parker told her.

"I love you too. Talk to you soon."

"Keep her safe, Sammy," Parker instructed before ending the call.

No one said anything for a few long moments. We all just bathed in the relief of hearing, that for now at least, Charlotte was okay.

The silence was eventually broken by a scuffle and some yelling on Parker and Jasper's end.

"What the fuck is this babysitting bullshit? I swear to God, Park, tell this goon to get his mitts off me. Only reason I haven't knocked him out is because I knew you'd be pissed."

I laughed at the sound of Louis, who by the sounds, had just arrived – with an escort – to Parker's house.

Even Tyler laughed.

"All these cross contaminated calls are getting too much for me," Ty told the guys down the line. "We're coming over and we'll call Charlote together again in an hour, sweet?"

"Yeah, man," Parker replied. "And thank you. Really."

We hit end on the call and all three of us breathed out deeply, almost in unison.

"Thank you," Tyler said, squeezing my hand.

I leaned my head back against the seat and closed my eyes so I didn't have to look at him while I lied. "Don't thank me; thank the genius that is motion pictures."

It had gone three in the morning by the time Sammy and Charlotte had finally gotten back.

We all crashed out in their spare rooms after plenty of tears and hugs from every single person in the room. Even Sammy teared up, and that guy looked like he was made of steel.

It had been a defining moment for me – it reminded me of how short life can really be and that if you have a shot at something real, you shouldn't just let that slip away.

Take the risk.

It made me want to hold on to Tyler tight and never let him go.

I glanced over at him and found him still totally out to it. I slipped out of the bed and shrugged on the hoodie he'd been wearing yesterday. Sunlight was streaming through the gaps in the curtains, so I assumed it was fairly late in the morning, but I still felt knackered. All the adrenaline from the previous day had taken a lot out of us all.

I tiptoed my way down to the kitchen, being careful not to make any noise that might wake someone up.

I heard voices as I got closer, and found Charlotte, Parker, and Louis – still in last night's clothes, all sitting around the dining table, each with a mug in their hands.

"Please tell me that's coffee?" I said hopefully.

Charlotte beamed at me. "Fresh pot right there."

"Thank god," I groaned. "I'm not sure I'd be able to function without caffeine."

"Sorry for keeping you up all night." Charlotte grimaced.

I raised an eyebrow at her as I poured coffee into the mug. "I'm not sure you're to be held responsible for a terrorist situation."

"What she said," Louis agreed.

She shrugged, still looking somewhat sheepish.

"Have they said any more about it all?" I asked.

Police had shot dead four of the six gunmen and the other two had surrendered. There were three others inside the van, one of whom was also killed.

Sammy had got Charlotte out of there about ten minutes before it had all gone down.

"They're reporting sixteen civilians dead so far and another one hundred and ten injured. There's still a lot in intensive care," Parker answered.

Tingles raced up and down my spine. Those poor people. Those poor families. I couldn't even imagine.

"I hope they torture those sons of bitches," Louis ground out, his hand tightly gripping his mug.

Charlotte tapped his arm. "I really like that mug, Lou."

He relaxed his grip and smiled at his sister. "Sorry, short stuff."

Jasper strolled into the room. "Morning," he said as he reached for a cup and held it out for me to fill.

"Can always count on Charlotte to have good coffee." He winked at me.

I filled his cup for him and escaped in the direction of the table. I still felt nervous around Jasper, like he'd somehow see it in my eyes that I was the woman he hired to find Hannah.

I sat down next to Louis, and he nudged my knee with his. "I hear you're an ideas woman."

I avoided eye contact with the lot of them and, instead, had a sudden interest in the liquid in my cup.

"I'm a movie addict you mean." I laughed, the nervous sound off to my own ears.

"I don't know what kind of movies you've been watching, but none of that shit made any sense to me," Parker mused.

I looked up at him and Charlotte; they were sitting so close together. He had his arm wrapped around her and he barely took his eyes off her.

I knew he wasn't going to be letting her out of his sight for a very long time.

I shrugged and took a sip of coffee. I needed my brain to turn on if I was going to have to be dodging questions on such few hours of sleep.

"I feel so bad for all those people," Charlotte said, thankfully changing the direction of the conversation and saving me from talking any more utter garbage.

"Me too, legs." Parker kissed her shoulder. "And I feel like a selfish prick for thinking it, but all that goes through my head is that I'm so glad you're not one of them."

Jasper strolled over to join us at the table, he paused near Charlotte, kissed the top of her head and then carried on and sat down on the other side of Parker.

"We should do something. Start up a foundation for their children or pay for the funerals. I don't know... I know it won't fix anything, but these people must be going through so much already, I'd hate to think that they might be struggling with money, on top of everything else. Some families will have lost their breadwinner."

"We can do both," Parker replied simply. "All of it. I'll do whatever you want, legs. Anything."

"*I* heard she wants you to come back to the boxing gym," Louis chimed in, grinning widely.

I sensed there was a story there, but I didn't ask.

Parker shook his head rapidly. "Anything but *that*... or getting in a car with your brother."

"I can second the car ride being a bad idea." My stomach lurched at the thought.

Louis chuckled. "Pussies."

"I want to do it," Charlotte announced, ignoring all the shit talk going on around her. "I want to do it today."

"I'll help," I told her.

"Me too," Jasper agreed.

"I want in," Louis piped up. "I missed all the action yesterday; you're not leaving me out again today.

Parker rolled his eyes at his brother-in-law. "Alright, legs, tell us exactly what you want to do."

Two hours went by in a flash. I hadn't even

realised how long we'd all sat there, slowly joined by Hannah, Floyd and eventually Tyler, as we planned out what Charlotte wanted to do for these grieving families.

I looked around the table at the people I was surrounded with. Smack talk and nonsense aside, they were some of the most caring, genuine and generous people I'd ever met in my whole life – they were a family – and I had no doubt there was nothing they wouldn't all do to protect the other.

I only wished I deserved to be a part of it.

CHAPTER 19

Tyler

"WHAT'S my future wife up to today?" Louis taunted me as he bounced back and forth on the spot, pendulum stepping to warm up for our workout.

I still hadn't figured out why I did this to myself. Setting foot in a boxing gym with Lou as a training partner never went well for me – last time I'd left with a bruise on my jaw and a fat lip. The time before I'd split my eyebrow clean open and had to go get stitches put in by Louis' medic.

Yet here I was, back for more punishment, like the sucker I was.

"Blow me," I retorted as I wound the last of the hand wrap around my wrist and secured the Velcro.

"Oh, come on, that's no way to talk to your favourite sibling." He smirked.

"We all know Charlotte is my favourite sibling."

She was. Always had been. But even more so since the attack. It'd been a couple of weeks now and the whole thing had shaken us, but also made us closer.

He clutched his chest. "Brutal as fuck."

"I'm not about to start lying just to make you feel good about yourself." I chuckled.

"You could at least hesitate like you had to think about it first."

I huffed out a laugh. "What's there to think about? You and your dipshit clone shave at least three years off my lifespan on a monthly basis with your antics. Charlotte is the only thing that keeps me ticking."

"I'm pretty sure Amarah is making you tick plenty... or do you purr, big fella?"

I scowled at him. "Please refrain from calling me 'big fella'."

His grin widened.

"And Amarah can make me do *whatever* she likes," I replied as I picked up a skipping rope and started skipping. "I'm not one to kiss and tell, but *damn*, there is no way you could handle a woman like that."

His step faltered for a second before he composed himself again and fell into the easy rhythm of the movement he'd likely done hundreds of thousands of times at this point.

"How you got a chick like that is beyond me."

It was beyond me too, but I wasn't about to agree with him.

"You're such a nerd. You're shit at boxing... can barely drive from A to B. You know, at least when Floyd gets a girl, I feel some type of satisfaction with it. He's an exciting fucker – handsome as shit... but you..." he taunted me, "all you do is sit behind a screen all day. Where's the thrill in that? Bring Amarah down here... let her see what a real man does when he goes to work."

"Oh yeah, I'm sure she'd love to see first-hand what a broken nose looks like, or how you can hardly breathe when you crack a rib... hey, maybe you could give her a real treat and spit a loose tooth in her direction."

He flipped me off, his mouth curved up into an easy grin.

I don't know how he didn't get tired of this constant banter. One afternoon with either of the twins, and I was exhausted. Mentally *and* physically, if it was an afternoon like this one was bound to be.

"Seriously though, shit talk aside for a second..."

I wasn't sure he was capable, but I allowed him to continue.

"Amarah is cool as, bro, you two are good together. You seem happy."

I nodded as the rope continued to loop over my head and under my feet.

"She's incredible," I agreed.

She'd won over my entire family, and that was nothing compared to what she'd done to me. I was up to my elbows in the feels with this girl, and I'd never been happier to find myself in deep shit.

We'd stayed up way too late last night, talking about nothing of any significance, yet somehow never failing to fill the silence. It was nice. It was easy.

I'd never been so *myself* with a woman before. There was a comfortableness between us, yet I still felt a thrill of anticipation whenever she was near. It was the ultimate balance between ease and excitement.

"Everything is so great with us; I keep catching myself waiting for something to go wrong."

He'd stopped his bouncing around and had strapped a pair of boxing gloves to his fists.

"Fuck that shit. What's going to go wrong? Just don't fuck it up and you'll be fine. She obviously likes you... for reasons unknown to me, but whatever, as long as she's happy."

I tossed the skipping rope to the side and grabbed my own gloves, putting them on in the same fashion as Louis.

"And if you do fuck up, bring her down here and let her take a few swings at you. Hitting your mug is bound to make up for whatever you did wrong."

"Condoning domestic violence; I bet your sponsors would eat that up."

"It's not domestic violence if you both consent." He winked.

"You have a warped sense of right and wrong, you know that, right?

"Maybe you're the dysfunctional one, did you ever consider that?" he asked before he started jabbing the heavy bag in front of him.

The sound when he made contact with the bag was enough to put the shits up me. Sure, I got in the ring with him for sparring reasonably frequently, but I knew damn well that he never hit me as hard or as fast as he was capable of – a rookie like me, I would have been lights out within seconds.

"You need to get a girlfriend, or a muzzle... whichever of the two is going to keep you in line more effectively," I suggested.

"Can't be tamed, bro... can't be tamed."

I just smirked at him and got to work on my own punching bag – Lou might have been right, and maybe he couldn't be tamed, but the majority of the world had thought that very same thing about Parker, and my sister had taken care of it with barely as much of a bat of her lashes.

It was definitely possible. And a guy could dream. The best thing that could happen to the twins was to meet a couple of women with their heads on straight who could get them to settle the hell down and act like sensible humans for five seconds.

That was the dream, but I sure as hell wasn't holding my breath. They were thirty-one years old and still acted like children eighty percent of the time.

I punched the bag repeatedly, practising the combos Lou had taught me over the years. That was half the problem in sparring with him, everything I knew – he'd taught me – he was my maker, and I was about to meet him.

"Five more minutes and we're in the ring," he told me between punches, his breathing not even the slightest bit ragged, and not a drop of sweat on him.

I was a fit guy, there was no denying it – but I was run fit. I did weight training too, but ring fit was another thing entirely, and I sure as hell wasn't it.

"Yip," I grunted back in response, already dreading it.

I loved it, I really did, it was a thrill, but I got my ass handed to me, without a doubt, each and every time – it was non-negotiable. If I ever did manage to get somewhat of a half decent shot in on Louis, he'd fire back, upping his pace and power – a not so subtle reminder to me of who was boss.

I needed this outlet today though. I was frustrated. Armageddon was pissing me the fuck off.

I was still no closer to finding out his real identity. I'd been fucking with him on the daily – messing up his work for clients and screwing around with anything external that I could get my virtual hands on, but it wasn't much – it wasn't enough.

After Amarah's successful suggestion on *that* day, I was tempted to ask her if she had any more ideas hiding in that brain of hers, but that would mean opening a can of worms I didn't want open. She didn't need to know about my petty rivalry.

I needed something more – something that was going to make an impact on this guy's real life, and the only way to do that, was to get close.

I had to get under this snake's skin, and I had the perfect way, sitting right in front of me – I knew where he lived... in the same building as my girlfriend – I just had to find my balls and use the advantage I had.

I smacked the bag over and over, hitting it like it owed me money.

I felt bad for even considering using my in with Amarah to get closer to this guy, but what she didn't know, wouldn't hurt her, and it's not like I was dating her because she lived in the building – I was dating her *despite* that fact. It was an endless source of guilt for me, and when it came down to it, I wasn't even technically doing anything wrong by her.

"Ty!" Louis' voice pulled me from my internal dilemma.

"Huh?" I asked, gasping for air as I finally stopped beating the shit out of the bag.

"Chill," he instructed. "You better save some juice for sparring, or I might legit knock you out this time."

He didn't look all that upset about the possibility,

but he was right. I needed to keep my head on straight. It was the only way I was going to come out of this situation alive – in the ring *and* the rivalry.

———

"What the hell happened to your face?"

I grinned, the small cut in my lip pulling slightly as I did. I shrugged. "You should see the other guy."

Amarah reached out and gently stroked her finger down my cheekbone, where a rather dark-looking bruise had already taken up residence.

"I'm going to go out on a limb here and say you tried to take on the pro boxer in your family? At least I hope that's the case; I don't feel like taking you down to the police station."

I chuckled. "No police required. You're right – Lou got me a couple of good shots."

"You guys are lunatics."

"It's fun."

She stepped aside and ushered me into the building. I crossed the threshold into the foyer, fully aware that this was the first time I'd officially crossed enemy lines.

She shook her head, her expression amused. "You and I obviously have different ideas of fun, but if you say so. I hope you at least got him a couple back for his trouble."

"I did," I replied proudly. "For once."

Louis was sporting an epic-looking shiner on his

right eye. I'd been too busy celebrating finally landing a clean shot on him that I hadn't seen the hook coming – hence the giant bruise on my face.

I followed her to the elevator. She pressed the up button and then glanced back at me.

My smile widened as I thought about it.

"Yip. Mental. My boyfriend is mental. Cool, cool, cool, cool, cool."

"No doubt, no doubt," I replied, the *Brooklyn Nine-Nine* reference falling from my lips without thought. "Wait." I paused. "Did you just call me your boyfriend?"

Her cheeks stained with colour. "I ah – I..."

"I'm your *boyfriend*," I crooned as the elevator doors opened and she stepped inside. "Fantastic use of a B99 reference there too. Your boyfriend rated that."

"Stop it." She swatted at my chest. "It was a slip of the tongue."

"No backsies," I replied, smirking as I took up residence on the opposite side of the elevator.

I'd considered her my girlfriend for a long while already, but we'd never officially had the chat.

She scowled at me; both our backs pressed to the opposite walls of the space.

My grin was so big my face hurt. I really liked the sound of being her boyfriend.

Her gaze rolled over me from head to toe, my grin slowly slipping as I felt her eyes touching every part of my body.

It was like an erotic caress, and she wasn't even close enough to lay a finger on me.

We just stared at one another, neither of us speaking as the elevator took us up to the fourth floor. I didn't know if she could feel it too, but the sexual tension radiating between us almost had me dropping to my knees.

The elevator dinged as we reached her floor and the doors slid open, but still, neither of us moved an inch.

"This is my floor," she finally whispered.

The sound of her voice pushed me over the edge.

I closed the space between us with a single stride, my body pressed firmly against hers as I cupped her jaw roughly with my palm.

She gasped as I lowered my mouth to hers and kissed her hard, forgetting all about where we were.

The doors slid closed again, enclosing us inside, and she kissed me back harder, her tongue slipping into my mouth.

I groaned as her nails sank into my biceps and she pulled me impossibly closer.

I tore my mouth away from hers, desperate for oxygen.

"I hate to be the one to kill the mood, princess, but if you keep kissing me like that, I'm going to fuck you, right here in this elevator."

Her breathing hitched, and the look in her eyes made me think that maybe that wasn't the worst idea she'd ever heard.

Dirty girl.

She raised a brow at me in challenge.

"I bet you fifty bucks that you won't let me fuck you here," I countered, smirking.

I wanted my fifty bucks – and bragging rights – back.

She reached between us and stroked my raging hard-on with the palm of her hand. "That's a risky little bet."

I groaned as she gripped me tight. "I've never been one to shy away from a challenge."

My hand slipped from her jaw to her throat, pressing just hard enough to make her gasp, while my other hand trailed down her body to slip beneath the bottom of the tiny little skirt she was wearing.

My fingers made contact with lace, and I stroked slowly back and forth over her most sensitive parts, teasing her.

"Oh my god," she whispered, "you're driving me crazy."

"Only seems fair," I grunted.

I dropped to my knees before her and lifted her skirt to expose her underwear to me before quickly sliding them to the side and pressing my mouth to her exposed flesh.

I was well aware of where we were, but I didn't care. The fact that the doors could slide open at any moment only gave me more of a thrill.

Her hands came down to my hair and tugged hard, the bite of pain only spurred me on further.

I licked, sucked and nibbled in all the right places, making her squirm, I reached up and gripped her hips, holding her steady as she came apart in my arms, her cry of pleasure ricocheting loudly off the elevator walls.

I smirked to myself as I got to my feet, my height making me look down on her.

"Still game, beautiful?"

She raised her chin in an attempt to look defiant, but all she managed was to look so deeply sated, it was entertaining.

She reached for the button on my shorts at the same moment the elevator lurched into motion, carrying us back down.

I smirked. "What's it going to be, princess? Shall I bend you over and give them a real show?"

We passed level three... level two...

She sighed and rolled her eyes. "Fine. You win." She huffed. "I can't do it. If it's the little old lady from down the hall, she'll probably die of a heart attack."

Level one.

I knew she'd cave – I was banking on it – exhibitionism wasn't exactly my thing, but a bet was a bet.

I straightened her skirt right as the doors began to slide open and grinned at her. "You owe me some cash, beautiful."

She muttered a string of cuss words at me, her face flushed as a couple with a dog entered the elevator.

They eyed us curiously, and I couldn't even

blame them; my hair was bound to be sticking out in one hundred different directions and my girl looked like she'd just had her world rocked.

Because she had.

It didn't take a rocket scientist to figure out what had been going on behind closed doors. Hell, it probably smelled like sex in here.

We stood in awkward silence until the doors opened at level four again, and this time we all but ran out, laughing like teenagers.

"You're a bad influence, Watson." She pointed at me as I followed her down the hallway.

As much as I didn't want to, I'd be lying if I said I wasn't taking in my surroundings.

I didn't expect this guy to have a sign on his door saying, 'Armageddon lives here, come on in', but I looked, just in case. It couldn't hurt to be optimistic.

"You're the one who started this bet business, I'm just an innocent bystander," I retorted.

She erupted into laughter. "You just got on your knees and made me come in a public place. You're the furthest thing from innocent there is."

I bit back a grin as I met eyes with the elderly woman who had just emerged from her doorway – and who was bound to have heard every word my girl just said – unless she'd forgotten her hearing aid, of course.

Amarah caught my line of sight and turned a deep red. "Mrs. McKlusky, I didn't see you there. Good afternoon."

"Afternoon, dear," she replied as she gave me the head-to-toe appraisal before smiling knowingly and walking away.

The old bird definitely heard.

I pissed myself laughing.

Amarah waited for her neighbour to be out of sight before she smacked me on the shoulder. "Oh my god, Tyler, I can't believe that just happened, I'm never going to be able to look her in the eye again."

"Look on the bright side," I choked out between laughs, "because you're a chicken shit, at least she's not going to get a free porn show when she gets in the elevator."

She groaned as she unlocked the door to her apartment. "You're the absolute worst, get in here before I have to move buildings."

CHAPTER 20

Amarah

"YOU KNOW any of your neighbours well?" Tyler asked from the living room.

"Well, I *did* have a reasonably good relationship with Mrs. McKlusky, but since she heard all about how you defiled me in the elevator, I'd say she's probably going to think I'm some kinky bitch with no self-control." I poked my head around the kitchen door to scowl at him.

He shook his head in amusement.

I rolled my eyes and went back to what I was doing, before emerging with two glasses and a bottle of wine.

"No one else? No friends or people in the industry?"

I froze for a fraction of a second before continuing to open the bottle of wine. "No friends and no technology geeks, as far as I'm aware... why?"

He shrugged. "Just wondering if any of the spaces were rented out as offices. Sometimes I get so distracted working from home. I've wondered if I'd be better off hiring a space to work from."

The line sounded rehearsed, as though he'd prepared it earlier. I knew why. I knew what he was doing – he was digging.

I eyed him cautiously. It wasn't that I didn't understand what he was asking, or why, but it made me suspicious of his motives.

"My building is a little far from home for you, isn't it? It's not exactly close."

He took the glass I handed him and eyed me over the rim. "It's close to you though, beautiful."

I felt my expression soften. I had to give him a virtual high five for that one, that wasn't something prepared. That was on the fly.

I knew he wasn't seriously about to rent a space half an hour from home, but the idea of seeing me every day would certainly have sweetened the deal if he were, it would seem.

"Aren't you just Mr. Smooth."

"I like to think so."

"And no, no friends in the building. I'll stop and talk to a few people, but I only really have the one really good friend, Jessie." I sank down next to him on the couch.

"The famous Jessie. Am I going to get to meet her any time soon?"

I grinned as I sipped my wine. "Trust me, meeting Jess is not something you want to rush into. She goes one hundred miles an hour, she says everything she thinks out loud and has zero ability to read a room."

He raised a brow. "Are you sure she's not a long-lost sibling of mine?"

I smiled wider. "I compared her to your brothers just the other day, actually. She's just as crazy."

"Did Wilder get her to go on that date? I haven't talked to him lately," he questioned.

"They're going out next week. She's making him wait," I replied with a roll of my eyes.

He chuckled. "And the logic behind that is..."

I waved my hand dismissively. "That's your first mistake, expecting to see logic in chaos."

He shook his head in amusement and reached out to rest his hand on my thigh.

Just that touch alone had my spine tingling.

"No, but really, I don't get it. She said that she's probably not going to be able to refrain from sleeping with the guy on the first date, so she wanted more time to 'make an impression'." I held my fingers up in air quotes. "I presume she's going to try and get him to fall in love with her over messages, so that when she does him on the first date, it's not such a big deal."

He chuckled. "Solid plan."

"*Ridiculous* plan," I argued, my tone amused,

"but that's Jessie. Best person I know, but undoubtedly batshit crazy."

"Her and Wilder might turn out to be a perfect match. He's completely unhinged at the best of times."

"Perrrrrfect," I drawled, grinning as I held my glass up to him for a toast. "To Wilder and Jessie, may they fall crazy in love, emphasis on the crazy part."

He chuckled and clinked his glass against mine. "I'll drink to that."

We both drank in silence, each of us just watching the other.

I didn't know how he did that – looked so completely and utterly appealing without even trying. He was looking at me the same way.

"You look like you're ready to finish what you started in the elevator."

"I was actually thinking that if that painting on the wall keeps staring at me like that, I might need a restraining order," he joked.

I glanced at the huge, weird-as-fuck piece of art that hung on my wall. "Oh, that's just Hernández. He's harmless."

"You *named* the creepy dude?"

"Nah, Jessie did. I think she Googled 'cliché Spanish name' and ran with it."

He huffed out a laugh. "Well, whatever his name is, he's making more eye contact than I'm comfortable receiving."

I giggled. "You wait until you see Sharese, then. That bitch knows how to stare."

"It gets worse?" He mock shuddered, ignoring the outrageous fact that I presumably had a piece of art I'd named *Sharese*.

"*So* much worse," I replied, clearly satisfied by this fact.

"I'm not going to lie to you, beautiful, you've got some weird shit in this apartment." He glanced around, taking it all in.

He wasn't wrong, I had a lot of stuff, and most of it was kinda quirky. I'd never seen an apartment that looked quite like mine – that was half the reason I loved it.

My smile widened. "I know. I love a good second-hand store, and heaps of this stuff reminds me of my mother and my grandmother. It's kinda chaotic in here, but it reminds me of home, and that makes me happy."

"Well, I like it, even if you are a little weirdo with pervy artwork."

I downed the last of my wine and sat the glass on the coffee table. "It's not like you can blame him for staring, I mean... *look* at you..."

He nodded casually in agreement. "I can't tell you how often I have creepy-looking Spanish men stop and stare at me in the street."

"It's the price you pay for that kind of perfection." I shrugged.

He chuckled.

We just stared at one another – I could have done that all day; he sure was easy on the eye.

He slid his hand slightly higher up my thigh, and I started to will it to go higher.

"I think it's time you gave me a tour of this place," he announced.

Giving him a tour of the apartment was the last thing I wanted to be doing. I'd have much preferred for him to be exploring my body than my living quarters.

"I can do that," I replied slowly, my gaze dropping to watch the deliberate path his hand was taking.

"Start with your bedroom," he instructed.

Thank god.

I nodded, unspeaking as his fingers slipped underneath my short skirt and made contact with the fabric of my underwear.

My head fell back slightly as he gently stroked. Something about his touch just felt *so* good.

"Your bedroom, beautiful." He smirked, enjoying the reaction he was giving me, just from a simple touch.

I was just like the keyboard on his computer; he knew exactly what to press… which keys to stroke to get what he wanted out of me. He'd quickly become an expert at writing my particular lines of code.

He slipped his hand out abruptly, and I groaned at the loss of contact.

He got to his feet and lifted me to mine,

pressing his body against me – showing me what I did to him. He was rock hard and straining against his zipper.

"You really liked Hernández, huh?" I teased, my breathy tone doing nothing to disguise how turned on I was.

"The guy just does it for me."

He growled as I reached between us, stroking him through his shorts.

"Bedroom," he snarled, his desperation showing.

I grinned, the smile slowly spreading across my face. I loved it when he showed how badly he wanted me. It made me feel like I was the most desirable woman in the world.

I turned, taking his hand in mine and finally, led him to my room.

———

This wasn't the first time he'd undressed me, but there was something about the look in his eyes that made it feel brand new again.

He was looking at me like he wanted to devour me, every inch, head to toe.

"Fucking look at you," he growled as I stood before him, totally stripped bare, in the middle of my bedroom.

He tugged his boxer briefs down, the last piece of clothing he was wearing, and kicked them across the floor.

I doubted I'd ever tire of seeing this man in all his naked glory. He was seriously hot.

Strong and toned, broad shoulders and defined muscles. He had a set of thighs on him that almost made me drool.

"You're giving me that look," he growled as he reached for me.

I gasped as he picked me up as though I weighed nothing and threw me across the room, onto my bed.

Oh. My. God.

His body was on top of mine in the next second, his hard length pressing against me.

He kissed me, frantically, and *fuck*, his kisses were out of this world. I'd never been kissed like this before. A few seconds of his lips on mine, his tongue in my mouth, his teeth sinking into my lip, and I was ready to go. His palm gripped my throat – it was the sexiest necklace I'd ever worn.

I pushed against his shoulders and even though I had no hope in hell of actually moving him, he complied, rolling onto his back, taking me with him so I was straddling him.

I moved down his body, kissing a path over his chest and stomach as I went, before reaching his cock.

I licked my lips and took him deep into my mouth.

He groaned, the sound of approval coming from deep in the back of his throat.

"Fuck that feels so good," he grunted as I bobbed

my head up and down, gripping what I couldn't get into my mouth, with my hand.

He reached down and ran his hands through my hair, collecting up the mass that surrounded me, as his hips thrust upwards, pushing him deeper into my throat.

I slipped him out of my mouth and ran my tongue from base to tip, and he shuddered. "Fucking hell, Amarah."

I smirked, pleased with myself for causing such a reaction within him.

I went to take him back into my mouth, but he pulled my hair, forcing my head up to look at him.

"Ride my dick, and don't stop until you come."

Hell, when he talked to me like that, it made me weak in the knees.

Outside of the bedroom, I was a strong, independent woman who had *no* intentions of doing something purely because a man told me to... but in the bedroom... there was nothing hotter than being bossed around.

There wasn't much I wasn't willing to do if he talked to me like that.

I climbed on top of him and guided his hard length to my opening.

I sank down on top of him and almost cried out from the feeling of him deep inside me.

"Fuck me, beautiful."

I didn't need to be told twice.

I started to move – bouncing, grinding and

rotating my hips to hit the spots I knew would have me coming undone quickly.

He gripped my hips tightly but let me lead and set the pace.

It didn't take long. I fell forward, crying out as my orgasm ripped through me. He wrapped his arms around my shoulders and took over, lifting his hips and making me feel like I was going to explode from the pleasure.

I rode it out until I couldn't take any more. "Oh my god, Ty, stop."

He stilled beneath me, a satisfied smirk on his lips.

"You all good, baby?"

"I'm *too* good. I feel like I'm going to combust."

He slapped my ass and turned me over, onto my back in one fluid motion, so he was hovering over top of me.

He kissed me again, his tongue sweeping into my mouth. "Take it," he growled into my ear before flipping me over onto my hands and knees and kneeling behind me.

"Oh fuck," I groaned, already knowing how much this was going to ruin me.

He slapped my ass again, *hard*, and I buried my face in the pillow in front of me to muffle my moan.

That is so hot.

He lined up and pounded into me, filling me in one fluid stroke.

It was so much; pleasure bordering on pain to the point I almost couldn't take it.

He started a relentless pace, hammering me over and over again.

"Oh fuck, I'm going to blow." He ground the words out.

"Yes," I hissed.

He groaned loudly and thrust so deep I literally saw stars.

He slowed, moving in and out as he milked the last of his release into me.

I collapsed, my arms no longer able to hold me up and he followed after me, laying on my back.

"Holy shit," I breathed.

"Agreed," he panted.

CHAPTER 21

Tyler

TYLER: **I bet you fifty bucks I can beat you in a running race.**

Amarah: Absolutely no deal. I've seen that body. You'd annihilate me. It'd be like taking candy from a baby.

Tyler: I do prefer my candy when it's been stolen from a small child. Tastes better. Gives it a little something extra.

Amarah: Not happening, Watson, you're not taking me for a ride with that one.

Tyler: I've got something else you can ride.

Amarah: THAT gives me an idea… I bet you can't go a day without making some type of sexual innuendo out of an innocent comment.

Tyler: Oh, you're on, beautiful. Easiest cash I ever made.

The fifty-dollar note had been passed back and forth between us about half a dozen times now.

Amarah bet me that she knew more lyrics to Eminem raps than I did and won herself the cash back. I was still shook up over that one – I'd been living my life thinking I was as close to the real slim shady as it got, only to be completely and utterly owned by my girlfriend.

I bet her that she couldn't eat an entire apple pie and won – she barely even made it through half. I chuckled as I remembered how disappointed she'd been in herself. She was adamant she was going to be able to demolish it, but I'd been solid in my belief that she wouldn't – she was tiny and that had been one hell of a pie.

Another time, she bet me that I couldn't do a head stand for a minute straight – I still didn't know why I took that bet, but I now knew that I couldn't do a head stand at all, let alone for a minute straight, meanwhile, she was apparently some type of yoga genius – I'd pushed her over after about three minutes of watching in bewilderment.

Needless to say, she now had the fifty dollars in

her possession... but I could go twenty-four hours without cracking inappropriate jokes like some type of horny teenager.

That cash was about to be mine again.

She'd started keeping a tally of wins on the note itself, in sharpie, so I couldn't risk losing again. It was basically a trophy with engraved names at this point. I wasn't in the mood to double her money, and I quite enjoyed this little back and forth banter we had.

She didn't reply to my message, but about an hour later there was an alert on the security system I'd upgraded to after Jasper had so charmingly let himself in a few months back.

That whole experience really had taught me a lot about the shortfalls in my security.

I pulled up the app on my phone and discovered who was approaching my front door right as they knocked on it.

Amarah.

I grinned to myself. I wasn't expecting her, but it was by no means an unwelcome surprise to see her on my screen.

I leapt up out of my chair and dashed across the room to get to her sooner.

I swung open the door with a huge grin on my face as I took a quick sweep of her, head to toe.

Fuck.

She looked sexy as sin. Tiny shorts and a cropped top were all that covered her insane body. She had a yoga mat stuffed under her arm and a bag slung over her shoulder.

"Well, well, well, aren't you a sight for sore eyes. Did I forget we'd made plans?" I questioned.

"Nope," she replied, popping the 'p'. "I just figured that I wasn't about to make this bet easy on you. Any fool can lay off the innuendos when they're alone, right?"

I smirked, delighted by this result. "So, you've come to torture me?"

She brushed past me, an extra sway in her step if I wasn't mistaken. She didn't need it; my eyes would have been glued to her ass regardless.

"That all depends on how you look at it, Watson."

Oh, I was looking at it, alright.

Dammit. I scolded myself.

She was right – I did turn *everything* into something sexual as far as she was concerned. It was hard not to when she looked like that. It was going to be a struggle to keep those thoughts from coming out of my mouth for the next twenty-three and a half hours, but I needed to win this bet.

She glanced back over her shoulder, a teasing expression on her face before she disappeared around the corner and down the hallway.

This was a well-played move by her – she'd upped the stakes considerably, merely by turning up.

I sat my ass down on the couch and waited for her to re-emerge.

She strolled out a few minutes later, her feet bare and a lollipop sticking out of her mouth.

Her eyes sparkled as she saw me watching her. Slowly, and very, very deliberately, she drew it from her mouth, her plump lips moulding around the lollipop, teasing the living hell out of me.

Fuck, I'm in danger here.

"You're going to make my life hell, aren't you?" I choked out.

She nodded. "That's the plan, boy."

"Just to be clear on the rules here, I can still fuck your brains out, right? I just can't make corny, cliché jokes and sexual references out of innocent statements?"

"Correct again."

"Sounds like I'm getting a pretty sweet deal here, Mara."

The smug smile on her face ensured me that she didn't agree with my assessment.

Her head tilted to the side. "You called me Mara."

"Yeah, no offence, but Amarah is kind of a mouth full."

She crossed the space between us and sat down in my lap. "My Grammy and all my aunties called me Mara when I was little."

I took the lollipop from her and stuck it into my mouth. I was going to lose my ever-loving mind if I had to witness her sucking on that thing any longer.

She pouted at me but didn't argue.

I ran my hands over her bare legs. Her skin was always so soft and smooth, and she had an exotic-looking tan.

"Is it alright if I call you that?"

I didn't know all that much about her family. I'd gathered she was close with them and missed them a lot, but my knowledge was basic at best.

She nodded slowly. "I like it."

"I like you."

She smiled. "I like you too, Watson."

"I'll like you a lot more when this bet is over."

She smirked and got to her feet. "You just carry on with your work, I think I might do some yoga."

I groaned as she rolled out her mat and bent down in front of me to touch her toes.

"You know, lots of stretching and bending."

One thousand different inappropriate comments filed through my brain, most of them involving me bending her over.

She smirked at me, waiting for me to crack, her ass high in the air, teasing me.

Stay strong I coached myself.

I turned around and went to my computer where I endured the most challenging two hours of my life to date. That gorgeous little she-devil twisted and turned and made endless comments that would have taken little to no imagination to construe into something sexual.

I became the master of nodding and smiling, the risk of opening my mouth to speak became too great.

She was *killing* me.

This was going to be the longest day of my life at this rate.

Those gym shorts were the shortest shorts known to man, and that raunchy-looking little sports bra – I was hard as a rock just watching her lounge around my space.

"We should go on a hike sometime."

"Mmm?" I questioned as I pretended to look at my screen.

"Yeah, there's a good one about half an hour from here, but I *have* heard it's long and hard."

Long and hard.

"That's it," I announced as I got to my feet and made a beeline for her. "You have to stop."

She grinned in triumph. "Only if you admit that you lose."

"How about an alternative that we'll both enjoy?" I bargained, clutching desperately at straws in a feeble attempt to still come out the winner.

She raised a brow from her position on the floor. "What did you have in mind?"

"If I can make you come all over my face, twice, then you let me off this stupid bet."

She leaned back onto her elbows and looked up at me with hooded lids. "Twice," she repeated. "On your face."

"You look so fucking tasty, it's making me *hungry*."

Her mouth dropped open before quickly snapping shut again.

"Deal," she breathed.

"Thank fuck," I muttered.

I dropped to the ground between her legs and tugged those barely there shorts down her legs and onto the floor next to me.

She stayed up on her elbows, watching my every move as I dove in between her legs, my mouth connecting with her pussy, through her g-string.

She groaned and her hips bucked.

I wrapped my arms around her hips and held her in place as I fucked her with my mouth.

"Oh my god," she moaned as I pulled her underwear to the side and snaked my tongue over her clit.

She bucked her hips again as I found the spot that drove her wild.

I reached down and freed my dick from my pants and stroked myself while I devoured her.

Her hands found my hair and tugged, hard.

I hummed against her pussy before diving in again, kissing, licking and sucking her in the way she loved.

She was on the brink in a matter of seconds.

"Fuck," she cried, "I'm so close."

"Come all over my fucking face," I demanded.

I let go of my dick and slipped two fingers inside her, hitting the spot that I knew would push her over the edge.

She fell apart in my arms, her orgasm ripping through her.

I rode it out with her until the twitching and squirming stopped. I released my hold on her and gently slipped my fingers out of her, before licking them clean. I sat back on my knees, my dick springing up, hard and proud.

"Fuck that's hot," she groaned, resting her head back against the floor.

I smirked in satisfaction. "One down, one to go."

"I give up," she panted. "You win. Take my money."

I wiped my mouth with the back of my hand. "Fuck no, beautiful, a deal is a deal."

———

"Yo, lover boy, I need assistance," Wilder replied when I answered the phone.

I chuckled and turned around in my desk chair to look out the window. "What have you done now?"

"I haven't done anything. I don't think..."

"I'd be willing to bet that you're wrong."

"Well then, smart guy, why don't you tell me what I'm calling about, seeing as how you know everything and all."

"Let me just get my crystal ball," I drawled. "I see woman troubles."

"Fuck," he snapped.

I chuckled. "So, I'll ask again... what did you do?"

I hadn't spoken to the man since the night of the gig, where he gave Amarah his number to pass onto her best friend. It wasn't as though he needed setting up, but I didn't blame him for playing his hand and trying something different – I'd seen pictures of Jess – she was a good-looking girl. Banging body. Cute smile.

She in no way appealed to me like the woman I'd scored did, but I could appreciate a pretty girl when I saw one.

"I thought I was doing the right thing..."

I waited him out, taking a sip from my water bottle while he arranged his thoughts.

"I wouldn't fuck her on the first date, okay. That's what's up."

The water that had just entered my mouth, exited it again in a far more dramatic fashion, spraying all over the window I was looking out of.

"What the hell was that?"

"Nothing." I wiped at my mouth with the back of my hand. "Continue."

I desperately tried to bite down my laugh as my mate launched into a detailed play by play of their first date and how it ended – which was apparently without sex.

"I'm not going to lie to you, bro, I don't get it. Were you not into her or something?" I asked him.

"I'm *definitely* into her."

"The fact that you turned down sex when she was offering, kind of suggests otherwise."

"I know that now, *fuck*... she wasn't happy."

I bit back another laugh.

"I like the girl. I didn't want to fuck it up by screwing her on the first date and then never seeing her again."

"Call me crazy, but you probably could have slept with her and then still seen her again. Wild concept, I know."

"I don't know why I bothered calling you, I should have known you'd be less than no help. You're paying me out exactly the same way I'd pay you out in the same situation."

I chuckled. "And yet you're mad?"

"Yeah. Because I'm not the prick anyone in their right mind would come to for advice."

He wasn't wrong there. Nothing about Wilder Hanson screamed 'I know what I'm talking about'.

"And I am?"

"Yeah, man," he replied, exasperated. "You've kept those brothers of yours alive and mostly out of trouble, I'd say you're the go-to Dr. Phil in our circle."

I most certainly had not kept them out of trouble, but he was right to a certain extent; they were still alive, and that had to count for something.

"*I'm* the resident advice giver. Well fuck me sideways and call me Susan."

"I'd really prefer not to," he retorted.

"Getting back to the problem here, if you still want my advice, that is?"

"Fuck yes, I'm clueless."

That he was. Wilder was a good guy, but he was still the same useless muso I'd known for years. He was shit with women – well, he was shit at *holding on* to women, he was more than adequately skilled at pulling them for one night.

But this conversation only confused me and my perceptions of him further. He'd done the opposite of what I'd always known him to do – and it'd still backfired on him.

Go figure.

"I'm no expert on women, but I'm pretty sure she'll be feeling rejected. Like you didn't sleep with her because you're not into her."

"I guess that makes sense, but it's fucked. I want her."

"You're pretty keen on this girl, aren't you?"

This was also new. I'd never known Wilder to care about... well, *anything*. It was just music for him – everything was all about the music.

"Yeah, I dunno what it is, but she's *different*. I want to talk to her all the time... tell her stupid, mundane shit about my day. It's all more exciting when I'm talking to her about it."

I could relate. Even driving down to the store to pick up supplies was way more fun if Amarah was in the passenger seat.

"So, call her."

"I tried. She let it go to voicemail."

"So, try again."

"You're a genius," he drawled, "why didn't I think

of that?"

"What I'm saying is keep fucking trying. Don't just give up if things aren't coming easy. Send her flowers, write her a long-winded message, show up on her doorstep... I don't know, bro, sing her a fucking song or something, and then when you get her attention – because you're bound to if you do all that, then fuck her brains out at the first opportunity you get."

"Romance and dick. Got it."

I chuckled. This unexpected conversation was certainly amusing, if nothing else.

"Basically, yeah. Think grand gestures. Chicks love those."

"And here I was, not letting her near my grand gesture. What a rookie."

"Not the grand gesture I was referring to, but you do you, bro. Let me know how it plays out. I'll try to put in a good word for you."

I was certain I was going to hear all about this from Amarah anyway, but it was bound to make for decent entertainment being delivered by Wilder and his severe lack of anything resembling tact.

"Talk me up hard."

"I'll do my best to sweeten her up for you, bro."

"Thanks, man, I gotta go, the band's here, but I'll work on a game plan."

"May the odds be ever in your favour."

I sat in my chair, the conversation playing over and over in my head. I never thought I'd see the day that Wilder Hanson chased a woman, but here we were.

I opened my messages and tapped out a message to Amarah.

Tyler: Tell Jessie to buckle up, Wilder is going to be coming in hot.

Amarah: WHAT HAVE YOU HEARD? TELL ME EVERYTHING.

Tyler: WHY ARE YOU YELLING?

Amarah: Sorry, Jessie is here and she's yelling and I got excited. Tell us everything!

I chuckled. I hadn't anticipated Jessie being there, but I knew damn well that Amarah would tell her anything I passed on anyway, so this just saved a step in the chain.

Tyler: He wants her. Bad.

Amarah: She looks like she's going to go into cardiac arrest. I don't think I can handle her on my own... you wanna come over?

Did I want to meet her best friend? Fuck *yes*, I did.

My reply was short and to the point.

Tyler: Be there ASAP.

CHAPTER 22

Amarah

"BREATHE. CHILL."

"I am breathing," Jessie snapped, as she paced. "I *am* chill."

"Yeah, you seem suuuuuper chill," I muttered under my breath.

"I heard that."

"Congratulations," I replied.

"Sorry." She flopped down onto the couch and then leapt back up and resumed pacing. "I'm just freaking out."

I was yet to figure out what the hell she was so worked up about. So, what... Wilder apparently wanted her, *and* she was about to meet my boyfriend for the first time... the woman needed to relax.

Maybe that's why she's so keen to get laid. She needs an outlet.

"What are you losing the gherkin about?"

"I've spent the past few days accepting the fact that nothing was ever going to happen with Wilder, and then just like that, I'm right back in the unknown."

I wanted to reply that she was full of shit, that she'd spent the past few days pining after the man, writing out – and then deleting – messages to him, but I decided I should practice some of the self-control I was always suggesting she use.

"Okay, but so what? You're so into this guy, Jessie, isn't this a good thing?"

"I don't know!"

"Tyler is going to be here any second, can you please try and take it down a few notches? I don't want him thinking my best friend is a total head case."

"Well, it's easy for you, you guys are all sweet and mutually falling in love, and I'm just over here getting cock blocked by my own date."

I pinched the bridge of my nose in frustration, my gaze tracking her as she made a solid attempt at wearing a track in my carpet. "Oh yeah, two sworn enemies, falling in love, that's real *ideal*, Jessie. And you don't have a 'cock'. *Jesus.*"

She paused, staring at me in shock, and I wondered what it was I'd said that had finally gotten through to her.

"You just admitted you're falling in love," she accused.

I gaped. I had. I said that.

"Did not," I lied through my teeth.

"Oh, did *so*."

There was a knock at the door. I pointed my finger at her in warning. "You shut your stupid big mouth, you got it? I swear to god, Jessie, I'll hunt you down and *end* you if you say a word about this to him."

A sly grin spread slowly across her face. "*Breathe. Chill*," she repeated my earlier sentiments back to me mockingly.

I flipped her off as I got up to cross the room and let Tyler in.

"See! It's like waving a red flag at a bull!" she called after me.

I muttered a string of curses under my breath.

You love her. I reminded myself. *She's your best friend. You can't kill her.*

Tyler knocked again.

The poor guy had no idea what he was about to walk into.

I swung open the door and there he was, all six foot, four inches of perfection, standing right in front of me. His cologne wafted in with the breeze and the smell made me feel weak; it took every last bit of my self-control not to lean in and sniff him.

I'd never met someone that smelled *so* good.

"I brought reinforcements." He held up a supermarket bag. "Charlotte told me that ice cream is only for break-ups, but I wasn't willing to risk showing up without it, and I got wine and chocolate too."

"You brought us food?"

He nodded. "I sensed some type of crisis was going down. I decided I'd rather be safe than sorry."

Be still, my beating heart.

"Marry him, Rah Rah, I swear to god, that's a smart man," Jessie called out from inside my apartment.

He smirked at me and held the bag out further in my direction. I took it from him, still a little bewildered that he'd not only thought about this in the first place, but then gone to the effort to stop and get what felt like an awful lot of chocolate, ice cream and wine.

He slipped past me, an amused expression on his face as I just stood there, slightly in shock about the man in my life.

This was a big step for me; a boyfriend meeting Jessie hadn't happened for a long, long time. She was like family to me, and with my actual family so far away, this was as close to meeting the parents as Tyler was going to get, without getting on a plane.

"Well, helllllooo, Tyler. She told me you were handsome, but hot *damn*," I heard Jessie say.

The comment snapped me back to reality, the reality where a guy I really, really liked – who I'd just admitted I was falling for – was about to get the full Spanish inquisition from my closest friend.

I slammed the door shut and rushed into the

room to see Tyler chuckle before he hugged Jessie. "And you're just as pretty as Wilder said you were."

She released him, stepped back and eyed him suspiciously, "Oh, I see how this is going to go, straight into bat for your friend, is it?"

"Hey, I came bearing gifts at least."

"It's cool, it's cool, bros before hos."

"You look like you could use some wine," Tyler suggested.

"Did you come here to bribe me with treats and wine, or to spill the goss about Wilder?"

"Well, I'm no expert on women, but I'm going to go ahead and say the correct answer here is *both*."

"Ty, this is Jessie," I interrupted, trying to save him from the theatrics of my friend.

"Jess, this is my...b-Tyler," I stuttered.

He smirked. "Your Tyler?"

"It came out wrong."

He shook his head in amusement. "Don't worry, I'll be *your Tyler* any day of the week."

I groaned but didn't even bother arguing.

Jessie gave me a look that told me she already loved him. "You get out the snacks, I'll get the glasses."

She disappeared into the kitchen.

"It's not even midday!" I called after her.

"It *is* somewhere," she called back.

I rolled my eyes at the same time as I heard Tyler laugh.

"I'd say I'm sorry about her, but honestly, an

apology won't even cover it. I really hope you're ready to dissect every single part of your conversation with Wilder, right down to 'what you think he meant by that tone'."

He sidled up to me and wrapped his arms around my waist. "I can't think of anywhere else I'd rather be."

"Not even naked in my bedroom?" I teased.

He chuckled and kissed my forehead. "Oh, that'll be happening after – you're going to owe me for this."

Owing this man was hardly a chore.

Jessie emerged from the kitchen, three mugs in her hands.

"Mugs?" I questioned, "I thought we were having wine?"

She shook her head, sat the three mugs down on the coffee table and beckoned us over. "The wine glasses were too small and delicate, this is serious."

I groaned into Tyler's chest, and he stroked my hair in a show of support.

"None of this cute stuff, you two, I'm not drunk enough."

"I get the feeling that's about to change," Tyler muttered.

That got a laugh out of me. He *was* a smart man.

"Okay, fine." I grabbed his hand and led him over to the couch. I handed off the bag to Jessie in defeat.

There was little point in arguing with the woman – no one ever won – poor Wilder had no idea what he was in for if he really was planning on making a solid play for her heart.

She grabbed out a bottle of wine and sloshed it somewhat evenly into the three mugs. "Right, start at the beginning, don't leave *anything* out," she told Tyler as she tucked her ankles up under her butt.

Tyler reached for one, handed it on to me and then grabbed one for himself.

I had to admit, I was pretty taken with how he'd just accepted his fate on this one. I doubted his plan when he turned up here at eleven in the morning, was to start drinking and dish on girly gossip, but he was taking it like an absolute champ.

"Alright, but I can't promise I'll remember every word."

"Every word, Tyler Watson. Every. Single. Word."

His eyes widened and a laugh slipped from between my lips.

"I warned you." I laughed.

"And yet, I'm still not prepared." He took a huge gulp of his wine. "Either look the other way or drink up, Jessie, I need to do something before we get started."

Jessie covered her eyes *and* took a drink, simultaneously.

Tyler grabbed me, his large hand roughly going to my throat before his lips landed on mine, kissing me in what was possibly the hottest, most possessive kiss of my life. I turned to putty in his hands – I'd never experienced anything like it.

Tyler Watson had been holding out on me.

"Um, newsflash, that's not 'cute', that's hot as fuck." Jessie was staring at us from a gap between her fingers.

I felt myself blush. Tyler chuckled – the man gave zero fucks.

"You know what, I *am* going to need more wine after all," I announced.

———

I woke up with my head pounding and my body overheating.

I didn't know at what point during the evening we'd decided it would be a good idea for the three of us to all share one bed, but that was the situation I'd found myself in.

Sandwiched between a snoring Tyler and a heavily breathing Jessie.

Tyler's leg was slung over mine, and it was so heavy I could barely move underneath it.

Whatever the guy did for leg day – it was working.

I tried to turn over, but my legs wouldn't move under his weight.

I grunted and struggled to push his thigh off mine.

"Urrrrrgggghhhh," Jessie groaned from next to me. "Who's making the world spin?"

"I don't know, but I need it to stop." I winced as I tried to lift my head off the pillow.

"Dear God, what is that noise?" she moaned.

"Tyler's snoring," I replied as I tried to will the incessant pounding in my brain to subside.

"Just kill him and be done with it."

I laughed, and then regretted it instantly.

I needed to get up and out of this bed – I was willing to bet that my breath smelled rank, and I needed a shower desperately. I also really required some painkillers and water before my skull exploded.

"I can't move, I'm pinned under one of his huge thighs."

"Bet you're the first woman to be complaining about it."

I shoved at his leg again, to no avail. His snoring continued.

"Just help me," I pleaded. "I really need to pee."

She pushed up to her hands and knees, grumbling and groaning as she did. I felt her pain, I really did, but I was seriously concerned about the state of myself, and I was becoming increasingly more concerned about my bladder by the second.

She leaned over and heaved his leg off me. "Get off her, you big, heavy bastard."

He grunted in his sleep, rolled over and within seconds, was snoring again.

Jessie collapsed back to the mattress, giggling and clutching her head.

"Thank you, thank you, thank you." I climbed out of the bed and made a beeline for the bathroom, my head killing me and my bladder about to burst.

I don't know how long I spent in there, but when I finally emerged, it was with fresh breath, a clean body and an empty bladder. My headache and squeamish stomach were another matter entirely, but I was just thankful that the urge I'd had mid-shower, to puke my guts out, had passed.

I'd lost track of how much I'd had to drink last night. In fact, a good portion of the evening was a total blur, but I did remember laughing – *a lot* – and having the time of my life.

We'd eaten chocolate and ice cream for lunch and ordered pizza for dinner.

I had a vague recollection of Jessie talking to Wilder on the phone, but what she'd said or done was anybody's guess.

Hell, what *I'd* said or done was anybody's guess.

I walked back into my bedroom and the smell nearly stopped me in my tracks. "This place smells like a brewery."

"I can't smell anything. Ew. I must be soaking in it," Jessie answered.

I crossed the room, pulled the blind and opened the window as far as it could go. "Honey, you *are* it."

She covered her eyes as the light hit her.

"Where's Tyler?" I questioned when I found his side of the bed vacant.

She yawned. "Woke up in bed with me, freaked out and left."

I rolled my eyes. "Liar."

"Yeah," she agreed. "The mad prick went for a run."

A run?

I grimaced. "Ew."

"That's what I said."

"That's fucked up."

She huffed out a laugh. "Apparently it's the best hangover cure there is."

"I very much doubt that, and there is no way I'm going to risk throwing up to find out."

"Agreed. Let's just eat deep fried food, watch crappy movies and hope for the best."

"It's the only thing for it." I nodded in agreement.

"You're going to have to deal with that peppy boyfriend of yours first."

I went into my wardrobe and slipped into some comfortable sweats and a cropped tee. "I can handle him, and if he wants to do fitspo shit and eat salad or whatever, he can take it somewhere else."

She held up her fist in salute.

"Have you done the check yet?"

She groaned. "No. I'm too scared."

"At least you don't need to find out your location or check your bank balance." I offered.

"Just checking text messages and my legs for bruises then." She sighed.

"The drunk-girl checklist. Get it done."

"RIP my dignity." She made a show of marking out a cross on her forehead and shoulders.

I sat down on the corner of the bed and watched as she located her phone from in the bed next to her and unlocked it. "Maybe I should start with the legs, how bad could that be... given we didn't even leave the apartment?" she sat up in the bed.

"You obviously don't remember dancing on – and then falling off – the coffee table."

She covered her face with her free hand. "Well, if I'm covered in bruises then surely that means I don't have any embarrassing messages to worry about then?"

I shook my head and grimaced. "I think there's also a strong possibility you've shat the bed on that front too. But maybe you should be more concerned about the phone calls."

She fell back, her head landing on my pillows. "Who let me have my phone in that state?"

"You say that as though you'd have listened to a word I said. Which, for the record, you didn't. I tried. You threw a fit and then we had a rock off to see what to do."

She groaned. "Let me guess, I won?"

"Well, your paper beat my rock, but whether or not you consider yourself a winner is another question entirely." I bit back a laugh.

"You're so mean; I'd never laugh at you if you made a complete disgrace of yourself like I'm bound to have done."

"You'd laugh *so* much worse than this and you know it. I'm showing restraint. Now just hurry up and look at your messages already, I want to know if we need more ice cream or not."

She scowled at me, but obliged, and unlocked her phone. "Ohhh *no*. He's messaged me this morning."

"Read it."

"I don't want to."

"Read it," I insisted. "Or I will."

She sighed and tapped her screen. She was silent for a few beats.

I reached for her phone, and she pulled it out of my reach.

"It says, '*You are balls to the wall crazy, Jessie girl, and I dig it.*' What. The. Actual. Fuck."

"Huh," I mused, "guess he likes his women completely crackers... and a lot drunk."

She ignored me and kept scrolling through her phone. "Oh, dear god, some of the messages I sent him are so embarrassing, and that's coming from *me*."

"None of that surprises me," I drawled.

What *did* surprise me, was that she hadn't managed to scare him off yet. Maybe this guy really was going to be the one for her.

I glanced around for my own phone. I had no idea if Tyler was coming back or if he'd gone home...

for all I knew, my own coffee table dancing had scared him off for good.

"Did Ty say anything about whether or not he was coming back here?"

I rummaged around under my pillows and eventually came up with my phone.

My dead-flat phone. I felt my forehead furrow into a frown.

"Relax, smitten kitten, he's coming back. He's so whipped it's almost embarrassing."

"He's bound to be giving himself a reality check right about now though... there's no way I'm going to get out of that binge drinking session totally unscathed."

"Relax, you're like a complete goddess, even when you're pissed and singing along to Mariah Carey."

I covered my face with my hands as the memories came flooding back to me. "Is there any chance I have the voice of an angel when I'm half a dozen drinks deep?"

She shook her head. "There is not."

"Mariah Carey? Man, that's a *bad* shout."

"I mean, it could have been worse, but I'm not going to lie to you, it could have been a lot better. Don't give up your day job."

"I think that's fair advice."

I heard the door to my apartment open and then Tyler's voice filled the space. "I'm back, booze hags! There's one hell of a day happening out there."

"Urgh, he's already too spritely for me. Make him shush," she grumbled.

I laughed and got up to go and see what my mad boyfriend was doing now.

"I'm going to shower, if I'm not out in an hour, send a search party. Hot tip, I'll be at the bottom of the shower, drowning in my hangover."

"Got it," I replied as I walked out the door.

I found Tyler in the living room, pulling his shirt over his head. My step faltered and I hovered in the doorway to watch him.

His bare chest was glistening with sweat, and his hair was dripping. Smelly and sweaty had never looked so good.

His baggy grey shorts were slung low on his hips, his defined torso on full display.

"Did you want to take a photo?"

My eyes snapped up to his face to find him smirking at me, that damn sexy fucking smirk that he executed so well.

"Shut up."

He wiped at the corner of his mouth with his thumb. "You've got a little bit of drool."

I raised my middle finger at him. "So, you caught me perving. Am I meant to be sorry?"

He shook his head. "I really fucking hope not."

He beckoned me over with his finger. I didn't need to be told twice.

"How do you look so good?" I grumbled as I approached him.

"I think you might be biased there, beautiful. I look like I just ran ten k."

I stopped in front of him, and he leant down to kiss the top of my nose. "I'd hug you, but I'm all sweaty."

"It's the only thing stopping me from licking your chest."

"What did you just say?" He chuckled.

I smiled up at him. "What did you hear?"

He just shook his head, his grin wide and those insane blue eyes sparkling with amusement.

"I can't believe you went for a run; I really should kick you out of here for doing something so unreasonable. I know you're new here, but we watch trash on TV and eat bad food when we're hungover. We wallow in it. We don't try to make it better."

He reached out and twisted a strand of my hair around his finger. "I'm sorry, I must have missed that part in my introduction packet. My mistake."

"I'll let you off this one time, but if I see it happening again, there's going to have to be consequences."

"I bet that one day you'll give in and come with me, your hangover will disappear, and you'll have to eat your words."

"Fifty bucks?"

"Of course. This one just might take quite some time to pay out."

I liked the sound of that. Truthfully, I liked the sound of anything that meant he was sticking around.

"You've got yourself a bet." I lifted my hand and he caught it in his, shaking it once.

"I think I should go take a shower. You pick the shitty movies, and when we're all ready, I'll drive you two to go pick up burgers and fries."

It didn't matter that my head was pounding, or that I'd sung Mariah Carey in what was bound to be an alarmingly, awful manner last night and no doubt embarrassed myself thoroughly... none of that mattered while he was here, and *nothing* sounded better than what he'd just described.

CHAPTER 23

Tyler

THE LOADED BARBELL clunked loudly as Floyd dropped it back into the rack of the bench press. We were working out without Louis today, and I was grateful – I wasn't in the mood to be lured into a punch up.

"So let me get this straight," he huffed out between breaths. He'd just benched a PB, and I wasn't about to tell him, but I was impressed. "You hung out with her and her best mate all night, doing like face masks and painting your nails and shit?"

He slid off the bench and I took his spot, fully prepared to match his weight. No little brother of mine was going to outdo me on weight day.

"Do my fucking nails look painted to you?"

He made a show of looking at my hands.

"No comment on the face mask though, *interesting.*"

"You can't get skin this glowing without some type of skincare routine," I clapped back, ripping the piss.

He chortled. "Don't be getting sassy with me, princess. I hear chick flicks and I immediately think face masks and fuzzy slippers."

"I think that says more about you than it does about me and how I spent my weekend. Are you going to spot me or what?"

He moved into a position where he'd be able to save my ass if it all went tits up.

I inhaled deeply and pressed the bar up before slowly lowering it down.

It was tough, but I matched Floyd's reps before racking the weights up again.

"So, your love life is going embarrassingly well, what's new with work?"

"Got that big client I was telling you about," I replied as I wiped the sweat from my brow. "I'm wrapping up that contract I had for the government; I'll be glad to see the back of that one actually."

"What about your petty little grudge that Lou was telling me about? You still tripping over yourself trying to beat some nerd?"

"He's probably no more of a nerd than I am."

"If the slipper fits, *Cinderella.*"

"Fuck you're a pain in my ass. Can you take a day off, just for once?"

"I guess I could give it a try."

I doubted that, *very* strongly, but if he was even willing to make one tenth of an effort then it had to be better than nothing.

"I've made no progress with Armageddon. Fucking nothing. Short of knocking down every door in Mara's building and seeing what I find, I'm running out of ideas. I've tried every trick in my magic box and this guy has had my number on virtually every single one of them. I need to think of something new... something that hasn't been done."

"Have you tried Googling 'new hacker tricks?'"

"At this point I'm willing to give it a try."

"I did it once. I was trying to figure out what you do behind that desk all day."

"And...?"

"And all I got was a sore head."

Unsurprised.

"I should ask around a little bit... see if any of my contacts know anything about him or what he does, because right now, I can't get in."

"Then lure him out," he offered as he slung a weight onto the squat bar.

"I've tried that. He took the bait once, but he'll be more careful next time."

"Then tempt him more," he said with a shrug. "Make that trap so enticing that he has no choice but to risk sticking an arm in."

Floyd was a lot of things – smart wasn't usually one of them – but he had a point here. I'd been so focused on trying to get in, that I hadn't put nearly enough effort into trying to get this guy to come out.

I could do tempting.

Armageddon wanted to fuck me over just as badly as I wanted to do the same to him, he wouldn't be able to risk taking advantage of me if the opportunity presented itself. I just had to find a way to make it look like I'd made a minor slip within a complex maze of skill and efficiency. That was the key here. I had to hope he'd be smart enough to find one small error in amongst a pile of flawless execution.

"I can't believe I'm about to say this, but you've actually proved useful to me today."

He puffed out his chest and made a show of strutting around like a peacock.

"What's new for you on the lady front? You found one worth settling down for yet?"

He stopped mid-strut. "Nope."

"What the hell are you looking for, man? I swear you're chasing something that doesn't exist."

"It does exist. I found it once."

This was news to me.

"Come again?"

He smirked, and I knew his mind had just gone to the gutter, but to his credit, he didn't comment.

"Forget it. We're here to lift weights, not have a deep and meaningful."

If I didn't know better, I'd have said my little

brother was squirming... over a woman. This was unchartered territory.

"No, no, no, we can do both, this is a modern era, bro, we can be strong *and* sensitive." A shit-eating grin spread across my face.

He flipped me off.

"Don't be like that, cupcake."

"You're not going to give this up, are you?"

"What do you think?"

"Fine." He huffed out a breath. "There was this girl... it was a long time ago... years even, we had this one, crazy week together. I was laying low for... reasons..." He shot me a sheepish look. "Anyway, I was holed up at this tropical resort and one day I went to the pool and there she was. The whole week is just a blur of her."

"What happened at the end of the week?"

"Something came up. I couldn't tell her about any of it; I didn't want to drag her into any of my shit... so I left. Never saw her again." He shrugged.

His words suggested it was no big deal, but there was something there, in his eyes that made me think this had hurt him more than he was letting on.

"Did you ever look her up? I could find her for you."

He chuckled and turned away to grab another weight. "Nah. It's all good, Ty, it was a long time ago and I doubt she'd ever want to see me again after I ran out on her. It's ancient history now."

Sounded to me like Floyd was a history major all

of a sudden, but it wasn't my place to push him. If he'd gone years without this chick, then maybe she wasn't the one for him after all.

If nothing else, it was reassuring to think that maybe he had it in him to find something more than a good time, one day.

I wanted that for both the twins, and not only so I could return the favour of giving them the endless shit they'd been giving me lately, but because I genuinely wanted them to find love. I wanted us all to have what Parker and Charlotte had.

"Do you reckon we can go back to sweating it out now? This sharing of emotions has been fun and all, but I reckon I'm going to get my period if this shit carries on any longer."

He slipped underneath the barbell and nestled it across the back of his shoulders in preparation to start his set.

"No worries, princess, last thing I want is you bleeding all over the gym floor."

———

"What are you nervous for? You've already met everyone."

"I know." She wrung her hands together as we approached Parker and Charlotte's front door.

They knew we were here; I'd had to buzz through to Sammy on the intercom to get past the gate.

"So then why do you look like you could puke?"

"I don't know, I was filled with liquid courage at the gig. Then we were all jacked up on adrenaline with that terrorist situation, what if they don't like me in a normal setting?"

"You *do* get less likable with time," I teased.

She swatted my arm. "That's not funny."

"Why are you smiling then?"

"Because you're so handsome, even when you're being a smart prick."

I certainly liked having my ego stroked by this woman. Praise from her was so much better than praise from anyone else.

"That just might be the sweetest thing you've ever said to me."

She rolled her eyes.

I opened the door and stepped inside. "We're here!" I yelled out.

"This house is honestly a mansion." Amarah mused as I ushered her in and shut the door behind her. "I remember it being big, but this is actually insane.

"Did you expect anything less from a rockstar?"

"How the hell do they keep this thing clean?" She peered into various rooms as we made our way to the living room.

I took her hand in mine. "It's cute you think they clean it themselves."

"Oh duh, of course not." She palmed her forehead with her free hand. "Rich as hell, I keep forgetting."

I could understand that; if you took away the security team and the screaming fans, Parker and Jasper were pretty regular guys.

My sister was pretty famous now too, but she hadn't changed a bit. The idea of them having children one day scared me. I had no idea what it would be like for a kid to grow up in the public eye like that, but I was sure Parker would have a plan to handle it. I'd seen how protective he was of Charlotte; I could only imagine how he'd be with his kids.

I glanced over at Amarah – she was chewing on her bottom lip nervously. "Relax, baby, they love you already. My sister hasn't shut up about you since the day she met you. The twins know I'm crazy about you and they're still plotting ways to steal you from me. You have nothing to worry about."

"You're actually pretty cute when you're not trying to wind me up."

"I'm cute as shit, beautiful. Now get that sexy ass in there and let my family get to know you even better."

I led her into the living room, where all heads turned to greet us. Parker and Charlotte were there, both the twins, Jasper and Sammy. Hannah was nowhere to be seen.

Charlotte rushed over and pulled Amarah into a hug.

"Nice to see you too, short stuff." I pouted; feigning hurt that I wasn't her number one.

She rolled her eyes at me over Amarah's shoulder. "You'll get yours in a minute, you big baby."

We did the rounds, with everyone hugging Amarah and making her feel welcome.

Hannah was apparently experiencing extreme fatigue, so she was next door – at her and Jasper's house, sleeping it off.

"See, this thing is epic, I can see everything she does." Jasper held up his phone and showed Floyd the picture of what I could only assume was their bedroom, with Hannah crashed out on the bed. "I got it for the baby's room, but until the kid gets here, I can use it to make sure my stubborn wife is looking after herself."

"Sex cam, that's cool, bro. I rate it."

Jasper chuckled. "You'll have a pregnant wife one day and you'll understand why I find that funny."

Floyd looked confused but didn't press him for an explanation on it.

"Do you want a drink? We're making cocktails," Charlotte told us excitedly. "Well, Louis is making cocktails but since he's back in training and can't drink them, there's more for us."

"I'm good at three things in life; punching, fucking and making drinks." Louis smirked as he shook the cocktail mixer in his hands from behind the kitchen island.

"That's too much information. My ears are precious." Charlotte shot him a disgusted look.

"I reckon you should put that on your Tinder profile," Floyd suggested to our brother.

"Who said it's not already on there?" Louis replied.

"Can you pay more attention to how much alcohol is going into that thing? If you get my wife as drunk as you did last time, I'm going to make you stay here so you can hold back her hair while she vomits." Parker frowned at Louis as he tipped a bunch of things into the mixer without measuring any of them.

I chuckled. Charlotte was about fifty-five kilos dripping wet, and an absolute light weight with alcohol.

"I did not vomit," Charlotte argued. "I just felt like I might."

"Ignore him, Little Red, you've got a new lease of life – may as well enjoy it drunk," Jasper chimed in. "I'm sure Amarah will join you."

"I'm not sure I can stomach any alcohol, not after last weekend," Amarah told them with a grimace.

"I heard you guys had *quite* the little party." Charlotte giggled.

"We had something alright," she replied.

My sister led Amarah over to the couch so they could talk. I couldn't really hear what they were saying, but I made out something about dancing on the coffee table and singing badly, and that got a smile out of me. Seeing them together, talking like good friends made me happy. I could see Mara fitting into my family with ease, and once the idea of her being part of my family had been planted in my brain, I knew it wasn't going to be leaving.

I didn't do things by halves and falling in love with Mara was proving to be no different. The idea didn't even scare me anymore.

It had only been a couple of months and I was right on the verge of being completely and utterly in love with her.

Parker chuckled, and I glanced at him, to find him watching me carefully.

"I wanna show you something," he said in response to my questioning look.

I followed him out the door, taking one last look at my girl, who was so deep in conversation with my sister, she hadn't even noticed me leave.

Parker led me down the hallway and into his in-home studio.

"Sit." He pointed to the couch. I sat.

He went over to the chest of drawers and rummaged around for a few seconds before pulling out a small tin box.

He carried it over to me and sat down on the edge of the coffee table, so he was facing me.

"I need you to do something when you get that woman of yours home tonight."

I raised a brow at him. "I gotta say, Park, I'm not sure where you're going with this."

"Not there." He chuckled. "I want you to take a

photo of her."

I frowned, not understanding. I had lots of photos of Amarah already, I didn't know what I needed one of her tonight for. "I don't get it."

He lifted the lid off the tin and took out a photo, before handing it to me.

It was of Charlotte. She was sitting on the couch in the apartment she'd once shared with Hannah. She wasn't looking at the camera, instead she was focused on the book in her hands, a small smile on her face.

"She has no idea that photo exists. I took it when it hit me that my future wife was right in front of me. I snapped it quickly before I told her I loved her for the first time."

I stared hard at the photo, understanding what he was telling me, but feeling unsure if I was really ready to hear it.

"This photo is one of the most important things I own, man. I take it out every now and then and just stare at it. She's fucking everything to me. I knew it then and I know it now. That's the last moment before she knew it too."

I cleared my throat and pulled my eyes from the photo, to meet his. "Why are you telling me this?"

"Because Amarah is your Charlotte. I can see it in the way you look at her. I'm telling you, that girl is going to be your forever. I'm not much into the sentimental bullshit, but if there's one possession I'd be willing to run into a burning building for, it'd be this."

I handed him back the photo and he looked at it again, smiled and then tucked it back into the tin.

I'd never really talked like this with my brother-in-law before; it wasn't something I was used to. My brothers came to me for advice, and my parents were virtually absent from my life, so I didn't have anyone *I* went to for advice. I had to admit, if I were to go looking for advice on love and how to be a good other half, I didn't need to look any further than the man in front of me.

"You really think we've got what the two of you have?"

He nodded. "There's a look in your eyes. You've got this awareness of her... maybe you haven't quite accepted it yet, but when you do... before you tell her... take the photo. You won't regret it."

He left me with that thought. I barely even glanced up as he put the box back in the drawer and walked out the door.

I was falling, hard, hell, maybe he was right, and I *was* already there.

The idea was a welcome one, but hearing it come from someone else was a reality check.

I'd never really bought into the idea of marriage too much. My parents never set a good example for me growing up, but when I thought of Amarah, and the idea of never being able to call her my wife, the idea didn't sit well with me.

"Shit," I breathed, the realisation sinking in. Maybe Parker *was* right.

CHAPTER 24

Amarah

"MY MUM IS CRAAAAZY. She's your traditional Hispanic woman; loud and all up in your business."

"Do you speak Spanish?" Jasper questioned.

I nodded. "Yeah, I'm fluent, but it's my second language. I was born there, but then raised here for about ten years before going back to Spain. I moved back here about six years ago – my family stayed in Spain."

Jasper, Tyler, Charlotte and I were sitting around in the living room. Parker was rummaging in the fridge for something to eat, even though we'd eaten a delicious home cooked meal, no more than half an hour ago.

"I've been trying to convince Hannah to teach the baby French once it's born," Charlotte told me.

"Only problem with that is that none of us speak French," Jasper drawled, his tone suggesting he was well and truly sick of having this suggestion broached.

"We could learn."

The look Jasper gave her let us all know what he thought of that idea. I was fairly certain myself that two internationally renowned musicians and their uber busy wives probably didn't have the time to learn a second language, let alone teach it to a child, but that wasn't my business.

It did make me think about *my* potential future children though. I couldn't imagine not teaching them Spanish the way my parents taught me.

I glanced at Tyler.

I wonder if he'd learn...

The thought caught me off guard. Here I was, thinking of this man as the future father of my children.

The idea was absurd. It didn't matter how right it felt, or how much I wanted to see what little mini versions of Tyler and me might look like, I was his secret rival. That glaringly obvious hindrance to our future hadn't changed.

It dampened my mood. I knew damn well it was the reality, but that didn't mean I wanted to accept it. Accepting it meant giving him up, and I had no idea how I was meant to do that.

"Ty, can you please come help me and Parker move that table? I sent the boys to do it about fifteen minutes ago, but I'm pretty confident they're playing pool; I can hear cheering."

"Why don't I just go down there and bang their heads together?" Parker's suggestion came from inside the fridge.

"I'm happy to help," Ty replied.

"With banging their heads together, or moving the table?" Charlotte questioned, getting to her feet.

"Both." Ty chuckled, following her. He paused to kiss the top of my head as he went, filling my stomach with butterflies.

Parker trailed out after them, a leftover chicken drumstick in his hand.

That just left Jasper and I, alone.

It was silly – given that he was the only person here, other than Tyler, that I actually felt like I really knew – but being along with him made me feel most nervous of all.

He took a pull of his beer and looked at me, his expression curious.

"You miss your family? Must be hard with them being so far away?"

"Yeah." I nodded. "I miss them a lot. I try and get over to see them a couple of times a year, but it's still tough. They're getting older now too. They don't want to be travelling to see me so much anymore, it's too much for my dad."

"Can't believe I'll have a kid of my own soon – I'll be the dad that's too old to travel before I know it."

"You'll be a great dad."

He really would be. He loved those close to him fiercely. I'd seen the lengths he'd gone to, to find and protect Hannah – to make sure she knew she was loved – I knew there wasn't anything in this world that he wouldn't do for his child – his own flesh and blood.

"What makes you say that?"

I shrugged, suddenly wishing I hadn't stated my opinion like the fact I knew it to be. "You just seem like you have a lot of love to give."

He sipped his drink again.

"That's all a kid really needs, right? Love," I rambled.

He nodded but didn't say anything. It was really making me anxious, the way he was watching me.

It was silent between us for the longest twenty seconds of my life. I could feel my palms starting to sweat. There was something there in his expression that made me think he knew... he knew who I was.

"You know, me and Tyler... we've had our differences, but he's a good man. He's crazy about you, you know that, right?"

"I know that," I replied cautiously.

He nodded slowly. "Can I ask you something, Amarah?"

This was not good.

I could feel my heart pounding in my chest as he

glanced around behind him to check we were alone, before leaning forward, his elbows coming to rest on his knees.

"Does the name Armageddon mean anything to you?"

He knows.

I swallowed deeply, my heart rate skyrocketing.

"You mean that old Bruce Willis movie?" I asked, my voice coming out in a whisper.

He didn't even dignify my question with a response. It was fair enough too; I was way up shit creek, entirely without a paddle, and we both knew it.

"*A?*" He said the nickname he'd called me many times before.

My heart whooshed in my ears.

He knows.

I covered my face with my hands.

Holy shit.

"I *knew* you seemed familiar. There was just something about you. Your voice... the way you speak... the other week when Charlotte was in trouble... I *knew* it."

I couldn't believe this was happening. No one had ever figured out my real identity – not in all my years in the industry. I was the best kept secret in my line of work.

No one knew who I was.

Until now.

Now, I was caught red-handed, and by the person

who had the reach to ruin the one thing I really, truly cared about, because that was the truth. Sure, my job was important to me, as was my anonymity, but the only thing that scared me – the only thing I really cared about losing, was Tyler.

And now that Jasper knew who I really was, that was bound to happen.

He *couldn't* say nothing, not now that he knew for sure. Not mentioning a suspicion was one thing but knowing something for certain and still saying nothing was different. He couldn't sit by and watch this happen and not say a word. He was a good person – a much better person than me.

"Is this all a game to you?" he asked.

I looked up and was surprised to find no hint of judgement on his face. He was curious – confused.

I shook my head quickly. "No. *No*. It's not like that."

"You better tell me what it is like, Amarah, and you better do it quick."

"I'm here because I have real feelings for him." My tone was pleading. "It might not have started out like that... he was at my apartment building, I didn't know who he was, but we met... he gave me his number and that was when I learned he was Tyler Watson – my rival. I thought he was playing me, so I figured two could play that game."

"Go on."

"I went out with him, got to know the real him... I'm falling in love with him, Jasper, he doesn't know who I am, and I don't know what the hell to do." I was on the verge of tears. Telling Jasper everything had made it all the more real.

He stared at me, thinking hard.

"You know what I think?"

I shrugged. "That I'm a terrible person and that you should rat me out the second he comes back into this room?"

The corner of his mouth lifted in a smile. "No. You're not a terrible person, A, you've made a fucking hash of this situation, but I don't think you want to hurt Tyler."

I blinked back my tears.

"I think that he *does* know who you are. He might not know your secret identity, but he knows the real you. That guy has got it bad for you."

I nodded. He *did* know the real me – one giant secret aside.

"I never meant for this to happen."

"You can't help who you fall for, I get that... but you're going to have to tell him."

"He'll leave me," I whispered.

He looked at me with sympathy. "What's the alternative? You marry the guy, have a bunch of kids? Wake up next to him every day, keeping this a secret? Call me crazy, but I don't think that's going to work out too well for you. You can't have those kinds of secrets, Amarah, not in a real relationship."

"I know."

I *did* know. This was nothing I hadn't already told myself one hundred times over.

I knew it was never my intention to hurt him, but I'd lied to him. I'd kept things from him. I knew it couldn't carry on like that forever, but the alternative hurt too much. I could barely even think about it anymore.

"Are you going to tell him?" I whispered.

There was a noise from down the hallway, and we both looked in that direction, but no one was there – *yet*. They would be soon though, and I needed to know if he was going to throw me under the bus or not.

It killed me to think this might be the last night I'd have with Tyler – the last happy memory we'd share.

"I don't know, A, he needs to know. *You* need to tell him."

"I will, but not right now, I just can't do it yet. Please, Jasper, *please* don't tell him. I'll do it. I just need a little more time."

He nodded, clearly not liking the answer but understanding. "Fine. Your secret is safe with me for now. I've got a lot of respect for you, but this is fucked up."

"I know. I'm sorry."

This felt like I'd disappointed one of my parents. I knew I'd let myself down. I knew I was going to hurt Tyler, but I didn't know what the alternative was.

Jasper was right; I couldn't go on pretending like this wasn't all going to blow up in our faces.

"You love him. He loves you. Maybe you'll work it out."

I wanted to argue that I didn't love him, that he didn't love me, but it would have been pointless, I now realised.

I do love him.

Somewhere along the way I'd fallen for the enemy. Not just fallen but dived headfirst into oblivion.

I was confident that Tyler loved me too. The way he looked at me was the same way my dad looked at my mum.

Tyler and Charlotte came back into the room, and Jasper leaned back in his seat, his posture relaxed and carefree, as though we hadn't just had a conversation that threatened to destroy my entire world.

"You ready to go, beautiful?" Tyler asked me, a look of pure adoration on his face.

I nodded, guilt swirling in my stomach as I got to my feet, being careful to avoid Jasper's gaze.

"Let's get you out of here." He smiled down at me.

I can't think of a better idea.

Tomorrow. I'd worry about all this tomorrow. For now, all I cared about was the man in front of me. The man that I loved.

CHAPTER 25

Tyler

I WATCHED FROM MY BEDROOM, looking at her in the reflection of the mirror in my bathroom as she brushed her teeth and cleaned her face.

Not a scrap of makeup on her face and she was still the most beautiful woman I'd ever laid eyes on.

Time slowed down as she shook out her hair and collected it up to pile it on top of her head in a bun.

So beautiful.

Sometimes I had to pinch myself to believe that she was really mine.

I took out my phone without even really thinking about what I was doing and snapped a picture of her doing her hair in the mirror.

I looked at the photo and felt the last of my reservations slip away.

I *loved* this woman. She was mine and if I had my way, she'd be mine forever.

This was it – the moment that Parker was talking about – the last moment before she knew how crazy I was about her.

I tossed my phone onto the bed as she came out of the bathroom.

She found me there, waiting, watching her.

"What?" she questioned, stopping in her tracks.

"Just fucking *look* at you." I shook my head in disbelief.

There was a slight blush staining her cheeks, and it was so fucking beautiful. "You always say that... Why are you looking at me like that?"

Here goes nothing.

"Because I'm in love with you."

I'd never said words I'd been surer of. I'd never told a woman how I felt about her, with so much conviction.

It was the most real, most terrifying thing I'd ever done in my whole life. Sure, I'd told women I loved them before, but nothing had ever felt like this.

A smile broke out across her face, and she rushed at me, throwing herself into my arms, which knew to catch her without my brain even registering the action.

"I love you too," she replied, her words muffled by her face being pressed into my shirt.

Her words, her *love*... it soaked into the very core of me. I let the feeling of loving and being loved in return wash over me as I held her tight in my arms.

"I can't figure out if I've known you for ten seconds or ten years and it's the best feeling in the world. I wouldn't trade this for anything, Mara."

"I know what you mean," she whispered.

Everything with her was so exciting, every moment felt like an adventure, but somehow, at the same time, there was this sense of peace and familiarity when I was with her that made me feel comfortable and like I could be completely myself.

I slipped my hand under her chin and tilted her face up so she was looking at me.

"I'm going to love you so hard, beautiful," I promised her.

I had no intentions of ever being without her. The world could throw whatever it wanted at us, but as long as I had her, I'd be a happy man.

She looked like she was about to cry.

"Will you love me through anything?" she asked, a slight wobble in her bottom lip.

"Anything," I agreed. I'd forever be in love with this woman, no matter what happened.

She pressed up on her tip toes and kissed me, her banging body pressed firmly against me as our lips melded together.

I didn't know how the fuck I'd gotten so lucky. It'd been nothing but a coincidence – the two of us meeting. If I'd left even a few minutes earlier, or not shown up looking for Armageddon at all, then I never would have met this incredible woman.

That said, it was time I told her the series of events that led me to find her. She'd never asked, and I'd never told, but it was time to be completely honest.

"Come sit with me, I want to tell you about something."

She looked at me curiously but let me take her hand and lead her over to my bed.

I sat down on top of the covers, and she climbed on after me, sitting cross-legged next to me, her knees touching my thigh.

"I never told you what I was doing at your apartment building the day that we met."

Her eyes widened, and I couldn't understand the panic in them.

"You don't have to," she replied quickly.

"I want to, Mara... I need to."

She nodded, unsure.

I took her hands and engulfed them in both of mine. "I kinda have this rival... you remember how I told you that I'd pissed off my sister by helping Hannah disappear?"

She nodded.

"Well, the guy that Jasper hired to find her... we kind of have this war going. It's been a back-and-forth situation for years now. Anyway, I finally found out where he's located... and it's in your building. That's why I was there that day – I was trying to figure out who he is."

"You were stalking my building?"

I felt like a psychopath. "Yeah... I was."

"What were you going to do if you found him?" She nibbled on her bottom lip, uncertainty etched all over her features.

"Honestly? I have no idea what I would have done. I'd just realised what a stupid idea the whole thing was, and I was about to get the hell out of there, when I saw you... *and* my battery went flat. You already know the rest of that story."

"Did you ever find him?"

I shook my head. "No. I even stopped trying for a while; I was too caught up in you. Then Jasper wound me up the night of the gig and I had another crack at it. I need to know who he is; it's gone on for so long... I just want it to be over, but I don't know how to give up," I admitted.

"So don't give up."

I shrugged. "I don't want this to consume me. It led me to you, and I'm grateful for that, and don't get me wrong, I love a bit of healthy competition, but I'm tired of constantly looking over my shoulder and worrying about when the next attack is going to come. It's probably not a bad thing, it keeps me sharp, but it's draining."

She nodded. "Tell me something... why did this rivalry start in the first place?"

"It was a long time ago, but I was monitoring this security company; a client of mine had used them and they'd failed to deliver what they promised, and his wife had been kidnapped and killed. It was my job to take them down. They were a big-time outfit, and every year they ran this competition, anyone who could hack into their system got paid a million dollars."

She squeezed my hands.

"So anyway, I knew if anyone was going to beat this thing, it was me. There was no one as good as me on the scene at the time – other than this one guy – Armageddon. Long story short and lots of technical shit later, I managed to get in, but I got stuck at a certain point... that's when I decided to try my luck piggybacking off Armageddon, and the one thing he'd figured out was the last piece of the puzzle that I needed."

"So, you got away with the million dollars and Armageddon got nothing?"

She was judging me, I could tell.

"No." I shook my head. "I took the money, but I gave it to my client's daughter – she'd lost her mother, but I figured a ten-year-old could probably take her mind off things by splashing someone else's cash around. So, I took their prize money and then I took them down. Ran them into the ground. I destroyed their entire operation. I'd done my research and my client wasn't the only one whose life had been ruined by their negligence. They were money-hungry crooks who deceived people into thinking their loved ones were protected, and then when things went wrong, they took no responsibility. I made them take that responsibility."

Her hand slipped out of my grasp, and she covered her mouth in shock.

"I didn't take payment from my client on that one either, chalked it up to public service."

"I can't believe you did that."

I shrugged. "I know it wasn't exactly legal and I'd have a huge target on my back if anyone ever found out that I was the one to shut them down, and I know I shat all over Armageddon in the process. I probably should have just reached out and explained, but I was arrogant back then. It never really occurred to me that my actions could have consequences for somebody else, I was so focused on my mission to even the score."

"And so, then it began?"

I nodded.

There had been little things over the years, but nothing on the scale of the fuck up with Hannah.

"I can't blame him for taking that job from Jasper and making me look like an absolute rooster, I deserved it, and I was sloppy enough or cocky enough to not see it coming."

"Why are you telling me all of this now?"

"I don't want any secrets between us, Mara, you're mine and I have nothing to hide. I want you to know everything about me."

"I want you to know everything too," she whispered, her emotions getting the better of her. "I really do love you, you know that?"

"I know that, and I love you too, beautiful."

"I bet you fifty bucks that I love you more," she teased.

"Deal," I replied quickly, pulling her on top of me and falling backwards onto the bed. "Oh, look at that, you lose."

She laughed and swatted my shoulder with her hand. "I do *not* lose."

"Judge's ruling..." I paused. "Official decision is that *I* love *you* more, hate to call you a loser, but..."

She pressed her lips to mine.

"I think we might have to agree to disagree on this one, Watson."

I'd never been happier to *not* see eye to eye.

———

Last night had been hands down, the best night of my life.

I had the woman I loved.

I'd been completely honest with her, and she hadn't looked at me like I was crazy. She'd just kept on loving me.

"Good morning, beautiful," I murmured.

She didn't reply.

I smiled to myself. It was rare she slept in later than I did, but I loved it when I got to watch her wake.

I rolled over to look at her.
The bed was empty.
My apartment was empty.
All her stuff was gone.
She was gone.

CHAPTER 26

Amarah

"BREATHE," Jessie instructed as we walked along the beach. "You need to chill the fuck out."

"I know, but it's such a mess and I know there's nothing I can do to fix it, and I'm going to lose him, Jessie, and I don't know how I'm meant to survive that."

"Okay, sit." She pointed to a patch of sand, and I dropped down to my ass. She lowered herself to the ground next to me.

"Why did the man of my dreams have to be him, Jessie? There's like, what? A few *billion* men in the world and I only want him?"

"Because the universe is a cruel bitch?" she offered.

Cruel bitch is an understatement.

"Just don't tell him?" she suggested.

I dropped my face into my hands. "I *have* to tell him."

"You could talk to Jasper again? Beg him not to say anything..."

I shook my head, already having thought about this idea and dismissed it just as quickly.

It would never work. I didn't want the love of my life to have no idea what I really did for a job. I didn't want secrets.

I'd always believed the only secrets between a woman and her man should be things like chocolate hidden in the back of the fridge or how much had been spent on a pair of heels.

I couldn't live happily ever after with Tyler with this hanging over my head.

"I can't carry on like this; I have to be honest with him."

She nudged me with her knee. "You never know... maybe he'll understand. He probably would have done the same thing, roles reversed. Don't write the whole thing off yet."

"And what would you do, if I came to you and told you that he'd lied to me, the way that I've lied to him?"

She grimaced, and then tried and failed to cover it. "I'm not sure you want me to answer that question."

"Exactly."

I picked up a stick and drew patterns in the sand with it.

"You have to try, Rah-Rah. You're crazy about him."

I am. So, so crazy.

"He's going to hate me."

"You don't know that. Be positive. Beg if you have to. What have you got to lose?"

"*Everything*," I whispered.

"I hate to break it to you, honey, but it sounds like you've got that to lose, either way."

She's right.

"He could expose my entire career, Jessie, and I wouldn't even blame him for it. Hell, I deserve it."

"No, you don't, you work harder than anyone I've ever met. He's just as responsible for this rivalry as you are. He messed with you too. The only thing you need to feel bad about is keeping it from him, but he's not blameless in this whole thing either. He showed up to your apartment building looking for you, that's next level stalker kind of shit. He's not been playing by the rules either."

I knew that was true, but the difference was, he'd been honest with me.

Guess it's time for me to be honest with him too.

"I know." I sighed. "I just wish things could have been different, that we both weren't who we are, and we could have had it all."

She wrapped her arm around my shoulders and pulled me close.

"That kind of feeling... that chemistry... the connection you share... that doesn't happen every day. It's something special and you need to grab it with both hands and hold onto it tight."

That was all I wanted. *He* was all I wanted.

"That might be somewhat challenging, given our situation."

"Just try, Rah-Rah, that's all you can do. Let him in completely and then the rest is up to him."

Letting people in wasn't exactly my strong point, but Tyler had busted down all my walls and made me fall head over heels in love with him.

"Okay," I whispered. "I'll try."

———

I tapped the keys on my keyboard with shaky hands.

I'm the worst kind of person.

There was no way I could keep doing this.

Especially not now that I knew his side of the story. Especially not now that I knew he was in love with me too.

I'd thought all along that he was the one in the wrong – that he deserved our constant dual after the way he shafted me, but once again, *I* was the asshole.

Yes, he'd done wrong by me back then, hacking into my server and stealing my hard work, but after hearing him talk about how complex it was, I doubt I ever would have got there on my own anyway.

His reasons were so genuine. Not only did he not

take the prize money for himself, but he didn't even take payment from his client.

He's practically a saint.

Then there was the fact that we'd unintentionally worked as a team, and that irony was definitely not lost on me. The more I'd thought about things these past few weeks, the more I could see us being exactly that – a team.

Ours was a lonely business to be in but having Tyler by my side would have made it so much less isolating. We could have worked together and taken on more than either of us probably ever thought possible.

But that's never going to happen.

Those were all naive, silly thoughts. There was no way Ty was going to overlook what I'd done – the lies that I'd told. That fantasy in my head was going to remain exactly that – a fantasy.

I knew I should have been doing this to his face, but last night and this morning only proved I didn't have the balls.

The shrill ring of my phone made me jump.

I didn't even look to see who it was. I already knew.

He'd called me half a dozen times since he'd found me missing from his bed.

I'm such a chicken shit.

I was going to crush him with this. I could see in his eyes last night how much he loved me. The way he'd held me, kissed me and touched me... he poured that love into me. I was almost coming apart at the seams, I was so full of it.

The ringing stopped and I got back to my work, my heart beating a million miles an hour.

I knew what I needed to do, but I had to be careful. I couldn't just leave myself wide open for anyone to expose me. I had to set this thing up so that only the best – only Tyler would be able to see everything when he eventually came looking – which he would. The last thing I needed was for my entire career to be exposed and ruined. I was going to lose Tyler soon enough; I didn't need to lose my livelihood as well. I just had to hope that Ty wouldn't stoop that low, once he learnt the truth.

I wrote and deleted code for what felt like hours before it was finally ready. My phone rang another half a dozen times and I let each and every one go to voicemail.

It'd been half an hour with no phone calls when I heard it.

His voice.

He was banging heavily on my door and calling out my name over and over.

I brought my knees up to my chest and wrapped my arms around myself, burying my face. This was torture. The man I loved was out there in the hallway, only metres away, and I couldn't go to him. He was clearly worried and distressed about not being able to find me. I felt like total trash. I'd have been beside myself if he'd disappeared like that on me.

Finally, after what felt like an eternity, the banging and yelling stopped and I pulled up the security camera feed for the building that I could tap into, and watched as he exited the building, jumped into his SUV and took off down the street at pace.

I didn't allow myself any more time to wallow, I had work to do.

———

I sighed as I finished. Just one more press of a button and this thing would go live. I had to admit, this was some of my better work. It was ironic really, that my best work was going to lead to my total undoing.

I picked up my phone from the desk, tears welling in my eyes. There was just one thing I had left to do and then I was going to turn this thing off. I knew damn well Ty could trace it if he really wanted to. I was protected, but not well enough to stop him eventually tracking my location – if he hadn't already.

I needed to apologise in advance for what I was going to do to him – for the hurt I was going to cause.

I typed out the message as the moisture overflowed from my eyes and ran down my cheeks.

Amarah: I'm so, so, sorry, I love you. I really do. I know this makes no sense now, but you'll see what I'm sorry for. I wish things were different. A x

Every last part of me wanted to wait for the reply I knew would follow, but I couldn't.

I powered off my cell and tossed it onto the desk before I broke down entirely.

———

There was a light tap at the door and it roused me from the spot where I'd fallen asleep on the couch.

I glanced around groggily, reality still catching up to me. I blinked a few times and felt the puffiness of my eyes.

It all came flooding back. I winced, hating myself and my actions as I heard the tapping again.

I crept over to my desk, and I was about to pull up the security feed when I heard her voice.

"It's me, Rah-Rah. Let me in."

Jessie.

I rushed to the door and flung it open.

Just the sight of my best friend took some of the weight off my shoulders.

She looked me over, her expression sympathetic. "You look like shit."

A sob broke free from my throat. "I know."

"Oh, *honey*." She stepped into the apartment and pulled me in for a hug.

"How'd you know?" I asked between hiccupping sobs.

"He called me, a lot of times. He's going crazy with worry for you."

I knew he would be, and I also knew it was only about to get worse.

"I couldn't tell him to his face, I wasn't strong enough. I've left a virtual trail of breadcrumbs so he can figure it out himself. He's going to hate me, Jessie."

She didn't answer. We both knew there was nothing she could say. There was nothing anyone could say. She just hugged me tight while I cried.

CHAPTER 27

Tyler

"I DON'T KNOW what the fuck to do, bro, I'm flipping out."

"No shit, I've never heard you this panicked. Take a couple of breaths, Ty, you'll wrap that car around a lamppost if you don't chill," Floyd warned me, his voice filling the car via my Bluetooth connection.

"Well, she's just disappeared, for fuck's sake, that shit isn't normal. She's not answering her cell. She's not at home. No one there has seen her; not even Jessie knows where she is. What if something has happened to her and I just go home and *chill*."

"Surely you can track her?"

Obviously.

"Did it already. Her cell showed she was at home, but she wasn't there. I banged on the door for fucking ages. Eventually found a spare key hidden on the top of a tall ledge and let myself in. There was no sign of her."

"Maybe she left it behind and went for a run or something? I dunno, bro, all I'm saying is that she's only been MIA for a few hours and there's nothing to suggest that anything bad has happened to her. Did you two have a fight or something?"

"No." I sighed. "Not even fucking close. "I told her I loved her. She told me she loved me too. We were right there in the thick of it."

He whistled long and low. "I really want to say I told you so, but I can appreciate this isn't the time. Maybe she freaked out about how serious it was getting? I know I've been there."

"Since when can you appreciate that *anything* has a time and place?" I questioned, momentarily distracted by my brother's sudden ability to have some self-control.

"No fun in kicking a man when he's already down. But seriously, Ty, maybe she just freaked out and needs some space."

I thought about it, but it didn't add up. That woman loved me. It was as plain as day to see. I knew there was a chance she'd bolted out of panic, but I just couldn't see it. Not Amarah. She wasn't some crazy chick who spooked easy.

She was my Mara.

"Maybe," I muttered.

An alert for a message popped up on my SUV's display and I nearly swerved onto the other side of the road when I saw Amarah's name pop up. The car coming towards me on the other side of the road tooted their horn at me.

"She sent me a message."

"Well, what the fuck does it say?" Floyd demanded.

I indicated to pull off the road and threw it into park as soon as I'd come to a stop.

I grabbed for my phone. I was so fucking scared, my hands were literally shaking.

Amarah: I'm so, so, sorry, I love you. I really do. I know this makes no sense now, but you'll see what I'm sorry for. I wish things were different. A x

"What the fuck is that meant to mean?" I hissed.

"What? What does it say?" Floyd yelled.

"Jesus. Calm down," I snapped.

I read the message aloud to him, and he was quiet for a few beats. "Yeah, I dunno, man, that's fucked up."

"This makes no sense now, but you'll see what I'm sorry for."

I couldn't make sense of it.

What the fuck does she have to be sorry for?

"What the hell am I meant to do with that?"

"You want to know what I think?"

Truth was, I probably didn't, but I was as curious by nature as he was stubborn, so we both knew he was going to tell me his opinion and that I was going to have to listen.

"Shoot," I drawled.

"I think you should just leave her the fuck alone. She's obviously going through some type of breakdown, and if she's apologising, that means she fucked up. I bet if you called her right now, her phone would be off. You don't need that shit. Let her do her thing and go focus on something that'll keep you busy."

I couldn't believe I was about it say it, but Floyd was right. I was none the wiser to whatever the fuck was going on with Amarah, and while I knew there was no way in hell I was going to be able to keep my mind off her for long, it couldn't hurt to try, and I had just the thing.

The honeypot.

I wound up the call with Floyd and then sat there in my car, pulled over on the side of the road as the rain started to trickle down on the windscreen, my head resting against the head rest and my eyes closed.

I didn't want to reply to her message, but I knew I would. I was pissed off and confused, but I loved her, I was totally smitten and most of all, I was scared.

I wasn't made of tough enough stuff to withstand losing her. Not now, not like this.

I opened my eyes and grabbed my phone.

Tyler: Talk to me, beautiful. I love you. I don't want to lose you.

I stared at the screen for a solid fifteen minutes, and when I didn't get a reply, I calmly put the phone down on the seat next to me – rather than throw it through the windscreen like I wanted to, and drove home to get to work.

———

I was in so deep it was making my head hurt.

This shit wasn't easy. I had to think like Armageddon, all the while, thinking like myself *and* trying to outsmart a system designed to get the better of people just like the both of us.

Floyd was right about one thing; getting my brain working was serving as the perfect distraction.

I typed furiously on my keyboard, endless streams of numbers, letters and symbols flying across my screens.

It was barely making sense to me anymore, but I was close to being done, I could feel it. I had a sixth sense when it came to hacking.

I turned to my other screen and went in search of Armageddon's server. It had been ages since I'd made any attempt to hack into it. I'd accepted that it wasn't going to happen – the guy was too good for that shit.

Only this time, I noticed something different. It wasn't something that most guys in this game would look at twice, but I wasn't most guys.

I virtually tiptoed in a little further, cautious. Armageddon might have been setting me up with his own honey pot, but I didn't think so. I'd seen it all before and this wasn't it.

What's he doing here...

I could feel my heart beating in my chest as I disabled the cyber security.

I'm so close.

One more click of my mouse and I'd be in. There was a chance this was a trap, but my instincts told me it wasn't. I'd made this very slip in my own system many moons ago, and it was so virtually unnoticeable, that thankfully, I never got caught out on it.

I crossed my fingers that Armageddon wouldn't have the same luck I did.

I took a deep breath, closed my eyes, and clicked the mouse.

Click.

My eyes flew open.

I'm in.

Holy fuck, I'm in.

He made a mistake. *Finally*, he'd made a mistake.

Now that I was here. In the place I'd been dreaming about for years, I didn't know what to do.

It was like when I went to that apartment building, I didn't know what the hell I would have done if I'd figured out who he was, but that was the whole point. I just wanted to know. He knew who I was, it was only fair.

That was what I wanted to do. *See* him.

I found the webcam and typed in the code

required to override the system and allow me access to view whatever the web cam could see.

My finger hovered over the enter key.

There was no going back. Once I pushed that button, I was going to see the face of my biggest rival.

My hand shook with nerves.

I didn't want to do this alone.

I grabbed my cell phone and hit call on the most recent number – Floyd's.

"Hey there, cupcake, how's the mood?" he answered.

"I'm in his computer." The words came out in a rush.

"For real?"

"For real. I'm about to get access to his webcam. I'll be able to look right at him."

"How do you know he's there?"

I didn't have time to attempt to explain any of this to Floyd, so I gave it to him in simple terms. "I can see him doing shit within his system."

"You're a real creepy motherfucker, you know that?"

"I don't give a fuck; I need you to just shut up and be there while I check this shit out."

"I can do that," he replied.

I had my doubts, but we were here now, and it wasn't as though hanging up on him and calling Louis would have been any more beneficial. Charlotte would have been the perfect person to hold my hand, but I wasn't willing to admit to her just how deep this rivalry went.

"Okay," I breathed.

"Okay," he repeated.

I pressed the enter key.

The screen flickered for a second, and then came to life.

What the fuck?

I gaped at the sight in front of me.

I couldn't believe what I was seeing.

"Ty?" Floyd questioned.

"Amarah," I whispered, shocked to my very core. "It's Amarah."

"You'll see what I'm sorry for..."

This is what she meant.

This is how she knew that stuff when Charlotte was in danger.

"What's Amarah?" Floyd questioned, confused.

"Amarah.   Armageddon.   Amarah   *is* Armageddon."

"What. The. Actual. Fuck," he replied slowly.

I was staring at the screen, watching her sitting there, her expression sad and tired as she worked on her computer. Her eyes were glassy and puffy. She'd been crying.

She sighed heavily as her hands paused over her keys and her eyes darted back and forth across the screen – reading.

She lowered her lids for a moment before slowly opening them again, and when she looked up, she looked directly into the camera, her eyes begging for forgiveness.

I heard myself gasp. She'd done this on purpose. She wanted me to finally know it was her. She knew I could see her right now.

She mouthed the words 'I'm so sorry'.

I could feel my heart beating in my throat.

She stared for a few more seconds before her hand came up and covered the lens of the camera.

Just like that, she was gone.

CHAPTER 28

Amarah

I COULDN'T SEE HIM, but my alerts had told me he was here, looking right at me.

I stared at the tiny, circle lens of my webcam and imagined the shock, hurt, betrayal... everything I knew he'd be feeling in this moment.

My heart was breaking – cracking further and further open by the second.

"I'm so sorry," I whispered.

I stared for as long as I could, covering the lens with my hand right before the first tear fell.

I didn't know what was going to happen now, but I knew one thing for sure, *something* was looming, and I wasn't going to like it.

———

My heart sped up to a gallop when I heard his knuckles rapping on the door.

I'd known he'd come, but I hadn't expected him so soon. I thought it would have taken him days, not mere hours to show up. I'd considered running – just packing a bag and going. I'd even pulled out my suitcase. But every time I looked at it, sitting there on my bed, the thought of filling it with my things and disappearing made me feel sick.

I need to see Tyler.

And now, I was about to.

I'd watched him on the security feed. I already knew he had on black jeans, a blue t-shirt and a black cap.

I knew his eyes were going to look so bright with that shirt on. I'd admired that very sight, countless times before. Today, it was bound to be my undoing.

I tiptoed towards my door. I was so nervous I was sweating.

"I know you're in there, Mara. Open up."

Big-girl pants.

I took a deep breath, turned the handle and opened the door.

CHAPTER 29

Tyler

"I THOUGHT YOU'D BE GONE," I stated.

"I thought I'd be gone too." Her voice was a whisper. She was a shell of the confident, self-assured woman I'd met and fallen headfirst in love with.

"Why aren't you then?"

"I guess I finally wanted you to be able to find me..." she whispered.

"It wouldn't matter where you went, Amarah, if I wanted to find you, I would."

She dipped her head and looked at her feet. I'd never seen her look so devastated. I was used to the sassy, smart woman I was crazy about.

"I can't imagine you'd want to look for me. Not after this."

I watched her as she stared at the ground. The toe of her shoe scuffed at the floor in what I assumed was a nervous gesture.

The silence enveloped us, and I wanted so desperately to reach out and touch her, but I knew it would be the wrong move.

I loved the woman in front of me, more than I'd ever loved anyone before her, but right now I had to protect myself.

If I held her, I'd forgive her, and I wasn't ready to do that yet – if at all. I needed answers before I did anything.

"I'm here, aren't I?"

She looked up and into my eyes. She was on the verge of tears, and I felt my resolve slipping.

"I don't know why you're here." She shrugged.

"I want the truth, Amarah, all of it. I need to know if this was all just a game to you."

"It's not," she interrupted quickly, looking up at me, her voice soft and scared. "It wasn't a game to me."

"Can I come in?"

"You want to know everything, right?"

I nodded cautiously, unsure where she was going with this.

"Come on then."

She slipped past me in the doorway, the scent of her perfume causing my eyes to close in appreciation.

I couldn't imagine never smelling that scent again, but if this all turned out to be some sick game, I would have to accept that as my new reality.

"Tyler?" she called from the door down the hall.

I took a deep breath and followed her.

"This is where I work," she explained as she swung the door open, revealing a setup very similar to my own.

Basic furnishes, a couch and table and chairs were the only other things in the apartment. It looked to me like she'd been sleeping on the couch.

"A second apartment – that's smart."

Credit where credit was due, it was a good idea, and something I probably should have done myself from the beginning.

I strolled over towards her cluttered desk. "You know, when I first met you, I was worried that you were connected to Armageddon in some way..."

Turns out I was more than right.

"Is that why you asked me out?"

I sat down in her chair and looked around at the random assortment of knickknacks on her desk.

There was a unicorn doing a handstand, a squirrel smoking a cigar.

She really was such an incredible and kooky woman; it sent a physical jolt of pain through me to think about how much I'd miss her if I had to let her go.

I shook my head in response to her question. "No, I asked you out because you're hot, and because you had a smart mouth. I liked you from the first moment

I laid eyes on you, and I've liked you every moment since."

"You don't like me right now."

She's got a point.

There was no way I was going to answer that question. She was fishing for information, and she deserved to squirm for a while yet.

She must have realised I wasn't going to answer her because she sighed.

"I know I have no right to ask, but do you still love me?"

Tears welled in those big, beautiful dark eyes of hers, and I had to coach myself through staying strong.

Every instinct I had told me to go to her and hold her while she was hurting, but I couldn't.

"I'll always love you, Amarah, but I'm reeling right now. I don't know who the fuck you are anymore."

"I don't know who I am either."

She crossed the room and sat down on the couch, amongst the assortment of pillows and blankets that covered it.

"I need you to tell me what the fuck is going on here, Amarah, because I honest to god have no fucking clue what just happened."

"I don't know where to start."

"The beginning," I snapped. "Start at the beginning and tell me everything, before I lose my mind."

She nodded her head a couple of times, the action a defeated one.

I hated seeing her like this, even though I was confused as hell, even though she'd clearly played me in one way or another, I still had feelings for her, and those feelings ran so deep that seeing her hurt, hurt me.

"So, you turned up here that day, trying to find me. I had no idea who you were when I helped you jump start your car, I swear to God, Ty, you were just a hot guy."

I nodded, willing her to continue. "It wasn't until you drove away, and I looked at your name and number on the piece of paper. I felt like I was going to have a heart attack."

"So why agree to the date then?"

She shrugged. "I guess I thought you were playing me. I thought you knew who I was, and you were trying to play me. I've never been one to shy away from a challenge, so I thought I'd give back as good as I was getting."

"You knew I was the bad guy, and you went out with me anyway?"

She nodded. "That's how the saying goes, right? Keep your friends close and your enemies closer? But then I liked you... I never intended to actually like you, and then you told me about your job, and I couldn't figure out if you were an expert at messing with me or if you really had no clue."

"I had no clue, Mara. Never once did I think *you* were Armageddon. *Never.*"

Not even for a second.

"And I'll admit it's a little sexist on my behalf, but I just didn't consider that you could have been female."

"You're not the first to make that assumption, and you won't be the last. To be honest, I like it that way, even if it sets women back about fifty years," she replied, her eyes rolling.

I felt the corner of my lip twitch with a hint of a smile. I bit it back down. This was no time for smiles.

"Anyway... I told myself I was going to end it with you, so many times... and then I'd try and find the balls, and I couldn't go through with it. You were too... magnetising. I'm drawn to you in ways that I can't even explain, Ty. I fell for you, hard."

"What was your plan then? Never tell me?"

"I don't know," she whispered. "I thought I could just leave it until it was a problem and then I was in so deep that I couldn't see a way out anymore. I kept convincing myself that I could end it – that I could do the right thing, but I lost the ability to get out a long time ago."

What a fucking mess.

"I feel like the worst person in the world. It's tortured me, Ty, but I didn't know what to do... I fell in love with you. I didn't want to lose what we had."

"So why tell me now?"

She sighed deeply. "Two reasons... the first is that

Jasper put the pieces together and figured out who I was. He and I became sort of friends when I took the job from him. I let my guard down and it came back to bite me."

This surprised me. They'd worked together to find Hannah. It'd shaken me to register that fact, but it never occurred to me that they might have been somewhat friendly. He'd obviously been let in on the secret of her gender, and that fact made me jealous – insanely jealous. I wanted to be the one who knew all her secrets – not some other guy.

I guess I'm hearing them all now. Ironic.

"So, he threatened to tell me, and you thought you'd better get in first?"

She tipped her head to the side, her eyes never leaving mine. "Yes and no. He thought I needed to tell you and I agreed. I'm sure I could have begged him for his silence, but I didn't want that."

"What's the other reason."

"Because you told me the truth about why you were at my building that day. You told me about the rivalry... I had no idea, Ty. If I'd have known why you stole my work all those years ago, I never would have held a grudge. I'm glad you took their money and then took them down. I'm only sorry it started this grudge match between us."

I was sorry for that too, but a part of me was grateful. I never would have met her if it wasn't for that. I wouldn't be here right now. And maybe she was lying, and this was all a game to her, one where she'd score the ultimate win by fucking me over, but if nothing else, my feelings were real. I'd experienced real love these past few months, and I couldn't find it within myself to regret that, no matter what happened next.

"I didn't have the strength to break it to you, to your face, especially not after the night we'd shared. But I knew you'd find your way in. You're the best at what you do, Tyler. There's no denying that... You win."

It sure as fuck didn't feel like I'd won anything – it felt like I'd lost everything that truly mattered.

"And I know you probably will *never* be able to forgive me for this, and I can't blame you for that, but I need you to know it was real for me too – all of it, Ty. I was me when I was with you... I've never felt more like myself and that's because of you. I love you, more than I've ever loved another person, and even if I never get to see you ever again, I want you to know that. You're the person I want to spend the rest of my life with, and I'm so, so sorry that I've hurt you."

She was looking at me with those big brown eyes full of emotion. She was on the verge of tears, and I didn't know how much more I could take.

"I need some time." I choked out the words, my own emotions threatening to take over.

A part of me hated her for what she'd done, but the rest of me... the rest of me loved her and those two parts were currently going to war with one another.

I needed to get out of here and away from her. I

needed to be somewhere where I couldn't smell her perfume or see her golden skin. I couldn't think straight while I watched her dark hair brush against her bare arms. There wasn't going to be any logical or reasonable actions until I got some space.

"Okay," she replied quietly.

"I don't know what to say. I can't even promise you that you're ever going to hear from me again. All I know is that I need space. Okay?"

"Okay," she repeated, broken.

I took one last, sweeping look at her, got up and walked out without even looking back.

CHAPTER 30

Amarah

"IT SMELLS LIKE MISERY IN HERE." Jessie greeted me when I opened the door to my office apartment for her.

She brushed past me, entirely ignoring the 'leave me the fuck alone' look I was giving her.

I closed the door behind her and rested my forehead against it for a few seconds – I contemplated smacking my head against it with force but decided against it – before turning to face my best friend. It wasn't that I didn't appreciate her showing up for me, because I did. I really, *really* did. I just wasn't good company right now and that made me feel shitty.

"It doesn't smell like *anything* in here. I took out

the rubbish. I showered. My hair is washed, my clothes are clean. Nothing in here *smells*," I argued.

"Fine, you're right, it doesn't smell," she agreed as she sat down on the couch, the neatly folded pile of blankets and pillows wobbling. "It *feels* like misery in here."

Fair enough.

"That's because I *am* miserable... and I don't do things by halves. I have *become* misery; misery has become *me*... me and misery are now one." I sighed dramatically.

She looked at me with sympathy. "He still hasn't called, huh?"

I sighed as I shook my head.

He hadn't called. He hadn't text. He hadn't even been sniffing around my servers.

He'd disappeared from my life as though he never existed in it in the first place.

It had been two and a half weeks since he'd come here and he'd told me he needed space, and it was the longest seventeen days of my life.

I had no clue if I was ever going to see him again. I lived in hope, but my instincts told me to lose that hope if I ever wanted to leave this depressed state that had become my new reality.

I doubted I would have come back to him if the roles were reversed, and he was a hell of a lot smarter than me, so my chances were slim, to none.

I knew I should have been trying to get on with

life, move on as best I could, but I didn't have the slightest clue on how to even begin doing that. I missed him like crazy. I couldn't and didn't want to, imagine my life without him.

My body ached for his. My fingers longed to touch his skin or run through his hair.

I wanted to snuggle up on his chest more than I wanted to take my next breath.

I was going insane here without him. I'd thrown myself into work as a distraction, but even that, I was half-assing. I'd been doing the bare minimum for weeks and the cracks were beginning to show.

I couldn't afford to lose my business at the moment, or to have my standards slip, but my motivation to care about anything much at all had gone out the door with Tyler when he'd left.

"Do you want me to get Wilder to talk to him?" she offered.

"No." I sighed. "*God no*. I don't want you guys getting involved. I don't want Wilder knowing anything more about this than he already does. You two are just starting out, the last thing you need is me and my bullshit getting in the way."

"You do bring a fair bit of bullshit to this friendship."

I went to my desk and sat down in my chair.

That was basically the extent of my physical activity at the moment. I hadn't been for a run in over a week. I was starting to feel like a sloth.

"I feel so lazy and gross. I need to get some fresh air, but the idea of running right now makes me want to stick pins in my eyes."

Jessie got to her feet. "I can't believe I'm about to say this, but go get ready, I'm coming with you."

That got a smile on my face. A real, genuine smile. "*You*. Running?" I even heard the sound of my own laugh for the first time in forever.

She rolled her eyes dramatically. "Yes, *me* running."

My smile got wider. "But you have a firm, 'I only run if a murderer is chasing me', policy."

"Yeah, well things have changed. I can't sit here and watch you mope around all down and shit, so go put on your shoes before I change my mind."

She made a show of getting up and doing what I presumed was meant to resemble a lunge.

I was confident that one run wasn't going to make all the difference here, unfortunately, but I was willing to give it a shot. This was the first time I could remember smiling in far too long, and if nothing else, watching Jessie attempt to run would be entertaining as hell.

"Thank you," I whispered.

"Yeah well, don't thank me just yet, I plan to do *a lot* of whining on this run." She mock shuddered.

I knew she understood. I wasn't just thanking her for right now. I was thanking her for tolerating me. It was for the hours in between messages. It was for forgetting to meet her for lunch. It was for having nothing exciting to say.

It was for being my person – when I needed her most.

CHAPTER 31

Tyler

I FEINTED a jab and came in hard with a cross, landing heavily on Louis' jaw.

He grinned, his mouth guard showing.

The prick was messed up in the head. He loved getting hit almost as much as he loved doing the hitting.

It was not normal – but I'd given up on expecting 'normal' from him a long time ago.

"You don't fight like such a girl when you're angry." The words were muffled with his mouth guard, but I heard the wind up regardless.

I ignored him and swung for his body but missed. He darted out of the way and then countered with an uppercut that missed my jaw by the narrowest of margins. It was nothing but good luck on my behalf that had that shot missing.

I grunted. That one would have been lights out if it had found its mark.

Louis was still grinning like the lunatic he was, and I was getting more and more pissed off by the minute.

It fucked me off when I was gassed as hell, frustrated as fuck, and he looked like he was having the absolute time of his life.

He dropped his hands low, goading me into hitting him.

I fucking hate it when he does that.

I lost all composure and went in swinging hard, throwing haymaker after haymaker. It was dangerous and stupid, but I'd given up caring.

I had rage and it needed an outlet, and unfortunately for Louis – he was that outlet – and I was out for blood.

He dodged and weaved, avoiding eighty percent of the messy shit I was throwing, which only made me wilder. I swung harder and faster. He hunkered down – wearing my erratic shots on the guard – unaffected.

I hit until I had nothing more left in me. Louis must have sensed that this had gone beyond sparring, because when I finally gave up and stepped back, my gloved hands hanging at my sides, he made no move to counter.

I was completely and utterly spent.

"You done?" he grunted.

I nodded, dropping down to the canvas to catch my breath.

He sat down next to me – barely puffing as I heaved in deep breath after deep breath.

I spat my mouth guard into my glove and lay back with my eyes closed, exhausted.

"You wanna talk about what the fuck you just tried to punch out of your system?"

I heard the Velcro of his gloves undoing and then the thud as he dropped them to the ground next to my head.

"Same shit, different day," I grumbled.

"That girl still playing on your mind?"

"It's more than playing on my mind, it's completely fucking with my head. And she's not just 'that girl' – she's *the* girl."

I opened my eyes and slowly sat up.

Louis was covered in sweat, but other than that, the bastard looked completely unaffected. He looked like he could comfortably get up and go another ten rounds.

Prick.

"What are you going to do about it, bro? Because, don't get me wrong, I love being your punching bag, but you're acting all kinds of fucking crazy."

I *was* all kinds of crazy and then some. I needed sleep. I needed to work. I needed to eat something that didn't come out of a packet. I needed my fucking stupid heart to be whole again, instead of this cracked-in-half mess that currently took up residence in my chest.

"I don't know what to do. I love her, man, but I don't know how to forgive her for this."

I looked down at my boxing boots. I was emotional as fuck, and given our location, I didn't want to risk any badass boxers seeing me with tears welling in my eyes.

I was no pussy, but this situation had me messed up, big time.

Louis knew the whole story, I'd spilled my guts to the boys, Charlotte and Parker, even Hannah and Jasper hadn't been able to avoid my oversharing.

Jasper was sheepish, but relieved that I knew the truth. Hannah was somewhat amused, and Charlotte was *pissed*. Parker and the boys were slightly more blasé about the whole thing – as they were about most things.

"Do you think she's really sorry?"

I nodded. I'd never seen someone look more remorseful. I'd never heard a more genuine apology in all my years.

"Alright, she kept you in the dark, so what?"

I went to open my mouth to give him an earful about how it was so much more than that, but he got in first.

"Can you honestly say you wouldn't have done the exact same thing, if you were in her situation?"

I went to say 'no', but my response faltered. I

hadn't asked myself that question in quite so many words.

I'd been so focused on 'she should have told me', that I hadn't really stopped to think what I would have done if she'd come into my life the way I'd come into hers, with me knowing exactly who she was, and having no idea if she was playing with me or not.

Truth was, I didn't know what I would have done. I'd wanted to beat Armageddon for such a long time, I could only assume that her desire to beat me would be just as bad. I'd like to say that I would have ghosted as soon as I realised who she really was, but truthfully, I wasn't sure. And then add in the fact that we had this insane connection between us, and I just wasn't sure how I would have handled things.

I glanced over at my brother, who was watching me carefully. There was a bruise blooming on his cheekbone, and if nothing else, that gave me some satisfaction – until I saw my own reflection in the mirror at least.

"You and I both know you would have gone out with her, and not just because she's hot as fuck, but because you *have* to win."

I could accept there was definitely some truth in that statement. I also wanted to knock his head in for calling my woman 'hot as fuck', but that was a whole other issue entirely – especially when I reminded myself that she wasn't my woman anymore.

"If you were handed your enemy on a silver platter, delivered literally to your door, you would have taken that opportunity and ran with it. Maybe she thought she'd just see you a couple of times, suss you out and then do a runner."

"But she *didn't* do a runner."

"Yeah, because she loves you, you rooster. Can't you see that? She fucked up, but she didn't set out to make you fall for her and then go 'oh, tricked ya, it was all a big joke', she fell for you too. Fuck knows why, you're such a whiny little bitch."

I huffed out a laugh. He was always trying to goad me.

"She lied."

"So did you," he pointed out.

"Why are you on her team all of a sudden?" I growled. "Shouldn't you be on my side?"

He jumped to his feet and picked up his gloves from next to me.

"Honestly, Ty, dealing with you is like trying to nail fucking jello to a wall. I *am* on your side. That's why I'm telling you to get over it and fix this shit so you're not such a miserable prick all the time. You love her – she loves you. Just kiss and make up already."

Nail jello to a wall. Rich coming from him.

He started to walk towards the ropes of the ring.

"It's not that simple," I called after him.

He turned back to look at me over his shoulder. "Nah, man, it actually *is* that simple. Forget your pride and figure out what you want the rest of your life to look like. I guarantee you can't even see it without her."

"But –"

"No buts, bro, she's human, we all mess up, just get past it and move forward. Or let her go and get on with your life. It's your call."

I lay back down on the canvas and groaned.

He was right, the bastard.

I didn't want a future without her, even with the mess we'd found ourselves in, I still wanted her more than anything.

I loved her.

I wanted her.

My heart already knew all this – now I just had to convince my head that it was okay to do that.

———

I waited for the phone call to be picked up, my knee bouncing nervously with each ring.

"Hey," she answered, her voice soft. It was that tone you used with someone who was skating on the thin ice of a total breakdown.

I felt better for just hearing her voice, even if it made me feel pathetic.

"Hey, short stuff."

"What's going on? I haven't heard from you for a few days. You doing okay?"

I shrugged to myself. "Not really. I think I'm

going insane. Let out some frustrations with Louis this morning."

I could practically hear her eyes roll through the phone line. "And how'd that work out for you?"

"Could be better," I admitted.

I was pretty sure the fucker had cracked one of my ribs.

She didn't reply.

"Yeah, okay, it was a stupid fucking idea, but it's not the first time and it won't be the last."

"You're meant to be the smart one." She sighed.

I had a feeling she wasn't just talking about my preferred method of frustration outlet anymore.

"What would you suggest I do?"

"I think talking to the girl would be a hell of a lot more productive than getting a hiding from Lou."

This was a new development from Charlotte. Only a few days ago she had been anti Amarah. I had no clue what had changed between now and then, but I wanted to hear it.

I was perched right on the fence right now, and truthfully, I needed one last shove to push me over either way.

I already knew I needed to speak to Mara, but I was torn about what that chat was going to look like. It wasn't until I heard my sister's voice that I acknowledged that part of my hesitation was because I didn't want to let Charlotte down by making the wrong choice.

I was a big boy, and I could make my own mind

up, but I wanted Charlotte to be part of my life. I didn't want some awkward divide separating us.

My sister's opinion meant a lot to me, and I was nervous to hear exactly what it was.

"You think I should talk to Mara? Since when?"

She sighed heavily. "Since Parker told me to pull my head in and stop being so unreasonable."

I stifled a laugh. I couldn't imagine Parker telling his beloved wife off, but clearly something had shifted her mindset.

"He reminded me of the fuck ups he made when we first got together and the fact that I gave him a chance to make things right. He also miiiiiight have sparked my memory about certain mistakes I made myself that he chose to overlook."

They'd certainly both made their fair share of mistakes, but they'd forgiven one another, learnt from those mistakes and come out stronger for it.

"But how am I meant to know if it'll be worth it?"

She laughed. "You *don't*, Ty, you've just gotta run the risk. If it's worth it, then it'll work out. Relationships are about forgiveness and compromise sometimes, and if you love her then you shouldn't just throw that away, not if you think it's the real deal. You just have to take a chance and see what happens."

"That scares the shit out of me," I admitted.

"It all comes down to whether or not you can get past it. It's simple really. If you can, and you love her, and you want a future with her, then go for it." She paused. "Don't be a baby."

I chuckled at the half-assed, tacked-on comment at the end.

"Thanks, short stuff."

"I know I probably haven't helped you much these past couple of weeks, but I've cooled off now and I think you should give her a chance – if that's what you want to do. Look at Jasper and Hannah; Hannah's always screwing up and they're two of the happiest people I know."

She was right, and the realisation that thinking about Hannah and Jasper brought me nothing but happiness, was the final push I needed.

I indicated and pulled over, before doing a U-turn and heading back in the direction of Amarah's place.

I was going to get my woman.

CHAPTER 32

Amarah

"*COMING*," I called out to Jessie after she knocked on my door.

I shrugged on my hoodie – an attempt to conceal the fact that I still wasn't wearing a bra – something she'd told me off for, several times already.

She knocked again as I crossed the room towards the door.

"I'm coming, you impatient bitch!" I yelled as I swung open the door and came face to face with the absolute last person I expected to see.

I'd given up monitoring the cameras a long time ago, probably around the same time I'd given up caring about anything much at all.

He smirked at me, and the sight just about made me tip over. He was so fucking hot. So, so gorgeous.

My hungry eyes roamed over every inch of him, totally unashamed at their blatant ogling – they had no fucks to give – they'd been deprived of the sight of Tyler Watson for too damn long. He looked like he'd just had the living shit beat out of him, and he probably had – he had a bad habit of taking on his brother – but *my god*, he was a sight for sore eyes regardless.

"I *have* been known to be an impatient bitch," he drawled.

My gaze finally came to rest on those incredible blue eyes of his. "I thought you were Jessie," I replied, sheepish.

He looked me up and down, and I cursed myself for not having my shit together. I looked like I was rocking some type of homeless chic outfit, that, combined with my ratty ponytail and total lack of makeup, and I was in no position to be entertaining a man – certainly not one this hot.

It was bold of me to assume that I was going to be entertaining Tyler in any way, but a girl could dream, and it certainly felt like I was in a dream with him standing before me.

"Do you want to come in?"

He nodded and stepped forwards. I stepped back, maintaining the distance between us. I couldn't risk getting close. Getting close meant smelling him. Hell, just looking at his hands made me think of the way they'd feel on my skin. I couldn't allow myself to risk touching him.

The corner of his lip twitched as he passed me, respecting the distance I was enforcing around myself, but being slightly amused by it at the same time.

He went and sat down on my couch, not waiting for any invitation to make himself at home.

I loved that. I wanted him to be comfortable here, I always had.

I didn't know whether to be excited or scared by the fact that he was here, sitting in my living room, looking the absolute picture of composure while I felt like a total wreck.

I had no idea why he was suddenly here, unannounced. I hadn't heard a peep out of him in what felt like years.

I racked my brain, trying to think if he'd left something behind... maybe that's why he was here.

I stood awkwardly in my own doorway while I ran through every possible scenario in which he'd have come here, ignoring only the ones that gave me hope.

Stupid hope.

"Sit, Mara."

"Bossy," I grumbled to myself as I moved to the armchair across from him and sat down.

He bit back a laugh.

We sat across from one another, neither speaking,

both of us just staring at the other, for a period of time that felt too long and too short, simultaneously.

"Why are you here, Ty?" I finally asked. "I'm not sure how much more of this I can take."

I got the words out without my voice cracking, but I could feel the moisture pooling in my eyes. My emotions were starting to get the better of me.

I looked down at my hands and blinked back my tears. I didn't want him to see me cry.

"I'm here for *you*, beautiful."

My eyes snapped up to look at his face. I must have been dreaming. He couldn't have just said those words to me.

He smiled at me so softly, so sweetly that I very nearly melted into a puddle on the floor.

"What did you say?" I whispered.

His smile widened. "I said I'm here for you, Amarah. For *us*."

Hope – stupid, *stupid* hope, blossomed in my chest, and I didn't have the strength to fight it anymore. I wanted him, I wanted to believe this was really happening.

"You want me?" I whispered.

"I *need* you," he replied, his gaze never once wavering. "It's so much more than want, Mara."

Holy heck.

"But... but, *why*? After what I did..."

I could feel tears running down my cheeks now, but I didn't care if he saw. I was a hot mess, but he was still looking at me like I hung the moon.

"Because I love you. I've figured out that people make mistakes, but sometimes it's worth putting in the work to get past them. So, if you really do mean what you say, and you love me too, then I want to fix this, Mara. I can't lose you."

I pinched myself on the arm. This couldn't be real. He'd just said all the words that every woman in the world wanted to hear, and I was the last person that deserved to hear them.

He got up from his seat and came to crouch right in front of me.

"Amarah, look at me. You might not be my first love, but you could be my last. I *want* you to be my last."

"I want you to be my last too," I whispered.

I couldn't believe this. I pinched myself again.

He chuckled. "Stop pinching yourself."

"I'm just making sure," I whispered. "I feel like I'm dreaming."

"You're not dreaming."

"That's something someone in a dream would say."

He looked at me, his expression amused, before turning serious again.

"But I've got one condition, Mara, and it's really fucking important. If you can't do this one thing, then I don't think we have a future."

Oh my god, what...

My heart was doing a good job of trying to bruise my rib cage. It was pounding against it in heavy thuds, over and over again. I'd never been so nervous in my life.

"What is it?" I whispered.

It didn't matter what it was. I'd do it. I'd have done *anything* at this point. He knew it. I knew it. Hell, anyone with half a brain knew I was a mess without this man and that I'd do whatever it took to get him back.

He didn't answer.

"Is it bad?" I stood up and then sat back down just as quickly. "It's bad, isn't it?"

He smirked; the bastard was enjoying my panic. He shrugged one shoulder, and I literally felt my blood whooshing in my veins.

"It's just one *little* thing." He took my hand in his.

"Just tell me what it is already," I demanded.

He paused, and I swore it was purely for dramatic effect.

"You have to tell me how to tell the twins apart."

My eyes widened.

Oh my god... this is... hilarious.

I covered my mouth with my free hand.

Oh, the irony.

He frowned at me, clearly confused by my bizarre reaction to what should have been a simple request.

Laughter burst from within me, filling the air.

"*What?*" he insisted. "Why are you laughing?"

"You're going to *kill* me." I howled.

His face had broken out into a grin as he watched

me laugh. "*What?* Just tell me your god damn secret, woman."

It feels so good to laugh again.

I managed to gain composure of myself... *just.* "I would tell you... I *really* would. But... I actually have no idea," I admitted.

"What? But that night at the gig... *what?*" he rambled, confused.

"We tricked you... Charlotte and the boys just played along, pretending that I'd guessed right. I had *no* idea which was which," I confessed.

Charlotte had told me the next time that I'd seen her that I'd actually only guessed right once, and that my last guess had been wrong, so the boys had had to wear each other's clothes and pretend to be one another for the rest of the night, just to keep up the façade.

Couple of troopers.

Tyler pointed a finger at me, his expression one of pure disbelief as he opened and shut his mouth, struggling to find the words he wanted to say. "*You.*" He gaped, outraged. "You owe me fifty bucks, you dirty little liar."

He was right – I owed him the fifty back. But I didn't care; it was the best feeling in the world to be back betting with him.

I laughed again, the sound still strange and unfamiliar to me. I felt happy and complete, right down into my bones – it was going to take some getting used to after being a depressed sack of shit for so long.

Sad had become my default setting, but I was ready to hit the restart button.

I pulled him in close by the scruff off his shirt and kissed him, hard. He kissed me back just as intensely. I couldn't speak for him, but I poured everything into that kiss; every moment I was lost without him, every second of missing him... *everything*.

"Fuck I missed you," he murmured against my lips.

His hands were in my hair, his body was pressed against mine. It was so much better than any of the dreams I'd had, because he was really here this time.

He pulled away a fraction, and I let myself drown in the sight of him. The taste of him on my lips. The smell of him. I soaked it all in.

"Played by my own siblings. *Unbelievable*. I hope they're not expecting Christmas presents this year – fucking traitors," he muttered, shaking his head.

I giggled. "Sorry, but you have to admit, it was well played."

His lips turned up into a grin. "You guys had me, hook line and sinker."

"You've got me, hook, line and sinker, Watson."

He chuckled. "Cheesy, but I'll allow it."

I draped my arms around his neck. "Oh, it could get *a lot* worse than that."

"Bring it on."

"Are you going to explain why you look like you took on a brick wall before coming here?" I asked as I gently ran a finger over his bruised cheekbone.

He smirked, straightened up and then winced.

"Let me guess..." I drawled, "I should see the other guy?"

He chuckled. "Just a bit of frustration release, that's all."

I raised a brow. "I can think of much better outlets for any pent-up frustrations."

"So can I, beautiful."

I could see the hunger in his eyes; I'd have been willing to bet the look in mine matched.

He kissed me again and it took every ounce of my self-control not to start undressing him.

"I love you," I whispered.

He looked at me so deeply I could feel it on the inside of my body. "I love you too."

I knew in that moment that he forgave me – really and truly forgave me, and I vowed to *never* let anything come between us ever again.

EPILOGUE

Tyler

THE FIFTY DOLLAR note she'd given me back when she'd admitted to rigging our first ever bet felt like it weighed a tonne in my pocket.

This was the most important bet to date, and the most ironic part of the whole thing, was that I wanted her to win. I wanted nothing more than for her to take this fifty bucks off me right now.

We'd been back together for six months now – there were no more secrets between us, and things were even better than before. I had every part of this woman.

We'd even started to work together on certain projects that were too big for either of us to take on, on our own. My woman had even more of a brilliant mind than I'd thought. She was seriously incredible.

Just when I thought she couldn't turn me on any more than she already did.

We worked well together. Turns out when we weren't each trying to ruin the other, we made quite the team. She was strong where I was weak, and vice versa.

We butted heads on occasion, but that was all part of the fun. I loved it when she fired up at me and put me in my place, and make-up sex after a disagreement almost made me want to pick a fight daily.

I watched Amarah laugh at something Hannah said, and my knee bounced up and down nervously.

"What the fuck are you all jumpy for?" Floyd scowled at me. "You're making me feel on edge."

"Mind your business," I snapped at him.

He made a sassy face at me. "*Precious.*"

I ignored him. He knew I was up to something, and he'd been trying to bait me all night. It was starting to piss me off.

Nothing new there when it came to my brother.

It was family dinner night, and although it had been a little awkward for Mara in the beginning, that was long gone now. She was part of the furniture like the rest of us.

Charlotte had surprised me and forgiven her quickly, and they were great friends now.

Amarah was also really close with Jasper. Now that I knew they had a friendship of sorts from before

I'd even met her, it made a lot of sense that they'd get along well.

The biggest surprise for me was how well Hannah and Amarah got along these days. Hannah was currently holding her and Jasper's baby girl and Amarah and Charlotte were fussing over her like they'd never seen something so perfect.

"Why don't you just ask her already?" Floyd said, capturing my attention.

"Ask her what?" I replied, my attention turning to him.

"To move in with you, cupcake – it's pretty obvious that's what's got you so nervous."

"How the fuck is it obvious?" I demanded, shocked that he'd hit the nail on the head.

His eyes lit up. "It wasn't." He grinned. "I took a punt."

"Fuck's sake."

"This is classic. What are the chances?" He laughed.

I groaned.

"Did you get her a key cut?"

"No."

He frowned. "Make a little effort, bro."

"Shut up."

"No can do." He grinned at me.

I had a sinking feeling in the bottom of my stomach that my dipshit, traitor brother was about to throw me under the bus.

"Hey, Mara!" he yelled across the room. "Ty wants to ask you something."

"I'm literally going to kill you dead," I growled at him as Amarah eyed me curiously.

"I'd only come back to haunt you," he replied, gleefully, as he strolled away without a single care in the world.

The asshole was so proud of himself, and I was about ready to put his head through a wall.

"Prick."

I couldn't wait for the day that he found himself a woman and I could return the favour of winding him up.

Amarah walked towards me, and I could have sworn my heart was trying to exit my god damn body. I had no clue why I was so nervous to ask her this. We spent pretty much every night together anyway; she had stuff at my house, I had stuff at hers – this made sense. It was time. I loved this woman, and I had no intentions of spending my life without her.

Hell, I'd had to hold back from buying her a ring when I walked past a jeweller the other day.

One step at a time.

"You look like you regret the day he was born," she said as she reached me, her expression amused.

"The very day," I said through clenched teeth.

"What do you wanna ask me?"

I could feel eyes on us, and I glanced over Amarah's shoulder to see everyone was indeed watching us in anticipation.

Fucking Floyd and his stupid big mouth.

"Come with me." I grabbed her hand and led her outside, onto the huge balcony off Parker and Charlotte's living room.

"What's going on?" she asked with a laugh as I fidgeted and shifted my weight from foot to foot.

Fuck, this wasn't like me. I wasn't a nervy guy, I was full of confidence, but the rules all changed when it came to her. Every single one of them.

"Are you going to ask me what you want to ask me or shall I give you a minute to find your balls," she asked, one eyebrow raised.

Fuck it. Here goes nothing.

"I bet you fifty bucks you won't move in with me."

Her mouth fell open as the words settled between us, then slowly, she smiled a devious smile.

"You think I won't do it?"

I shrugged a shoulder, playing down how much I was dying to hear her say that she would.

She took a step closer to me, and then another one, until we were toe to toe.

She lifted her chin to look up at me, her eyes sparkling.

"You owe me fifty bucks, Watson."

ALSO BY

Love like Yours Series

Rushed – Book 1

Pierced – Book 2

Hunted – Book 3

Chased – Book 4

Love like Yours Box Set – Books 1-4

All Access Pass Series

Paper, Scissors, Rock – Book 1

Hide and Seek – Book 2

One for the Money – Book 3

My Heart Duet

My Heart Needs

My Heart Wants

Every Last Beat – The Heart Duet Box Set – Books 1 & 2

Calendar Boys

Mr. January

Mr. February

Mr. March

ACKNOWLEDGMENTS

As always, thank you to the readers, it's been a long time since I added anything to this series, so I appreciate you picking back up where we left off!

Huge thank you to Stacey, Bianca and MV who are always encouraging and supporting me.

Thanks for always being only a message away.

The fantastic editors at Spell Bound – thanks for making it readable!

Thanks again to anyone who picked up this book and took a chance on reading it, I hope you liked Amarah and Tyler's story as much as I do!

N x

ABOUT THE AUTHOR

NICOLE S. GOODIN is a romance author and mother of two from Taranaki in the North Island of New Zealand.

In mid-2015, she started to write about a group of characters who wouldn't get out of her head. Her first book, Rushed, was published in mid-2016.

Nicole enjoys long walks on the beach, pillow fights and braiding her friends' hair. She dislikes clichés, talking about herself in the third person, and people who don't understand her sense of humour.

Please feel free to contact her either via her website, email, Instagram, Twitter or on her Facebook page, she would love to hear your feedback. If you're feeling really game, you can even sign up for her newsletter.

www.ingramcontent.com/pod-product-compliance
Lightning Source LLC
Chambersburg PA
CBHW030830110726
47900CB00006B/1827